I Carry Your Heart

Barbara A. Luker

Black Rose Writing | Texas

ISBN: 978-1-68433-890-0
PUBLISHED BY BLACK ROSE WRITING
www.blackrosewriting.com

Printed in the United States of America
Suggested Retail Price (SRP) $20.95

I Carry Your Heart is printed in Plantagenet Cherokee

*As a planet-friendly publisher, Black Rose Writing does its best to eliminate unnecessary waste to reduce paper usage and energy costs, while never compromising the reading experience. As a result, the final word count vs. page count may not meet common expectations.

For Mom,
who encouraged me to try.

I
Carry
Your
Heart

Chapter One

"You know Nan, we could have waited until your actual birthday for the party," the young woman said as she helped her grandmother down the steps to the waiting car.

Even as yet another birthday drew near Abigail was still as fit and trim as she had always been, but there had been extra pep in her step lately making the offer of assistance down the stairs more of a courtesy than a necessity.

"No we couldn't," the older woman insisted. "I'm going to be busy on my birthday."

Spread across the country, it wasn't often the entire family was able to gather together for an event; however Abby's eightieth birthday had changed all that. Beloved by family, friends and neighbors alike, Abigail Lillian Peterson Ward had spent her lifetime doing for others. Now, just days away from a momentous birthday celebration, the family had been understandably confused when she had insisted on celebrating beforehand.

"What? Do you have a hot date or something? Pops has been gone for a while now and it's not too late to find yourself some charming silver haired fox to spend your time with."

"I might just do that," Abby said with a wink at her granddaughter.

With a dozen grandchildren it would be difficult to have just one favorite, but if Abby could be coaxed into admitting she had one, youngest grandchild Krista was it. Living in the same small town just a few doors down from each other helped, but the two were as alike as peas in a pod and enjoyed each other's company enough to spend hours together each week.

From the moment of Krista's birth comments had been made on the remarkable resemblance to her grandmother and as the girl grew into a beautiful young woman she became the mirror image of her grandmother at the same age. Decades later Abby was still a beautiful woman with snow white hair framing a face unlined by the many experiences of life. Deep chocolate eyes still sparkled with laughter and love and she was rarely seen without a smile on her face. Indeed time had truly been kind to Abby; so kind that many who met her would never guess she was nearing octogenarian status.

Good health and aging well wasn't what brought the impish smile to Abby's face today though. She had a secret; one she had kept for almost sixty years and which her family was about to discover. Today's party would be lovely of course, but for Abby at least, it was just the precursor to the real celebration.

Pulling up to the party venue, Abby scanned the crammed parking lot for a hint of who waited inside. For many years her birthday had brought about regrets of another year and another wasted opportunity; so much so she had come to dread the day of her birth. There really was only one day she had ever looked forward to and it would be here soon enough.

"I know you're not that fond of birthday parties Nan, but Mom put a lot of work into this so I hope you'll have a good time," Krista told her as they got out of the car. "Oh wait; I almost forgot your corsage."

"Now I look like an old lady," Abby said as Krista pinned the small corsage on her grandmother's stylish dress.

"You are an old lady," Krista told her with a laugh before giving her a peck on the cheek. "But you're a beautiful old lady who I happen to love with all my heart."

Trying to seem stern Abby had a quick response. "Aren't you the cheeky one today? Whomever did you learn your manners from?"

"You of course. Now let's go in."

A packed room filled with extended family and long-time friends exploded in applause as the pair walked in. Abby's aversion to being the center of just such a moment was quickly forgotten as guest after guest enveloped her in a hug or offered kisses and a personal birthday wish.

Deborah, Krista's mother and Abby's first-born, had certainly gone all out for the party. Decorated with more balloons and streamers than a fourth of July float, the room was ablaze with color with each place setting painstakingly set with real china and expensive flatware. The scene brought a smile to Abby's face as she looked across the room and caught her daughter's eye before giving an appreciative nod that brought a sigh of relief to the woman's face. Of all the relationships in Abby's life, only her relationship with Deborah had tested her patience and all too often had left Robert to serve as referee between mother and daughter.

Robert always said the pair was too much alike to get on and while that may have been true, Abby often suspected there was more to Deborah's churlish behavior. At first they had shared the typical mother-daughter bond, but somewhere in her late teens Deborah began to look at her mother in a different light and things were never the same between them. After years spent trying to force Deborah to admit what had changed, Abby simply gave up and it became one of those regrets she knew she would take to her grave.

Since Robert's death, their shared grief at first seemed to ease things between mother and daughter, but it wasn't to last. Eventually they drifted further apart even as Abby's relationship with Deborah's own daughter became closer. Still, the effort Deborah had put into the party, which came as a surprise to the entire family, might well be the beginning of a new relationship between them.

It seemed the entire town had shown up for the event with many sharing stories of how Abby's generosity through the years had been a blessing to their families. Whether offering a meal to a family too poor to feed their children, or organizing clothing drives, bake sales, and the like for those less fortunate, Abby was the one woman in town who could always be counted on to extend a helping hand to someone in need. Her advancing age hadn't diminished those efforts one bit although these days Abby left most of the heavy lifting to those a bit younger.

After a long enjoyable evening, the meal complete, toasts long recited, one by one the guests said their final farewells leaving immediate family to clean up while Abby, relegated for the first time to being simply a guest at a family function, watched over it all with the pride of someone who had lived a fulfilling life with a family she loved. Grandchildren ranging in age from mid-twenties to their forties manned the kitchen clean up as their parents gathered at the table with the family matriarch.

"Thank you all for such a lovely evening," Abby told them before her gaze settled on Deborah. "Thank you most of all Deborah. I realize how much time and money you spent on this party and it meant the world to me. Thank you."

"It's okay Mom. You only turn eighty once," Deb told her as if she was trying to make peace at last. Few at the table believed it even as all wished for it. "I only wish Dad could have been here."

An image of Robert, strong and healthy and full of life flashed through Abby's mind. In the end his slow and painful death from cancer had left him a shell of the man he once was, but it was the vibrant man she married that she remembered these days. She missed his companionship every day.

"As do I", she said wistfully. "Your father always loved a good party and at the risk of ruining a nice evening, I have to tell you he would have loved that you were the one to plan it all for me."

"He knew," Deborah said quietly, unable to look her mother in the eye.

"Yes, I'm sure he is looking down on all of us," Abby said hesitantly. There was something about the look on her daughter's face that put her on guard.

"No, I mean he knew. He made me promise before he died that I would make this birthday extra special. I don't know why, but it was really important to him that you be reminded of your family on your birthday and that we all were here. I wonder why that is."

The comment was offered as a challenge directed at her mother. Each of the siblings stopped their own conversations as the atmosphere between Abby and Deborah once again turned tense.

"I couldn't imagine," Abby said hesitantly, unwilling to start yet another argument with her daughter but for a brief moment wondering if Deborah knew something she shouldn't.

"Daddy loved you more than anything. Did you know that?'

"Of course I did. Why would you ask such a question?"

"Deb, what are you implying?" Matt asked. As the oldest boy in the family, he had become very protective of his mother after their father passed away and had always had little patience for Deborah's behavior towards Abby.

"I'm not implying anything," Deborah snapped. "I'm simply asking a question and want to know if Mom realized how much Dad loved her. He put her first in everything in his life and I'm not so sure she did the same. Did you even love him? It's a simple question."

"Deborah stop it," Abby said with tears in her eyes. "Of course I loved your father. We were married fifty-eight years and you don't stay together that long without loving each other. I don't understand why you're even asking me the question. Did your father say something to you? Did he tell you I didn't love him?"

"No," she admitted. "It's just . . . I thought . . . "

"You thought what?" Abby asked tenderly.

"I don't know. I just thought maybe . . . I don't know. I guess I'm just being silly. He was so insistent about this party but he wouldn't explain why it was so important. I guess my mind was going crazy places. Just ignore me like usual."

"Deb I think you've said enough," her husband Steven told her. "Let's go home before this gets out of hand."

"That's not something any of us are going to forget Deb." Matt told her. The anger in his eyes hadn't dissipated one iota. "Mom are you ready to go? We can give you a ride home."

"That's okay Uncle Matt," Krista said as the grandchildren, finished with their kitchen duties, joined the older group. "I'll take Nan home when she's ready."

"Thank you all once again for a lovely evening. I am truly blessed to have such a wonderful family around me and I love you all," Abby said as she gathered her things.

How Abby could say that after what Deborah had said left an unsettled feeling amongst the family as Deborah and Steve walked quickly to the door without saying goodbye.

"I'm sorry Deb ruined your party," Matt told his mother. "Sometimes I wish she'd just stay home instead of making everyone miserable each time we get together."

"Nothing was ruined," Abby said firmly. "Deb has a right to her own opinions about me. Maybe I wasn't the best mother, but I like to think I did my best by all of you."

"Of course you did," Mary insisted. "Deb was just a brat and I can't stand to see how she treats you."

"Whatever her problem is with me, that's between the two of us," Abby insisted. "Now, we're all tired after such a big night so it's time for me to say thank you and goodnight."

With a final round of hugs and birthday wishes, the group slowly made their way out to the parking lot for the drive home.

"Did you have a good time?" Krista asked as she carefully navigated the dark streets in no hurry to end the evening.

"It was wonderful," Abby admitted. "But my birthday's not over yet."

"I know that and so I would like to take you out for lunch on your birthday. I'll be back in town then and it can be just the two of us."

"Sorry sweetheart, but I can't."

"Oh, are you doing something with your friends?"

Abby's list of friends, young and old alike, was legendary. Everyone in town claimed her friendship and rightly so.

"No, but I have other plans that I've waited a very long time for."

"What does that mean? What are you going to do?"

"You'll just have to wait and find out with everyone else, but suffice it to say, my life is never going to be the same."

"Come on Nan, you can't say something like that and not tell me more. What are you doing?"

"Sorry Krista, as much as I love you, and I love you more than words can say, even you will have to wait to find out."

Pulling into Abby's driveway, Krista put the car in park and turned to look at her grandmother; receiving only a mysterious smile in return.

"I guess you're entitled to your secrets, you've earned them after all, but promise me it's nothing dangerous like jumping out of an airplane. That might have been fine for the President on his birthday, but it would devastate me if something happened to you. I need you with me for a very long time and don't you forget it."

"I'm not going anywhere sweetheart and there are no parachuting adventures in my future I can assure you. Now, it's time for this old lady to get to bed. You've got that work conference the next couple of day's right?"

"Correct, but I'll stop over when I get back in town. Do you want me to help you into the house?"

"Thanks honey, but in case you have forgotten, I'm still in my seventies and I can make it myself," Abby said with a chuckle before leaning over to plant a kiss on Krista's cheek. "Thanks for being my date tonight and have fun at your conference. I love you."

"Love you too," Krista said before Abby got out of the car and made her way into the house. It wasn't until a light came on and the front door closed behind her grandmother that she slowly backed out of the driveway and headed home.

•　　•　　•

Changing into her nightclothes, Abby was too keyed up from the party and the thought of what the next few days would bring to sleep. Making herself a cup of tea, she settled down in her favorite armchair and turned on the television before flipping through the hundreds of channels in search of the classic movie station and one of the many movies featuring her favorite actor. Luck was on her side when his handsome young profile lit up the screen in a movie she and Krista had recently watched together. For one so young, Krista claimed to love the classic movies as much as her grandmother and it had become a shared passion.

Settling in to watch, with slippers on her feet and a warm throw across her body, a wave of indigestion washed over her as she carefully put her cup of tea to the side and touched her palms to her chest.

"That's what I get for eating such rich food at the party tonight," Abby said to the empty room as she waited for the pain to pass.

It was some time before she felt it lessen and reached for her tea cup once again. Pulling the blanket to her chin an intense pain erupted throughout her arm sending the tea cup flying to the floor where it shattered into tiny shards. Abby gasped for breath at the intensity of the pain coursing through her body. Struggling to stay upright, the horrible realization hit her that her long-awaited plans for her birthday would never be realized. A handsome face filled the television screen as tears slid down Abby's cheeks and finally, everything went black.

Chapter Two

"Nan? It's Krista", she said as she pounded yet again on the door.

Even with the windows tightly shut she could hear the television going in the back of the house. Abby's hearing had steadily diminished over the years but she had never before not answered the door after the first knock and a sudden feeling of dread came over Krista. Racing around to the back of the house on grass made slippery by a mid-afternoon rain shower, she nearly went down in the mud in her haste to make contact with her grandmother before reaching the relative safety of the back deck. From that vantage point she could see the television screen, but not much else.

"Nan, it's me, please answer the door," she said as her fear ratcheted up at the continued lack of response. Moving to another window, she finally saw what she had been dreading. A broken tea cup on the floor, her grandmother's arm hanging limply from the chair.

It had only taken seconds for the 911 call to generate response from local Police followed closely behind by the volunteer ambulance. In such a small town everyone knew everyone else and the emergency personnel exchanged sad looks when they got a glimpse in the window. Krista stood by helplessly as one of the Officer's broke into the tightly secured home and confirmed what Krista had been dreading. Abby had passed away.

"I'm sorry Krista," Officer McMillan said as he steered her back out of the house. "She's gone."

"She can't have died on her birthday," Krista cried. "It's her birthday today. Please let me go to her."

"I'm not the medical examiner," Officer McMillan said gently, "but it looks like she died a couple of days ago. That's not how she would want to be remembered and anyway I can't let you go in there. Let's go to the kitchen and call your folks while the EMT's do their thing okay?"

Carefully blocking any attempts Krista might have made to go to her grandmother, the Officer directed her to the kitchen and helped her to a seat at the table while the other emergency responders tended to Abby. He was right, there were calls to be made and with tears flowing freely down her face, Krista placed the first call to her mother and tried to choke out the words.

"I don't know what happened. Maybe a heart attack or a stroke. They won't let me see her. They think she's been dead for a couple of days. That means she died after I brought her home from the party. How could that be? She looked so healthy and happy."

Abigail Ward was known as one of the strongest willed members of the community and everyone in town knew Krista took after her grandmother, but still the Officer watched her carefully in case she had a breakdown. Shock had a funny way of hitting people when they least expected it.

"I don't know," Krista said into the phone. "I suppose they'll take her to the mortuary…"

"Hospital. We'll take her to the hospital first," the Officer said quietly. "For any unexplained death there will need to be an autopsy." At the look of horror on Krista's face, he regretted his bluntness. "Sorry," he said sheepishly.

"Mom, Officer McMillan said they are taking her body to the hospital to try and find out why she died. Can you meet us there? What do you mean after you get your hair done? Nan's dead. Do you not get that? Can't you put aside your differences now that's she gone?"

Throwing down the phone in disgust Krista was embarrassed when she realized the Officer was still watching her. Tired of making apologies for her mother's behavior, she offered a sad smile.

"Apparently getting your hair done is a higher priority than dealing with your mother's death," she told him.

"You don't have to explain to me," he said as he took a chair opposite her. "Everyone deals with grief in their own way. Your mom's probably in shock."

"I wish that was the reason," she told him as she shook her head. "Nan and Mom never had what you might call a picture perfect mother-daughter relationship.

"It wasn't exactly a secret in town," he admitted. "I don't want to embarrass you, but I personally witnessed a number of dust ups between them myself back when your grandmother was still running the restaurant. My dad always called it bad blood. He said there was some sort of bad blood between the two that Abby could never figure out."

"I hoped that maybe after the birthday party the other night whatever was between them could be forgotten, but I think it actually just made it worse."

Like the rest of town Officer McMillan had also been in attendance at the party but had left before the harsh words between mother and daughter at the end of the night.

"That's too bad. Now your mom will have to live with that regret with your grandma gone and all."

"I'm not so sure she'll care," Krista said before she started to cry yet again.

The thought of her beloved Nan dying all alone was more than she could bear and soon the cries turned into full-fledged sobs as the ambulance personnel began to wheel her grandmother's shrouded body out the front door. Neighbors from blocks away; many with tears on their own faces, lined the sidewalk as the somber procession made its way to the ambulance.

Officer McMillan put his arm around Krista as they followed behind before Abby's body was carefully secured in the ambulance.

"Why don't I give you a ride to the hospital? There won't be much you can do there but if you want to be with her you can sit and wait." he suggested. Krista seemed at a loss for what to do next.

"I appreciate that, but I better go back in the house and start making some calls. I'm not sure Mom can be bothered."

"If you want some help, I'm off duty in a half hour or so. I could come back and help."

The pair had known each other since childhood, and while his offer of assistance was appreciated, Krista just wanted to be alone with her thoughts before the rest of the family swooped in.

"Thanks Alex, but I'll be okay. I just need a moment to compose myself and I'm sure my family will be here soon. I appreciate everything you've done for Nan today."

"We all loved Abby and she will be missed more than you know," he said before pulling Krista into his arms and hugging her tightly. "She loved you very much."

"I know but thank you for reminding me."

•　　•　　•

If there was one person who embodied all of the good in the world, Abigail Ward was that person for the hundreds of people who packed the small Presbyterian Church on the day of her funeral. It had been the same at the wake the evening before as hundreds of mourners waited patiently in line for well over an hour just for the chance to express their condolences to Abby's family. The funeral service that would normally have taken thirty minutes stretched to double that as people lined up to speak of Abby's goodness; leaving the family alternating between tears and laughter as stories they had never heard before came to light and continued well into the luncheon that followed. If ever a woman was more beloved it would be hard to find her and the family realized not for the first time how blessed they were to be part of Abby's legacy; although it provided little consolation in their grief.

With a final thanks to the church ladies for hosting the luncheon, the family gathered together back at Abby's house. Ties removed, belts loosened, shoes kicked off, the stress of the last few days fading, there didn't seem to be much more to say.

"So what are we going to do with all her things?" Matt asked. "The thought of selling it all breaks my heart. Everything in here has some kind of memory from my childhood."

Indeed the house where Abby had raised her five children seemed a shrine to the life she and Robert had shared - the still visible record of each child's height on the pantry door; the window pane needing replacement after an errant baseball sailed into the dining room; and the third step of the staircase that each of the kids had tried so hard to avoid when sneaking into the house past curfew.

The grandchildren had their own memories of the house - the early morning aroma of Nan's homemade bread pulled hot from the oven to be slathered with homemade grape jelly; Pops' gum jar which always sat prominently on the counter just out of the reach of little hands who were taught to ask politely before taking a piece of the minty gum; and the matching recliners sitting just close enough in front of the fireplace so Nan and Pops could reach out their hands and touch each other. Every corner of the house held a special meaning for each of the family members now gathered together and having to say goodbye to those memories would be difficult.

"Kevin, I think you have something to tell everyone don't you?" middle daughter Mary prompted. With a quick smile at his wife, Kevin stood from the couch and moved to stand in front of the fireplace as he faced the group.

"Kids if you'd all come in here, I have something to tell you," he shouted into the kitchen where the younger generation had congregated. As everyone found a place in the crowded living room, he pulled out some papers from the briefcase he was never without.

"Some time ago Miss Abby came to see me," he started. Kevin, a Georgia boy whose marriage to Mary had transported him further north, had always referred to his mother-in-law as "Miss Abby". Along with his southern accent, it was a habit too ingrained to change even after all these years.

"I wasn't her lawyer; you all know that Charles Browning did the legal work for your folks, anyway she asked me to draw up a new will just a few months ago."

"Why would she do that?" Matt asked quickly.

"She never explained, but she was pretty insistent on it."

"I suppose she wanted to cut me out of the will," Deborah said bitterly. "I mean it wasn't like we had the best relationship after all."

"And whose fault was that?" Kyle interjected. "Isn't it about time you let it go? She's gone for Christ sakes."

Seeing her husband so upset, Casey touched his arm and tried to get his attention. "Honey calm down please."

"Ahem . . . " Kevin said to bring everyone back to what he was trying to tell them. "For the most part, except for some very specific bequeaths to each of the grandkids, her estate is being divided equally between you five kids. You'll probably be as shocked as I was to learn that through some pretty astute investing your folks had a substantial nest egg saved over the years. We'll have a forensic accountant go over everything to make sure, but the five of you will be splitting a boatload of money."

"Nice legal jargon Kevin," Matt said with a smile. "Although I'm surprised there is a lot of money, that doesn't sound any different than her old will."

"Matt's got a point," Charlie said. Youngest of the five kids, and the only single one of the bunch, he was also the least interested in the family drama. "By why are we arguing about this? It's not like any of us need the money. Whatever Mom wanted is fine with me."

"I agree," Kevin said as he shuffled through some more papers, "But there's one substantial change and it involves you Krista."

At the sound of her name, Krista's eyes locked on her uncle. "Me? What are you talking about?"

"Miss Abby asked that after today, the house be locked up tight and that you be the only family member allowed back in. She would like you to go through her things from basement to attic and everything in between. You will have final say in what happens to the house and all its contents. She said and I quote . . . '*In this house you will discover the story of my life and the love we shared.*'"

"Honey what does that mean?" Mary asked. "I thought we knew everything about her. What is left to discover and why would Krista be the only one to go through her things? It's too big of a job for one person to handle."

"I'm not sure. I know Miss Abby was incredibly close to Krista, but other than that I'm as clueless as you all are."

"It's just Mom playing games with us is all," Deborah said as she got up from the couch and grabbed the papers from Kevin's hand looking through them ostensibly to find some way around the condition. "She always wanted to be the center of attention and she's doing it even after she's dead. There has to be a way around this right? Krista shouldn't be the only one with a say in what happens to the house."

"And you think you should?" Krista asked so quietly that at first many in the room didn't even notice. "Do you really think after the way you treated Nan all those years that you should be the one to go through her things? I don't understand why she picked me either, but she sure as heck wouldn't have picked you."

"Watch your tongue young lady," Deborah said sternly.

"I'm sorry for being so blunt, but Mom you have to realize the way you treated Nan was horribly undeserved. Whatever problem you had with her didn't justify all the tears you caused. Nan loved you more than anything. You had to know that. Dad back me up on this will you?"

Steve had played peacemaker between his wife and daughter much like his father-in-law had between mother and daughter before him but he was ready for it to end.

"Come on you two, no fighting today of all days. What's done is done. I'm not saying we should try, but Kevin is there any chance that a challenge to the will could be overturned by the courts?"

"Unless there was some proof that Miss Abby was not of sound mind when she signed the will it's ironclad I'm afraid and you should know that as her lawyer and son-in-law, I would not support any action to contest the will. Miss Abby has always had valid reasons for everything she has done even if we haven't agreed with them. Why would we question her now?"

"You're right honey," Mary said as she moved to stand next to her husband before taking his hand in her own. "Although I must admit, I never understood the solo vacations every year. For a woman who claimed to love her family so much, the need to go on a vacation by herself was a little odd don't you agree?"

"I totally understand why she did it," Matt's wife Anne said. Normally quiet and withdrawn in the middle of such a large and gregarious family, Anne usually only spoke up when she had something important to share. "Look at the life she lived. She single handedly ran that restaurant for decades while at the same time making a comfortable home for all of you and still having time to save every wayward stray that came through town. She barely had five minutes to herself each day. The woman needed a break from all of you. After being part of this family for so long I wish I would have thought of it myself!"

"You have to admit it was like she was a new woman every time she came back," Mary pointed out. "I can remember her telling me how all that solitude renewed her love for life."

"And how many of our plays and concerts and ball games did she miss being gone that week each year?" Deborah interjected. "I can remember begging her to delay her trip so she could see me in my senior play. I had the lead for Pete's sake, but she wouldn't even consider changing dates and she missed it all."

"From what I remember she didn't miss much. That play sucked," Matt interjected before receiving a death stare from his older sister as everyone else laughed. "Kevin's right though. Mom has always had her reasons for what she does and we have to accept that this time is no different. No one is contesting anything and that's that. Krista will let us know if she needs our help and until she does, the house is off limits to everyone else in the family . . . and that includes you Deb."

"Let's go Steven," Deb demanded angrily as she rose from the couch and gathered her things.

"Come on Deb," Kyle implored. "This might be the last opportunity we have together as a family. Don't go."

"I'm sure you all have plenty you'd like to say about me behind my back, so have at it. Kevin you know where to send the check."

There was no further discussion as she strode out the front door leaving Steve to offer a look of apology before he followed.

Chapter Three

Up early the next morning, Krista cradled a cup of strong coffee in her hands while looking at her grandmother's photo on the front page of the paper. For a small town newspaper the amount of front page space afforded the article on Abby's death was impressive. The stories of Abby's kindness shared during the funeral had been repeated in the publication for the entire world to see and would remain there for future historians to discover. Even so, they would never know the woman herself.

Remembering her Grandmother's words from the will Krista wondered if any in the family truly knew her either. "*In this house you will discover the story of my life and the love we shared.*" Abby had seemingly been an open book to all those around her, especially to her granddaughter, so what could be left to discover? Going through the house would take weeks but luckily Krista had the summer free from her teaching job.

Despite her mother's insistence that she be allowed back in Abby's house, Krista would stand her ground knowing how important it apparently was to her grandmother. Before everyone went their separate ways the night before, she had promised to keep them updated on whatever she might find. She also promised that things in the house, many of which hadn't been bequeathed to a family member but nonetheless held special significance to some, would not be sold but instead divided among the family. Abby certainly never meant for her things to go to strangers, especially when items held a special memory for those she cherished the most.

Dressed in shorts and a t-shirt, long hair tied up in a ponytail against the building summer heat, Krista grabbed a note pad and pen before walking the few doors down to the house. Pulling out her grandmother's keys, tears welled up in her eyes at the "World's Best Grandma" keychain. It had been twenty odd years since the grandchildren at that time had jointly presented the birthday gift to Abby and she had pretended to be blown away by the inexpensive drugstore gift. Where some may have discarded it as quickly as possible, Abby had used it every day since then. It was the type of person she was.

Entering the house alone for the first time brought about a fresh set of tears. Never again would she hear her grandmother's lyrical "Krista dear is that you?" when she came over. Never again would she smell her perfume or hear her humming in the kitchen while she cooked. All that remained were her things; lovingly cared for with never a speck of dust to diminish their value. Nan and Pops had never accumulated possessions simply for the sake of owning something, but over nearly six decades and five children together they had accrued an impressive household of goods.

The simplest way to deal with it all would have been to let each family member take whatever they wanted and sell the rest, but that wasn't what Abby wanted. More so than that however, was Krista's growing excitement over the secret to be found in the house. Wiping the tears away she opened all the windows to catch a cooling breeze or two before heading for the basement. Like her grandmother before her, Krista was comfortable tackling projects in an organized and logical way and would work from the bottom floor to the top.

It had been years since she had spent any substantial time in the basement. As with many old homes, the concrete walled basement was dimly lit and musty smelling yet the cobwebs that seemed to appear overnight in her own basement were non-existent in Abby's. Opening the smaller basement windows for a bit of fresh air helped minimize the musty odor, but it would most likely be unpleasant work. Fortunately for Krista, Abby was an exceptional organizer and entering the first of the many storage areas in the basement she discovered stacked tubs that would be easy to go through. Pulling the string on the single bare overhead bulb, the light swung wildly above her head as the beam bounced off the walls before settling down again.

"Well Nan, let's see what you've tucked away," Krista said to herself before digging into the first box.

Krista found herself strangely disappointed when the tub revealed nothing more than old women's clothes. Pulling each carefully folded garment out of the tub, she suspected the clothes were from her grandmother's younger years. Many of the items appeared to be handmade, but all were in incredibly good condition and many would be considered retro chic. Consignment shops in the city would certainly purchase them and if not, a deserving soul could have a new, albeit retro, wardrobe. As each tub was opened before the items were once again carefully refolded and packed away, the room yielded a fashion history of the family's life. Abby had always been particular about her clothes. Expensive but well made to last a lifetime was the motto she had lived by and knowing how Nan and Pops had struggled to support their growing family during lean years, that motto stood the test of time and set a great standard. Now they might well last another generation.

The next storage room contained similar tubs filled with the memories of children; board games, drawings and programs from school events and letters written from summer camp by both children and grandchildren along with thousands of photographs all carefully categorized in albums labeled with each child or grandchild's name. Pulling up a tub to sit on, Krista slowly paged through each album seeing hundreds of photos for the first time; smiling more than she thought possible knowing the task at hand, but wishing so much her Nan had been there to explain what was happening in each photo.

For hours she sat in what she now thought of as the "memento" room, paging through the albums before carefully placing them in boxes for distribution to the appropriate family member. More than just mere photographs, they were memories of times gone by and laughter shared between loved ones that shouldn't just sit in a box. With the sun having set, the shadows in the basement had taken on an ominous feel as Krista reached for one last album to page through before heading home. Turning it over she was surprised that unlike all the others, there was no name on the cover. But that wasn't the only difference. Unlike the others, which seemed fairly new and untouched, the edges of this album were faded and worn, like someone had gone through it hundreds of times.

Opening it carefully lest one of the pages crammed with photos were to fall out, she discovered a series of pictures, many with a lake in the background, and all featuring a very young Nan. Nan fishing, Nan cooking over an open fire, Nan hanging laundry on a clothes line while waving at the camera, Nan swimming in a lake. There were no dates on any of these photos, but judging from the cars in the photo and Nan herself, they appeared to start out in the 1960's. Obviously Nan and Pops had spent time at a lake on their vacations, but why were there only photos of Nan? Was Pops the photographer? It was a running joke in the family Pops never liked having his photo taken. Apparently his aversion went pretty far back.

Carefully studying the photos Krista was struck by how intensely happy her Nan looked even as she aged in the photos. Flipping through the album the progression of age was slight, but her smile and happiness was apparent in every one.

But something was off. It took some time, but upon careful examination she figured it out. Nan's ever present locket was missing. Fascinated as a child by the tiny picture of her Pops in his military uniform, Krista spent hours on Nan's lap begging to see the inside of the locket which her grandmother always seemed to caress when in deep thought. Did she take it off at the lake to keep it safe? At some point in the future, if her mother was in an amiable enough mood, she would ask her about the photos. Carrying the boxes of albums upstairs to distribute to family members in the coming days, she made one final trip to the basement to collect the unusual album and turn off the lights before heading home.

· · ·

Over the next many days, every inch of the basement was gone through. Working from sunrise to sunset each day, Krista's only breaks came when she delivered the albums and other things of note to her cousins and aunts and uncles. Item's to be given to her own mother had begun to accumulate in Nan's garage as Deborah had consistently been unwilling to meet to look at things; her petty squabble with Abby continuing even after she was gone.

"Just what should I do with Mom's things?" Krista asked her father. Deborah's resentment of her daughter for the provision in the will had continued and the two were barely speaking. It seemed safer to have the conversation with her father at the local coffee shop.

"I'd love to pick them up, but the mood your mother's been in lately I think it's safer if you just leave them at Abby's house for now. If she discovered them at our house I'm afraid she'd just toss it all out and regret it later when she calms down."

"Do you really think that's going to happen?"

"Tossing it all out?"

"No, I mean will Mom ever calm down? After all these years you must have some inkling of what went so wrong between her and Nan. What could be so bad that it continues even after Nan is gone?"

"Believe me honey, I wish I knew, but I learned years ago that the easiest way to start a fight with your mother was to bring it up. Finally I just gave up and for you and I at least, life was a whole less stressful. I'm hoping that whatever you find in the house will put an end to it."

"Why would that be?"

"Honestly I have no clue, but I'm tired of your mother being angry all the time. If she could just let this all go she might actually enjoy her life."

"I wouldn't count on that, but at least things are going smoothly at the house."

"Have you discovered any deep dark secrets yet?"

"Nothing close to a secret. Everything I've found so far, with maybe one exception, has been pretty routine. Nan was a pretty good pack rat, even if she was an exceptionally organized one."

"What was the exception?"

"It's probably nothing, but Nan had a ton of photo albums, all very carefully organized starting from the earliest year to the present. There were albums for each of us with our name on the front. The pictures were all labeled with the date or year taken and names of who was in the photo, but there was one album that was different. No name, none of the photos were labeled and all were pictures of Nan from I think vacations she and Pop took at the lake. There was no one else in any photo."

"Maybe she ran out of time to complete it," he suggested.

"I don't think so. This album seems to be much older than the rest. It certainly looked well worn. I was thinking I would ask Uncle Matt if he knew anything about it. I'd ask Mom if I didn't think it would end up in another argument."

"Don't give up on your mom, sweetheart. After all these years of being angry, I'm not sure your mom can just let go of those feelings, but I'm hopeful that at some point she'll figure out that whatever she's angry about no longer matters and then maybe we can all find some peace. Just remember, as much as you two butt heads, she loves you more than anything."

Krista had been their miracle baby after years and years of trying for a child only to be told they would never conceive. Her arrival was joyous news to her parents and Deborah had doted on her daughter from the moment of her birth. But, much like Deborah and her own mother, things had soured in the last few years and neither seemed to be able to find their way back to the close relationship they used to enjoy.

"I know you're right, but for now at least, it's easier to avoid her."

"Why don't you come over for Sunday dinner?" he asked. "I know she's dying for an update on the house but she's too stubborn to ask."

"Okay," Krista agreed hesitantly, "But if it all blows up, it's your fault!"

"Great, now I better get back to work. Some of us don't have the summer off," he teased before kissing his daughter on the forehead and throwing a few bills on the table.

"See you Sunday Dad and thank you for the talk."

"Any time sweetheart."

•　　•　　•

Starting on the main floor of the house the working conditions were about the only thing that was better. Unlike the basement, where everything was neatly packed away in tubs, the main floor where Abby spent the majority of her time was much less so. Here things were for daily living and everything needed to be carefully packed away and labeled for its eventual destination. Krista spent the first day going from store to store begging for cardboard boxes and hitting up neighbors for old newspapers to use as packing materials. With stacks of the materials on hand, it finally was time to dig into the eclectic collection of household items garnered over almost six decades of marriage.

If the basement had served as a reminder of time past, the main floor was a never ending reminder of present day. The numerous knick-knacks and kitchen goods and hundreds of well read books had all been part of Abby's every-day life. Everything on the main floor had been touched at least once a week and Krista had only to close her eyes to picture her grandmother with any number of objects. It was here on this floor where Nan came back to life and in many respects that made the work harder. Thinking her grieving process well past, she was surprised when tears came as easily as the day of Abby's death making the work more challenging at least from an emotional level, especially in Nan's bedroom.

Neat and tidy, just as the rest of the house, Krista remembered the hours she had spent in the room as a child; playing dress up in Nan's clothing, trying on different pieces of jewelry and, when she could get away with it, trying out Nan's latest shade of lipstick. She packed the items with loving care knowing a large percentage of what she was placing in each box would be cherished by the other grandchildren as well as herself. By the time she got to the closet she had steeled herself to pack away the most personal of all Nan's things. Pulling each garment out of the closet she held it out in front of her while visions of Nan in each piece filled her mind. Abby had always taken extra care with her clothing and it was rare when she bought a new dress so it was surprising when Krista discovered just that. Tucked in the far corner of the closet, still in the garment bag, was a new dress; but it wasn't just any old dress.

Unzipping the bag, the extraordinary beauty of the garment was revealed. This was a special occasion dress, in the softest and loveliest shade of dove grey, accentuated with what appeared to be hand stitched crystals at the hem and collar. Laying the dress carefully on the bed, Krista stared at it wondering why it remained in the closet. Surely if

Nan had something this special, not to mention this expensive, she would have worn it the night of her party, so what was it for? It seemed such a waste to pack the dress away but Krista put it once more in the garment bag and left it hanging in the closet. Maybe one of Nan's lady friends could provide insight about the dress but that would be something to deal with later.

•   •   •

Every now and then Krista's work was interrupted by the ring of the doorbell or the shriller ring of the not yet disconnected phone. Neighbors, noticing lights on in the house or Krista coming and going as she carried boxes to the detached garage, occasionally stopped by with offers of assistance or to share yet another story about Nan. By now the gossips in town had gotten wind of the reason Krista worked alone in the house and everyone wanted to know how it was going. Occasional disruptions were fine, but as the week's continued with no sign of whatever her grandmother expected her to find, Krista was growing more anxious each time she picked something up and she just wanted to get on with it.

She wasn't the only curious one however. Since starting to go through Nan's things, she had become the most popular member of the family. Aunts, uncles and even cousins called on a fairly regular basis wondering how things were going; disappointed to discover that she had no news to share. The only one who wasn't calling was her own mother, but Sunday dinner was sure to change all that and Krista wasn't sure she was ready to face her mother after weeks of silence between them. When the day finally came she nearly cancelled, but out of respect for her father and his attempts to broker a truce between the women in his life, she made her appearance at the appointed time.

Walking in the house without the formality of knocking, she headed straight to the kitchen at the back of the house where her mother, still dressed in her church clothes, stirred a pot at the stove. With her back to the doorway Deborah was unaware of her daughter's presence and Krista did nothing to change that. As a now young adult on her own, Sunday dinners had become a rare event in Krista's life and watching her mother she realized how much she had missed her as a wave of love for her mom washed over her. Steven had been right . . . the two women loved each other very much even though they couldn't see past the angry words that were all too often exchanged between them these days.

As Krista watched, Deborah began to sing quietly as she worked. She had always had a beautiful voice, but had never had the temperament for singing in public much to the chagrin of the church choir director who could have used her deep rich voice to bolster up the alto section. Many times Krista had walked in on her mother singing only to have her immediately stop in embarrassment and no amount of cajoling could get her to willingly start again. Recognizing the rare treat for what it was, Krista stood transfixed as her mother finished the hymn.

"That was lovely Mom," she said quietly so as not to startle her.

"Oh Krista, you're here. Why didn't you say something?" Deborah asked.

"You know why. If I had you would have stopped singing and I wanted to hear it."

"Don't be silly. Have you said hello to your father yet? He was out back in the garden last I saw him."

"I will in a bit, but I wanted to talk to you first if that's okay."

"If it's about your grandmother and her things I don't want to hear it," Deborah told her. The tender moment listening to her mother singing disappeared in a flash; replaced by the biting responses that were becoming more commonplace between them when discussing Abby.

"That's not it. It's been so long since we talked I was going to ask how you are."

"I'm sure your father has filled you in."

"Mom, I'm just trying to say I miss you. I know things have been a little tense between us, but you're still my mom and I love you. That's all," Krista said dejectedly.

Even something as simple as asking after her mother's well-being was becoming more effort than it was worth. For a brief moment Krista thought about walking out, but deep down she didn't want to give up on her.

"Can I help with something?" she finally asked when her mother turned away from her and continued with the meal preparation.

"Dinner's nearly ready, but if you'd like to set the table that would be helpful. You know where everything is."

"Would you like to use the china?" Sunday dinners had always been formal affairs for the family and the question was unnecessary, but there was a method to Krista's asking. It was a surefire way to get her mother to talk to her.

"Of course. Did you know that your dad got me that china when he was in Navy? He brought it all the way from Japan without breaking one single piece."

"Really?" Krista asked. She had heard the story a dozen times already but wanted to keep her mother engaged in the conversation. "Was that before or after you were married?"

With a safe subject to discuss, mother and daughter continued their banter until Steven came back in the house to discover a smile on his wife's face for the first time in weeks and prompting a whispered "thank you" to his daughter. On a solid and congenial footing for the first time in weeks, dinner was pleasant enough almost to the end.

"So Mom, I don't know if you've heard, but I have been delivering boxes of things to the family from Nan's house . . . things I think they would like. I've accumulated quite a stack of boxes for you also."

The change in her mother was instantaneous. Gone was the smile replaced with a frown and angry eyes.

"I told you I didn't want to talk about it," Deborah snapped.

"But Mom, I . . . ."

"No means no Krista and you of all people should realize that. I want none of Mother's things. Now if you'll excuse me I have a headache and I'm going to lie down."

Pushing herself away from the table with such force she tipped over a water glass, Deborah stormed out of the dining room before slamming her bedroom door with such force the pictures on the wall rattled.

Father and daughter looked at each other in resignation.

"I'm sorry Krista, but I told you it was too soon," Steven said.

"No, I'm the one who should be apologizing Dad. We had been getting along so well and for a moment it felt like Mom was back again. God how I miss having a mother who laughs and smiles."

With a wry smile Steven admitted his own regrets. "I probably shouldn't share this with you, but it's getting harder and harder to live with your mother. It's a lot of strain to be with someone who is so unhappy."

"Are you saying you and Mom might get divorced?" Krista asked with tears in her eyes. The thought that questioning her mother during lunch might be pushing her father into such an action was heart wrenching.

"Hey, don't cry my darling," Steve said as he took Krista's hand in his own. "I'm just thinking out loud and whatever happens between your mother and me isn't your fault. At some point though your mother is going to have to start considering what her anger is doing to you and I. If she can't do that, then I might have no choice but to leave. After all these years of marriage though, it won't be something I do on a whim so don't spend your time worrying about it. Since it looks like your mother won't be coming back to join us, what don't you help me clean up?"

Chapter Four

Back at Abby's house after the disappointing dinner with her parents, an unexpected knock on the door the next afternoon came as a welcome relief for Krista after one very long day.

"Oh Alex, hello," Krista said as she opened the door to find a familiar face.

Unlike his previous visit to the home, Officer McMillan was dressed as casually as Krista albeit with much less dirt covering him. Alex was a childhood friend and opening the door to see his friendly face was a pleasant diversion.

"Hi Krista. Long time no see," he told her with a smile. "I hope I'm not interrupting."

"Actually it's a welcome break. I've been digging through Nan's stuff for weeks now and today is turning into a particularly emotional one. Everything I start to pack is bringing back memories. But how can I help?"

"Actually I was wondering if I can be of any help to you. It's no secret in town you've been going through Abby's things on your own, but could you use some help from a friend? It's a lot of work for one person and I've seen the lights on well after dark each night when I'm on patrol."

His offer was not entirely unexpected. Both single, Alex had always had a difficult time hiding his interest in Krista since she moved back home after college. But dating a cop and having to worry about his safety wasn't something Krista was interested in leaving her to downplay her own interest in him rather than start something with the man even as her Nan had tried everything under the sun to push the two of them together. Nan had tried to play matchmaker between the two ever since Krista graduated from college and yet neither of them ever admitted they knew what she was doing.

"Uncle Kevin did say I could hire people to help as long as they aren't family, but I was trying to stay true to Nan's wishes," she said hesitantly. "Why don't you come in for a drink while I think about it?" Opening the door wider to allow him to pass, the pair walked into the kitchen.

"What would you like? Coffee, tea, a beer?"

"I'd settle for lemonade if you have some," Alex said with a smile as he took a seat at the well-worn kitchen table and Krista opened the fridge to pull out an ice cold pitcher of lemonade. "Boy not much has changed in this house over the years has it?" he said as he looked around the as yet untouched kitchen. "I remember your grandma inviting me in for lemonade on hot summer days when I was delivering the afternoon paper. She always had some fresh baked cookies for me. Those were the best cookies ever and I sure missed them when she closed the restaurant."

"I know what you mean," Krista told him as she took a seat across the table. "Nan's baking was pretty legendary. Too bad that gene didn't get passed down to me."

"Really? That's not what Steve tells me. He said you're an excellent cook."

Krista raised an eyebrow at his comment.

"My dad? You had a conversation with Dad about my cooking?"

"Well not specifically about that, but it's come up. We have breakfast at the diner each morning and talk about a lot of stuff."

Her father had a long-time habit of going to the local diner each morning for breakfast. Deborah had always liked to sleep in and when it came to cooking breakfast for himself or finding a professional to do it for him, Steve opted for the latter.

"So it's just the two of you?" Krista asked wondering if this was Alex's way of getting closer to her.

"No, there's a whole group of guys who meet every morning...well not on Sunday obviously, but pretty regularly. I'm actually the youngest in the group and was surprised when they invited me to join them. Anyway, how's it been going here?"

"At first it was kind of exciting . . . finding all sorts of cool things in the basement I didn't know Nan had, but when I got to this floor it's been hard emotionally. And on this level, everything has to be packed carefully away and boxes labeled with what's inside. The basement rooms were all neatly packed already. It must have taken Nan months to do."

"Why do you think she wanted you to be the one to do this? Was it because you two were so close?"

"I suppose, but it was interesting how she said it in the will . . . "*In this house you will discover the story of my life and the love we shared*'. To me that sounds like there is some big surprise that I'm supposed to discover and other than a few unexpected things, I've found nothing."

"What kind of unexpected things?"

"There really was only one, but I've been thinking about it ever since I found it. I'll be right back."

Rising from the table, Krista went to the pile of boxes near the front door where she had placed the photo album before placing it on the kitchen table in front of her.

"Nan had dozens of photo albums in the basement, all carefully labeled with a family member's name and the dates and who was in each of the photos, but this one was different. See for yourself."

Turning the book towards Alex, she crossed her arms and sat back in her chair as he carefully began opening the overflowing album. Turning page after page, he said nothing until he was half-way through the album.

"I don't get it," he told Krista. "It's an album. What's so strange about it?'

"Okay...first of all, there is no name on the cover and none of the photos have dates or even any clue to where they were taken. And look how worn the cover and the pages are. It's like someone was constantly going through the album while all of the other's looked brand new."

"Maybe she didn't have time to finish this one. And since she seems to be the only one in the photos, she probably knew exactly when and where they were taken."

"But why are there no pictures of Pops? You'd think that she would have taken at least one picture of him on these vacations. I don't really remember them going to a resort on a lake, at least not since I was alive, so where was this? If you look at the photos carefully it looks like the same place over and over. And here's another thing . . . Nan's locket is missing in every single photo. She never took it off, but it's not there and I've looked through the album a dozen times already myself."

Taking a more careful look this time, Alex once again went through the album, trying to find what was so confusing for his friend.

"You're right, there are no pictures with the locket, but maybe Abby didn't want to risk having it fall off at the lake," he admitted.

"I already thought of that, but it just doesn't make sense to me. Dad suggested I ask Mom about it, and I tried to yesterday at Sunday dinner, but she stormed out of the room. Trying to get any kind of an answer from her is hopeless."

"Maybe your aunts and uncles could help?" he suggested as he continued to page through the album.

"That's my next step. And by the way, the answer is yes."

Stopping what he was doing, he looked at her in confusion. "I'm sorry?"

"Yes, I would love your help with the house . . . that is if you can spare the time," she told him.

"I have ten days off before my next shift. If we're not done by then I'll have to go back to work, but until then I'm all yours. What would you like me to do first?"

"You can say no if you want, but I need a break from all this. Would you like to go the movies with me tonight? It would be on me as a way of saying thanks for all the hard work I'm going to put on you in the next few days."

The unexpected offer came as a surprise to Alex, but the smile on his face was the only answer Krista needed.

"I'd love that," he said softly.

"Terrific, but I need to get cleaned up first. Could you pick me up at my house in an hour?"

"It's a date."

Getting ready for her outing with Alex, still not comfortable calling it a date but warming to the idea of going out with him, Krista wondered if that was Nan's intention with having her clean out the house. Alex had been such a help to her grandmother when she was alive, she probably knew he would offer to help Krista in her duties. Was it possible bringing the two of them together was the "secret" Nan was hiding? But it didn't seem to fit with the message in the will. "*In this house you will discover the story of my life and the love we shared.*" The phrase reverberated in her head. No, it definitely was a secret about Nan and Pops and the next few weeks should finally bring it to light.

•　　　•　　　•

"Krista did you want this entire box as donations?" Alex asked as he struggled to affix packing tape on an overly full box.

They had been working on the last room of the main floor all day and were hoping to finish the kitchen before midnight. Since their movie date a few nights back, they had spent most of each day together and Krista discovered that even after a long hard day going through her Nan's things, there was a smile on her face that hadn't been there before Alex started helping. Not quite ready to admit that her Nan might have known a good relationship when she tried to create it, Krista was still happier than she had been in months and it was all down to Alex.

Having him around had eased the emotional strain of going through Nan's things and it was easy to see he would be a pleasant companion in the best of times and an emotional rock in the not so good. Each time Krista had begun to get weepy about a new discovery, he was quick with another story about Abby that lifted her spirits and because of it, their work was going smoothly.

"I think so, unless there's something in there you need?" Krista answered with a smile. "I know how you like all those kitchen gadgets Nan was so fond of."

"Now I know you're teasing me," he said with a laugh. "Most of the stuff in here looks like utensils of torture instead of something to cook with. But are you sure no one in the family would like them? I'm willing to bet some of this stuff is from the restaurant."

Nan had been the sole owner of "Abigail's" restaurant for nearly fifty years before she retired and the establishment was razed to the ground. In the end, real estate located near a state highway was much more valuable than the actual business even if a buyer could have been found for the restaurant. It was a bittersweet day for the Ward family when they gathered to watch the demolition and say their good-byes. The business that had supported them all during the recession years and the lean years when Robert went for months without a job, was missed by not only the family, but everyone in town as well.

"Even if it is," Krista told him, "it's mostly junk. Everyone in the family had a chance to take a piece of the restaurant before it was demolished so I think we're safe in donating it."

"I never asked," Alex said as he taped up the box, "but what did you take?"

"Nothing of value, at least not monetary value. I got Nan's recipe box. Inside are fifty years' worth of recipes and memories from the restaurant all wrapped up in one small metal box."

"Didn't you tell me once that Abby didn't use recipes?" he asked in surprise.

"Technically she didn't…everything was in her head long before I was born, but when she first started she collected recipes like some people collect figurines. Every time she ate something extraordinary she begged the restaurant or the cook for the recipe and then tweaked it just enough to make it her own. After making the dish for so many years, she knew the recipe by heart. I think she always hoped that one of us grandchildren would continue with the restaurant, but as much as it was part of our family, we all had other goals in life. She never said so, but I think it broke her heart a little."

"I can see that, but it was pretty easy to see she was proud of each of you even if you didn't follow her into the business. She bragged on you a lot. She was definitely one proud grandmother."

Without actually saying anything Krista's warm smile as she thought of her grandmother indicated her agreement with Alex' assessment.

"Hey isn't that Abby's cell phone?" Alex asked as he picked up the phone from the counter.

"Oh yeah, I was going to take that home and try and find a charger that works. I want to make sure there weren't any messages from old friends who might not know she passed away. I suppose I'll have to remember to cancel the account before long. Just put it by my keys if you would please. It looks like that's the last of the boxes for this floor. Let's go upstairs and see what's what before tomorrow morning."

"Sure."

It was a relief to have the main floor of the house completed, but the upstairs should be easier. None of the upper bedrooms had been used for a very long time and the work was sure to go quicker. As they opened closets and drawers they realized the entire floor could probably be completed in just a day or so and after a long day finishing up the kitchen, they agreed to start a little later the next morning.

"I think I'll join the guys for breakfast then," Alex said. "Why don't you come too?"

"And be the only female in your men's club? I think I'll pass," Krista said with a laugh as they both made their way downstairs. "Enjoy yourself and tell Dad I said hi. If you want to give him an update on our progress I'm okay with that too. I'm going to take another look through that old photo album, but I'll see you tomorrow morning. Thanks for your help today."

"See you tomorrow," Alex said before unexpectedly landing a kiss on her cheek that surprisingly seemed natural to them both. It was the first of that type of physical contact between them and while a faint pink stain appeared on Krista's face, she smiled back at him before he left.

"Oh Nan, what have you gotten me into?" she said looking skyward before once again reaching for the album and settling into a comfortable chair.

Opening the album, she gazed sadly at the first photo of her very young and very beautiful grandmother before running the tip of her finger over the page. Lately it seemed snatches of loneliness for Nan would come over her at the most unexpected times and the feeling of missing her was stronger than ever. This time, like others before it, she felt truly blessed to have time alone in the house to say goodbye. Unlike the rest of the family, Abby and Krista had seen each other nearly every day and now that she was gone, the grief was as potent as it had been the day Krista found her lifeless body.

Paging through the album, the loneliness was slowly replaced with a growing curiosity about the as yet still undiscovered secret hidden somewhere in the house. She was half-way through her task and had found nothing concrete that would justify the work she was doing. Was it possible she had missed something?

"Oh Nan, what was going through that beautiful head of yours when you changed the will?" Krista wondered aloud in the empty room. Half expecting some kind of answer and disappointed when there was nothing, she closed the album before heading for home.

•　　　•　　　•

Krista's assessment of the upper floor of the house was spot on and within two days, everything had been gone through with boxes distributed to family and Goodwill, leaving nothing but furniture in each of the four bedrooms.

"One floor left," Alex pointed out as they stood in front of the door leading to the attic. "I've always loved poking around other people's attics. You never know what kind of treasures they hold. Should we go up?"

"Do you realize what's behind that door?" Krista asked as she stared straight ahead.

"What do you mean?"

"Whatever it is that Nan wanted me to find has to be up there somewhere. We've been through the rest of the house and found nothing. That means it's up there somewhere. I don't mind telling you I'm a little nervous about what we'll find."

"Are you expecting something bad?" he asked before moving just a bit closer to her as if to protect her from something.

"Certainly not. How could Nan have anything bad in her past? It's a nervous excitement . . . like being unable to sleep on Christmas Eve because you're excited about what's waiting under the tree. Before we go up, there's something I need to tell you."

Turning to look at Alex, Krista took his hand in hers and looked deep into his eyes. "Thank you."

"For what?" he asked.

"Thank you for being part of this with me. I couldn't imagine going through this with anyone but you and I just wanted you to know is all. Whatever we find up there will mean even more to me because I shared it with you."

"You know when all this is over I hope you and I can go out every once in a while," he said shyly.

"I wouldn't have it any other way," Krista said with a warm smile. In that moment, they both knew Nan had succeeded in bringing them together even if she wasn't alive to see it. "Here goes nothing."

Hand in hand, they made their way up the rickety attic stairs and looked around at six decades worth of clutter. The two small windows at either end of the space did little to illuminate the many nooks and crannies all filled to the brim with long forgotten items. Dust and cobwebs covered every space making it hard to breathe as Krista felt along the wall looking for the light switch and a dim light that barely penetrated the gloom came on.

"I think I can prop those windows open to get some fresh air in here," Alex said before making his way to one end of the space.

"Nan would never let us up here and I'm shocked to find everything in this condition," Krista said as she continued to wander around being careful not to touch anything. "She always told us that it was too dangerous up here and now I see why. Some of this stuff looks like it hasn't been touched in decades."

Indeed most of the items that were visible seemed to belong in a museum and not a private home. It would take weeks to go through everything and the only thing that prevented Krista from throwing in the towel and hiring someone to haul it all away was the promise of finding her Nan's hidden secret.

The fresh air cutting through the mustiness as Alex opened the window did little more than create a cloud of dust and the window was quickly closed again. It was going to be a rough few days.

"I don't know what you think Krista, but there's so much stuff up here we should probably start closest to the stairs and as we go through things, take it down right away to give us more room to work. Eventually it will all need to come out anyway."

"That's a great idea," Krista told him before they got started.

Being careful not to dislodge the piles of treasures, each of them pulled out a box from the fringes of the piles.

"It's kind of like a giant Jenga game," Krista said with a laugh. "If we pull out the wrong piece, the whole thing is going to come crashing down on top of us and they won't find our bodies until next spring!"

"Do you think all this really was your grandparent's stuff?" Alex asked. "Maybe the attic was full before they even bought the house."

"I'm not sure. Some of this looks familiar to me, but most of it just looks like junk."

It didn't take long to discover that the amount of dust covering every square inch of the attic and its contents was easily disturbed making it hard to talk and even harder to breathe sending Alex to the local hardware store to pick up masks and gloves before the work continued. In such cramped quarters the work was hard, dirty and tiring and with only a quick stop for lunch, they had barely made a dent in the space by the time the sun went down and they gratefully made their way downstairs.

"I was going to suggest we go out for a nice dinner tonight," Alex said, "but I'm embarrassed to say I am wiped out after today."

Chuckling as she looked at the dirt mixed with sweat on his face, Krista couldn't argue the fact for she was equally exhausted.

"Maybe I should have started from top to bottom," she said as she grabbed clean dish towels so they could wipe their faces. "You only have a couple of days before going back to work and then I'm on my own again. I'm not looking forward to that."

"So, you'll miss me?" Alex asked with a wink of his eye.

"Of course I will. You're great company and a hard worker. I just hope we find Nan's secret before you have to go back to work."

"If it's hidden somewhere up in that attic she must have really wanted it to remain hidden, but now that I'm so invested in the whole thing I hope I'm around when you find it too. Do you want a ride home? You look like you're asleep on your feet."

"Thanks for the offer, but I think the walk and some fresh air will do me good after the day we've had. See you tomorrow?"

"It's a date."

Chapter Five

Even with both Alex and Krista working hard the next two days, they still hadn't found Abby's secret and a disappointed Alex was back on patrol leaving Krista to continue the quest on her own. Without the extra pair of hands, work was slower than ever and it was another week before the first half of the attic was cleaned out. Much of what they discovered, including an ancient baby stroller, some old pieces of furniture, paintings and light fixtures, had been hauled down to the garage and folks from the local historical society had finally arrived to look them over. From the smiles on the faces of the historians, it was easy to tell they felt they were looking at the motherlode.

"I should have more for you to look at in a couple of weeks, but this is all I've been able to go through so far," Krista told them as she shook hands with the group and they began to load the materials in a large trailer.

"Even when she's gone, your grandmother continues to do good," one of the women said with a wide smile. "She was a lovely woman and you have our condolences."

"Thank you," Krista said with tears in her eyes. "I'll give you a call in a few weeks when I've gone through the rest and I look forward to seeing Nan's things in an exhibit."

As the group pulled away from the curb, Krista nearly jumped out of her skin when a police siren sounded right behind her. It was Alex back on duty in his patrol car and she smiled at him even as she wagged her finger at him for scaring her.

"You almost gave me a heart attack", she said as she leaned in the driver's window.

"Sorry about that," he told her even though he looked anything but sorry. "It's a little police joke. I saw all the stuff in the trailer. Does that mean you've finished the attic without me?"

"Heavens no. Without you things are going even slower. I'm about half-way through but at least now I have room to move around."

"Any sign of Abby's big dark secret?"

"No," she said with disappointment. "I'm beginning to think it wasn't her secret."

"What does that mean?"

"I think you know as well as I do that Nan spent years trying to get you and I together and now that it looks like she might have succeeded, maybe that was her point."

"But she couldn't have known I would show up to help right?"

"Well not for sure, but she knows how helpful you have always been and I'm sure she expected you to offer your help."

"So I wasn't as smooth as I like to think in hiding my feelings for you huh?" he said with a laugh. Now that their mutual attraction was out in the open, there didn't seem to be any reason to be coy anymore.

"You were about as subtle as a bulldozer my friend. I think I was way more discreet."

"Discreet?" he said with a laugh. "You came right out and said you would never date a cop. So what changed your mind?"

"It was Nan actually. After she passed and all the stories were told about how much she meant to people, I knew that I wanted someone to feel that way about me and you were the only person that came to mind. Still I might not have acted on it if you hadn't shown up at the door that day. And we have Nan to thank," Krista told him before leaning in and giving him a kiss not caring who might be watching. "I think she'd get a kick out of the fact that after all this time, we have admitted our feelings to each other at the side of the road. None of that romance nonsense for her."

"Maybe not for her, but I'm a romantic kind of guy. What do you say I take you out for a fancy dinner and champagne tonight…maybe a little dancing?"

"I'd love that. Pick me up at seven?"

"Okay," he said before his radio crackled with a call. "Better go, see you tonight."

As Krista stepped back, the patrol car sped away with lights and siren blaring. Resigned to the need to once again enter the sweltering hot attic, Krista grabbed a cold glass of water and headed back upstairs determined to make headway before the day was done.

It was several hours later when the box caught her eye.

•   •   •

There was nothing special about it, but there was something different. Unlike all the other items in the attic, this box was almost clean, as if it had recently been handled. Looking down at the floor Krista also noticed a pair of footsteps easily visible in the dust. Too small to belong to her or Alex it was obvious that at some time in the recent past, someone, her Nan most likely, had been in the attic standing in nearly the same spot. But why? With so many other things up here, why would anyone be standing here? She hadn't noticed footsteps before but maybe she and Alex had walked over them in their earlier exploration of the attic space. And the box . . . why was it relatively clean when everything around it was covered in dust? Was this Nan's secret?

Excitement began to build in her and with shaking hands she carefully reached for the box pulling it slowly from the pile until the full beauty of the deep mahogany wood shone back at her. Running her hands carefully over the surface, she marveled at the deep shine and the rich luster of the wood grain of the oblong box. Heavier than it looked, the box was approximately a foot long and half that wide but almost a foot deep. Placing it carefully on top of an unopened box, she took a deep breath before opening the clasp to lift the heavy lid.

Gasping in surprise, her hands flew to her mouth. There, nestled in a bed of royal blue velvet, lay a golden Oscar, the coveted statue synonymous with the movies. The gold surface captured the faint light coming in through the window creating a brilliant juxtaposition to the grey dirt and grime everywhere else in the attic. Afraid to touch the statue itself, she could only stare in surprise. Could it possibly be real and if so, where did it come from? But more importantly, what was it doing here of all places? There was nothing to indicate who it belonged to and only the year 1962 was engraved on the plaque at the bottom. Krista immediately suspected it was a fake. Oscar winners didn't just forget they had one and no one in their right mind would have hidden away a real Oscar in the attic for who knows how long.

An unexpected surprise, but if Nan had been the recipient of an Oscar, surely someone in the family would have known about it. And if not, why would she ever have kept such a secret? Thinking back to the words in Nan's will, doubt that this was the secret began to creep into Krista's mind. *"In this house you will discover the story of my life and the love we shared."* Had Nan been an actress? Was it a love of acting that she shared? That couldn't be it. As exciting as finding the statue was, it just didn't fit with what she had said. There had to be more to this story.

"Hey Krista are you up there?"

Hearing Alex's voice Krista cast a quick glance at her watch and realized she was late for their dinner date.

"I'll be down in a minute," she said before carefully closing the box. Tucking it securely under her arm she made her way down the steps to the kitchen.

Seeing Alex dressed in his nicest suit, hair freshly washed and the faint fragrance of a new cologne permeating the air, the smile on her face faded away.

"Oh my god Alex, I am so sorry!" she exclaimed at the look of disappointment on his face when he realized she had forgotten.

"I thought we were going to have a special night out?" he said quietly before putting down the bouquet of flowers he had been hiding behind his back. "If you changed your mind you should have just told me."

"I didn't change my mind," Krista quickly assured him, "and I'd give you a kiss right now if I didn't think I'd ruin your suit. I'm really sorry, but time just got away from me. Wait until you see what I found."

The excitement in her statement was the only thing that wiped the disappointment from Alex's face. Noticing for the first time the box she carried under her arm, he followed her to the table.

"Is that the secret? Have you finally found it after all this time?" he asked.

"I don't know if this is what Nan was talking about, but it was one heck of a surprise nonetheless," Krista told him. Grabbing one of the few remaining dish towels in the house, she placed the box on top of it so the contents would face Alex when opened. "Maybe you should sit down for this," she suggested with a smile that stretched across her face. "It's not something you see every day."

"Stop being so mysterious and show me for Pete's sake," he encouraged.

Slowly lifting the clasp, Krista pulled the box open and waited for his reaction. She wasn't disappointed.

"Jesus, Mary and Joseph," he exclaimed before looking back at her. "Is that what I think it is?"

"I think so, but don't ask me where it came from. I think we're looking at a bonafide Oscar."

It was one thing to see it in the midst of the attic clutter and another to look at it in good light with a witness. Each passing moment was more exciting than the last.

"But how . . . ?" He asked looking once again at the golden statue.

"I don't know! Everything you're asking yourself right now I've been asking myself for the last hour or so. That's why I was late. I couldn't believe what I was seeing. Can you tell if it's real?"

Carefully picking up the box he turned it every way possible. "It's pretty heavy, but I have no idea if it's real or not. Was Abby an actress or something?"

"No, that's the thing. If she was, someone in the family would certainly have known about it especially if she won an Academy Award. That's just not something people keep a secret. So if it wasn't hers who does it belong to?"

"There's got to be some way to trace it," he said. It was easy to see the excitement building in him also. "Maybe there's a BOLO out for it."

"A BOLO? What's that?"

"Oh sorry, it means 'be on the lookout'. I don't want to speak ill of the dead, but maybe it's stolen."

"Seriously? Can you imagine Nan harboring stolen property in her attic? There has to be another explanation."

"Well as exciting as your discovery is, I doubt we'll figure it out tonight. Unfortunately, I think we've blown well past our reservations, but if you're hungry we can settle for pizza if you'd like."

"Sure, but obviously I'll need to get cleaned up first. What should I do with this though? Now that we've found it, just leaving it here doesn't seem like such a good idea."

"If you trust me, I could put it in my gun safe at home while you're getting cleaned up. The safe's too large for a thief to carry away and if the department thinks it's secure enough for my guns, I think it should be safe enough for this guy."

"Of course I trust you and your safe sounds perfect, but one thing before we go . . . " she said with sudden seriousness. "I want to keep this between you and me for now. Can you imagine the stories this might start in the family, not to mention the rest of town?"

"It will be our little secret," he told her with a smile. "Now go change and I'll pick you up at your house in say forty-five minutes? You kept me waiting so long I'm starving!"

"Let's say half an hour," she told him before carefully planting a quick kiss on his cheek and checking to make sure she didn't get him all dirty.

●   ●   ●

Having agreed to keep it a secret, the excitement over their find was still too enticing to ignore and they spent the rest of the evening discussing it while being careful to change the subject when others were close by.

"Did you notice the dried flower petals tucked in by the statue?"

"Is that what that was?" Krista asked as she wiped pizza sauce from her mouth. "I wasn't sure if it was dirt or what. Maybe Oscar winners back then were given a bouquet of flowers too."

"What do you mean...back then?" he asked.

"Didn't you notice the plaque on the bottom? It had the year 1962 engraved on it. Why do you suppose if they went to the trouble to engrave that, it didn't say who the Oscar was given to and what the category was?"

"Maybe it hadn't been awarded. Maybe it was stolen before the telecast and that's why it was hidden away."

"Are you saying that Nan and Pops were thieves?" she asked in surprise.

"No, I'm not," he said hastily. "We don't even know if everything up there was theirs or if it came with the house. You said you found it at the back of the attic so it could have been tucked away there decades ago."

"But what I didn't tell you is that when I first spotted the box, it was almost clean; certainly not covered in the thick layer of dust everything else up there was. Someone, Nan I suppose, had obviously been up there and handled the box recently. And there were small footprints in the area that were probably Nan's."

"Well this just gets more interesting as it goes. So let's look at what we know . . . Abby had a secret she expected you to find; you've been through almost the whole house and other than the album, this is the only thing that stands out."

"Except that I'm not done yet. I have about a third of the attic left to go through."

"Except for that. But then there's the fact that someone, for now we'll assume it was Abby, had recently been up in the attic in the same general area of the box."

"Not just the general area, but right there in front of it."

"Noted. So where does that leave us?"

Having asked the question Krista was expecting an answer from Alex, but he said nothing as he drummed his fingers on the table with a frown on his face.

"Well?" she finally asked.

"I got nothing," he admitted. "Right now there is nothing concrete. It may be real or maybe it's fake. Or maybe it's stolen. We just don't know enough, but there has to be some way to trace these things and tomorrow I'll spend a little time researching that very thing."

"Can't we start tonight?" Krista asked disappointedly.

"I'd love to say yes, but I have to be on duty tomorrow at six for a twelve hour shift and I know you . . . if we get started on this you're not going to want to stop until we have an answer. I'll bring my laptop over to your house tomorrow night and we can take a crack at it okay?"

"I guess. We'll be just like Rizzoli and Isles."

"You do realize they were both women right?" Alex asked with a laugh. "And not only that, one of them was a coroner."

Laughing along with him she couldn't help but tease, "So which one do you want to be?"

"All right, I think someone has had a little too much wine and not enough sleep lately. How about I take you home?"

"Aye, aye Captain," Krista said giving him a quick salute. "But I seem to remember someone promised me dancing."

"How about a rain check?" he asked as he pulled his slightly tipsy date to her feet.

"I'm going to hold you to it and if you help me solve this mystery there might even be a bonus in it for you if you know what I mean?"

Having indeed drunk just a bit more than she should and her flirtatious manner being totally out of character, Alex knew exactly what she was suggesting, but after years of flirting with each other, when the time came to take their relationship to the bedroom, it would be something they would both want and more importantly, both remember.

•   •   •

Only the wine helped lull Krista to sleep that night. If she had been sober, her thoughts would have been consumed with the Oscar, but as it was, she slept like a baby and spent the next day working as hard as possible to put it out of her mind. Rather than disappoint Alex again, she set the alarm on her phone to remind her to finish up on time and when the knock came on her front door at around seven, it was an eager, fresh from the shower young woman who greeted Alex.

"Hey there," she said as she opened the door fully and stepped aside to let him enter. "Right on time as usual."

"You smell nice," he told her as he walked by. "It kind of reminds me of your Nan. She always wore a fragrance that smelled like that."

"That's because it's hers. I kept the bottle thinking that I would smell the perfume every now and then when I was missing her, but I decided to put some on. Glad you like it. But don't keep me in suspense, what did you find?"

"Aren't you going to feed me first?" he teased.

Turning a pleasant shade of pink Krista looked back at him in embarrassment.

"I'm sorry. Of course. Dinner's all ready," she said before turning to the kitchen as he followed.

A fragrant aroma of baked chicken permeated the room as she reached into the fridge to grab a couple of beers.

"That smells just like the chicken from Abby's restaurant," he said as he took a swig of the ice cold lager.

"It should," Krista said with a smile. "It's Nan's recipe. If I'm remembering correctly, it was what you always ordered when we were teenagers."

"I can't believe you remember that after all this time," he told her in surprise.

"It's because you always left such a big tip. We waitresses remember all the big spenders."

"Well at least you remember me for something," he said with a laugh.

By the time they had finished dinner and the kitchen was put back in order, Krista could contain her curiosity no longer.

"So what did you find?"

Laughing at her eagerness he pulled out his laptop and fired it up. "Not much. Here is the list of Oscar winners from 1962 and it's a long one. I also checked the database to see if there are any cases involving stolen Oscars, but they are all solved, which pretty much brings us right back to square one with no clue."

"But didn't I read somewhere that they made duplicates of each of the Oscars?" Krista asked. "Maybe this one is a duplicate."

"I see someone wasn't content to wait until I got here to do her own research," he teased. "I did read something about that, but that didn't start happening on a regular basis until decades later when a whole batch of them were stolen before Oscar night. Unless the plaque on this one is a misprint, I think our only option is to contact each and every one of the winners that year and see if their Oscar is missing."

"And just how should we go about doing that?"

"Well I have access to a lot of data bases, but honestly, it would be illegal of me to use them for this purpose. And even if I could, you would have to consider that maybe half of the winners from that year have passed on, gotten married, divorced, or whatever and they may not even have the same name. There's a couple of people on this list that I recognize, like the guy who won Best Actor and the guy who won Best Director, but they have to be pretty old by now."

"The guy who won Best Supporting Actor was one of Nan's favorite movie stars. We used to watch him all the time."

"Yeah, well he's probably as old as she was by now and it would be highly improbable that they knew each other."

"So are you telling me there's no way to track down the real owner?" she asked, her disappointment punctuating every word.

"It's not impossible, but the odds are probably not in our favor."

After all the excitement of finding the Oscar, the thought of never solving the mystery was more than Krista could take and tears began to well up in her eyes. When Alex noticed, he stood to put his arms around her.

"Please don't cry Krista. It was always a long shot and you had to know that."

"I know, but I've knocked myself out going through this house and to come to such a dead end is really disappointing. What could Nan have been thinking?"

"Hey wait a minute," Alex said before releasing her. "Come on, we're going to my house."

Grabbing his keys and Krista's hand, they rushed to the car.

"What's going on?" she asked in surprise as she got in beside him.

"I'll tell you when we get to my house."

Putting the car in gear, he pulled away from the curb faster than either of them expected. By the time they arrived at his house, and made their way to the basement where the gun safe was stored, they were both out of breath. Taking the box carefully from the safe, he adjusted the light on his work bench and turned to Krista.

"Something has been nagging at me ever since you showed me this. Look at how deep the box is, but yet the Oscar is much smaller. I'm willing to bet my truck that there's another compartment beneath the statue."

Reaching to lift the Oscar from its secure bed of velvet, Krista reached out a hand to stop him.

"Wait a minute; I've seen this in museums. You shouldn't touch it with your bare hands, but since we don't have any gloves, at least pick it up with a cloth or something."

"You're right," he said before using his shirt as a barrier between his hands and the statue. Carefully removing the Oscar from the box, he placed it upright nearby before ever so carefully pulling back on the blue velvet. "I think I'm right about there being more to this box…the material isn't even secured."

He was right as the velvet came easily out of the box revealing a plain wooden shelf it had been resting on. A bit more careful examination and he discovered a latch that when pressed would allow the shelf to be removed. Before he did so though, he looked at Krista.

"Looks like we're about to discover Abby's real secret," he told her. "Are you sure you're ready?"

"Just open it," she said. "The suspense is killing me."

"Here goes nothing."

With that proclamation, Alex pressed on the latch and carefully removed the wooden cover as they both peered in to see bundles of envelopes tied together with several different colored ribbons.

"Are those letters?" he asked.

"There must be hundreds of them," Krista said as she pulled one of the bundles out of the box and carefully untied the ribbon. "And they all seem to be addressed to Nan. But look at this, they were sent to a post office box but there was no return address. Nan didn't use a post office box for her mail. It comes right to the house."

"Maybe there was a reason for that," he suggested.

"Like what?" Krista asked as she turned to face him.

"Don't get upset, but in my line of work some people with post office boxes have something to hide. I'm sure that's not the case with Abby, but you never know."

"Should we read them? I'm curious of course, but it seems like such an invasion of privacy to read a private letter."

"That's up to you remember? Your Nan asked you to go through her things. Wait a minute! If all these letters are addressed to Abby, then the Oscar must be hers. Why else would they be in the same box?"

"None of this makes any sense," Krista told him as she shook her head and carefully retied the letters before placing them back in the box. "There's something not right about all of this and I think we should just put it all back and forget we saw it."

"You're not serious are you?" Alex said with more than a touch of disappointment in his tone. Like most good cops, once he got wind of a good investigation it was going to be hard to let it go.

"Yes . . . no . . . I don't know. I'm going to take the box home with me and think about it some more."

"Are you sure?"

"Yeah, I think so. I'll let you know what I decide."

"Well I guess that's it for tonight then. I'll get my keys and take you home."

"Thanks, but I think I'll walk. It'll give me time to think."

Chapter Six

If Krista thought the walk home would bring clarity about the situation, she was sadly mistaken. Instead all it did was make the dilemma harder and by the time she walked into her own house and carefully tucked the box away in the bottom of her bedroom closet, she had no more idea what to do with her discovery than she had before. Sitting on the end of the bed staring at the closet door, all she could do was shake her head in confusion.

Alex was right. Nan had obviously wanted her to find the box and everything in it or she wouldn't have changed the will, but why not just come out and tell her instead? The two were together every day with ample opportunity for Abby to share with her granddaughter, so why put her through all this?

Nerves on edge Krista found herself pacing the house until well into the wee hours of the morning; stopping every so often to stare at her favorite photo of Nan on the mantle while wavering between excitement and anger at the position her grandmother had put her in. Her imagination ran wild with the secrets the letters could contain and questions about why, after all this time, any of it was a secret. It was rare to find a handwritten letter in this day and age, but to find hundreds of decades old letters all nicely tied in bundles had to mean whomever penned the notes had been important to Nan.

It was that thought that finally prompted her to go back to the bedroom and once again remove the box from the closet. Taking a seat on the floor by her bed, she opened the box, carefully removed the Oscar and the velvet surrounding it before removing the bundles one at a time and spreading them out on the floor in front of her. The postmarks went back as far as 1960 and continued every year until one letter that was postmarked as recently as two months ago. Selecting the bundle with the oldest postmark, she estimated there were a couple dozen envelopes in the group and she finally admitted to herself that not reading them had never seriously been an option. For whatever reason, Nan had chosen her for this task and she couldn't let her down. With shaking hands, she gently pulled out the single sheet contained in the first envelope and began to read the strong masculine handwriting.

"My dearest Abby . . . it's only been a week since I last held you in my arms, but it feels as if a lifetime has passed . . . "

'Oh my God," Krista said to herself. "It's a love letter! But from who?"

Quickly turning to the back page, it was signed simply "T" and she turned back to start it over.

" . . . and I lay in bed at night wishing that you were here at my side. I miss everything about you. Your sweet smile, the way you tuck your hair behind your ear when you're stressed, the smell of your perfume and most importantly the taste of your lips on mine. Will it really be the last time we see each other? I can hardly believe so for even though we've only know each other a few short weeks you have become part of me and I will always love you and always long to have you with me. Through your kindness and love I have my life back and I will never be able to repay you for that, but I will never give up trying either. Someday we will be together my love and only then will I once again be complete. Yours always and forever . . . T"

Holding the letter tightly to her chest, tears sprang to Krista's eyes at the words of love and longing shared on the page and she tried to imagine Nan reading the letter for the first time. From the well-worn page and the tattered edges of the envelope, Nan had obviously read the letter more than once and there was no longer a doubt in Krista's mind that this was indeed the secret her Nan had meant for her to discover. The letter was dated August 12, 1960; quick calculations revealing it was well before her grandparents had been married and for that she was grateful. As her Nan had most likely done, she read the letter again before carefully placing it back in the envelope and pulling out the next one.

Dated just a week later, the second letter contained even more words of love and loneliness, but unlike the first one, it also contained what may have been the first hint to the person's identity.

"... the place is small but grand and for the first time in my professional life I am working with other professionals, all hoping for that one big break where the rest of the world will realize what we have to offer. Of course even this wouldn't be possible without you and I find myself once more in debt to you for all the kindness and the love you showed me. There will never be a more loving, compassionate woman on the face of the earth and for that reason alone I will always cherish you my love."

It was the same with the remaining letters in the bundle; words of love and longing, but never anything to indicate who the man was, how they had met, or where they were at the time. By the third letter it was obvious that Nan had responded to the man and soon began a correspondence that, if the number of letters in the box were any indication, spanned decades. But who was he and why was he so important to Nan especially after she married Pops? She wouldn't know the answer until she had read them all, but the excitement of her discovery had been exhausting and she fell asleep in the middle of her bed surrounded by Nan's love letters.

•   •   •

The jarring ring of the phone woke her the next morning and cracking one eye open, she saw just how late it was before reaching for the phone.

"Hey kiddo, it's Dad."

"Oh hi Dad," she said sleepily as she struggled to sit up in the bed covered in letters.

"Did I wake you up?" he asked. "Does the fact that you are sleeping in mean you're done at Abby's house? Alex said you were getting close. Did you find the secret?"

Without making a conscious decision to lie about it, the word "no" came out. Something told her it was too early to share her findings with the rest of her family . . . even her dad.

"I mean, I am not done, but it shouldn't be too long now. That attic is packed full of things and every single piece has to be looked at and then carefully packed away."

"I ran into the curators from the museum, and they said you donated so much stuff they are thinking of having a special exhibit just to display it all."

"That would be cool, but I'm sure there will be more before I'm done. How's Mom?"

It had been days without any contact with her mother after the disastrous end to Sunday dinner and Krista was anxious to try and mend fences but had a sneaky suspicion the discovery of the letters would instead cause more problems.

"She's fine but I think she really regrets how things ended the other day. Why don't you stop over and say hi?"

"Now's not really a good time," Krista told him. Looking at the letters covering the bed all she could think of was finishing them. "Is that the reason you called?"

"Actually no. My lawn mower is on the fritz and I wonder if I could borrow yours while mine is being repaired."

"You don't even have to ask. I'll leave the garage door unlocked when I leave this morning. Stop over whenever you want."

"Thanks sweetheart, and think again about stopping in to see Mom . . . she might surprise you this time."

"You know Dad, I've had enough surprises lately, but I'll think about it. Now I better hop in the shower and get over to Nan's or I'll never finish. I'll talk to you soon okay?"

"Love you."

•   •   •

Freshly showered and ready for a new day, Krista gathered all the letters from her bed and placed them back in the box before putting the box back in the closet. More than anything she wanted to go back to the letters, but as the tone of the correspondence became even more personal, it felt like a betrayal to her grandmother to read on. What she really should do was finish up in the attic, but what she needed was a break from everything having to do with Nan's secret.

Making her way down to the kitchen she started a pot of coffee. Lack of sleep the night before had left her feeling almost hung over and it was going to be a hard day without copious amounts of caffeine. As the coffee began to brew, she noticed Abby's cell phone still sitting on the counter reminding her of the need to check Nan's contact list before cancelling the service. Nan had carried the old flip style phone for years and as much as the family cajoled her, she had steadily resisted trading in her ancient technology for a brand new smart phone. Unable to find the original charger for the phone in her grandmother's house, Krista began digging through her junk drawer hoping to find one that might work. It took a while, but eventually she found one and plugged it in before setting the phone aside to deal with later.

Her thoughts interrupted by the ringing of her own cell phone, she looked at the caller ID to see Alex' name. Most likely he wanted to know what she had decided but she wasn't ready to admit she had read the letters. She let the call go to voicemail as she stared out the window thinking once again of Nan and the man who had penned such heartfelt letters. It didn't take a rocket scientist to figure out the man was deeply in love with Nan, but who was he? There was only one person who could tell her that and grabbing the phone and turning off the coffee pot, she locked the house up tight and headed towards the cemetery; hoping for some inspiration from her grandmother.

•　　　•　　　•

Seeing Abby's name on the newly engraved headstone brought tears to Krista's eyes. She knew her grandparents were buried side by side, but it was still a punch in the gut to see concrete evidence of her final resting place. A fresh bouquet of flowers adorned the grave and she wished she had thought to bring her own flowers for Nan. A gardener with the greenest thumb she knew, the flower beds in Nan's yard had served as a year round feast for the eyes. Even so, she loved being the recipient of an unexpected bouquet of flowers. Whomever had visited the grave before Krista must have known that.

Carefully brushing the dead grass away from the headstone, Krista sank to her knees not caring who saw her talking to a dead woman.

"Oh Nan, I wish you were here to answer my questions. You said the house contained your secrets, but instead it seems I'm left with nothing but questions. Who was your mystery man? Did Pops know? Knowing how much you loved each other I wouldn't think so, but if you weren't having an affair why would you carry this secret with you for sixty years?"

The emotional roller coaster Krista had experienced since the night of Nan's birthday party was suddenly more than she could bear and a flood of tears erupted from her as the few other mourners nearby shook their heads in sympathy. Whatever answers Krista had hoped to find at the graveside never materialized and finally, with no reason to stay, she wiped the remaining tears away and started the long walk home.

Turning up her front walk, a neighbor shouted out a greeting as she walked by with her tiny dog.

"Good morning Krista."

"Hi Nancy, how's Roscoe today?" The aging dog had begun to spend more time at the vet than most.

"So much better and thank you for asking," the woman told her. The dog was her life and Krista feared for her emotional well-being should anything happen to her beloved pet. "Did you know there was a man on Abby's front steps? We just came by there and I thought you would want to know."

"That's odd," she told her neighbor, "but thanks for letting me know."

In minutes she was crossing the lawn to Abby's front door just as an elderly gentleman with a full head of snow white hair knocked heavily on the door. Dressed in an older but impeccably tailored suit and the style of hat rarely worn by men these days, he carried himself upright and strong, belying his apparent advanced years. An expensive gold watch adorned his wrist as he knocked firmly again.

"Can I help you sir?" Krista asked as she approached the porch.

At the sound of her voice, the man turned towards her with a smile on his face.

"Yes, thank you. I'm looking for Abigail Peterson. Do you know if she lives here?"

The deep rich timbre of the man's voice was intoxicating and something about him looked oddly familiar to her, but she couldn't quite place it.

"Peterson? No, I . . . wait a minute, do you mean Abigail Ward? I'm her granddaughter."

"Of course, sorry about that. Old habits die hard I guess. Abigail Ward. Is this her house?"

"Are you a friend of hers?" Krista asked. It had been weeks since she had been forced to break the news of Abby's death to someone and she dreaded having to go through it again.

"In a manner of speaking. She and I had an appointment a few weeks back and she didn't make it. I've been trying to contact her ever since without much luck and I thought I'd take a chance and stop at her home. Is she in?"

There was no easy way to break the news. "I'm sorry to tell you, but my grandmother passed away a few weeks ago."

The man seemed to crumble in front of her and she raced to his side before he collapsed. "Whoa there, let me help you." Grabbing his elbow she quickly steered him into the house before helping him to sit.

"I'm sorry to just blurt it out like that. I thought we had notified all of Nan's friends, but apparently not. Let me get you a glass of water."

Quickly returning with the water, she handed it to him and noticed his hands were shaking.

"What did you say your name was?"

"James, Theodore James. And you must be Krista."

"How did you know that?

"You look just like her and your grandmother talked of you often."

"How did the two of you know each other?

"We've known each other a very long time and I thought we were about to reconnect, but now…" he trailed off looking wistfully around the room before his gaze settled once more on Krista. "How did she die?"

With most people Krista simply said Abby died from a heart attack, but he looked so devastated by the news, she found herself telling the entire story starting with the birthday party.

"It was just so unexpected. If I had known something was wrong I never would have left town that day. And the worst part was she was really looking forward to this birthday for some reason. She wouldn't let us plan anything for the day which was unusual, but she insisted she had plans."

"And it was just before her eightieth birthday?"

"Yes."

"How unfortunate. A promise never fulfilled," he said as he shook his head sadly and tears gathered in his eyes.

"What do you mean?"

"I better be going. Thank you for your hospitality and for telling me about Abby."

The man who had seemed so strong and virile when she first saw him now got unsteadily to his feet before walking slowly to the door.

"Please, why don't you stay? I have so many questions I'd like to ask you about Nan."

"As much as I'd like to discuss your grandmother with you my dear, I don't think that's wise. Maybe if life had worked out differently, but we can't change it now."

"You're talking in riddles. Please don't go. You're obviously not from around here. Why don't you stay here for the night and in the morning maybe we can chat? Nan would love having an old friend in her house."

"I already have a room at a bed and breakfast not far from here and then I suppose in the morning I'll be heading back to California. It was wonderful to meet you. Oh my, you do so look like her."

Somehow, as he looked into her eyes before reaching out an unsteady hand to gently caress her face, Krista knew that it wasn't really her he was seeing, but more likely her grandmother and she stood there not knowing how to respond. In the end he sighed deeply before walking out of the door and driving away with a last slow wave her direction as a squad car pulled up and Alex got out. She hadn't returned any of the numerous messages Alex had left on her cell phone and his frustration was apparent as he walked quickly up to the house.

"What's going on? Why haven't you called me back?"

"Hello to you too," she replied although she knew perfectly well why he was irritated with her. "I'm sorry I didn't call you back but it was a late night and I just needed a break today."

"A break from me? Well you could have just told me if that's what you were thinking," he said angrily.

"That's not it at all!" she interrupted before he got really angry. "I didn't mean I need a break from you. I meant I need a break from all this - from Nan and her secret. It's been overwhelming, but you," she said putting her hands on his shoulders, "You have been my rock and I couldn't have done any of this without you. I'm sorry I didn't call you back, but can we please start this conversation over?"

"I'll forgive you this time, but in the future, just a text or a quick call to let me know you're okay please? So, hello...how is your day?"

"Let's go inside and get something to drink. I have a lot to tell you."

"You read them didn't you?" he said without a hint of surprise.

"Not all of them, but enough to have figured out Nan's secret was bigger than we thought."

Over glasses of lemonade and store bought cookies that would have made Abby cringe, Krista told Alex everything she had discovered.

"Judging by the postmarks, their correspondence carried on from before she married Pops to just months ago although I've only read a handful of the letters. Whomever this man was, he was deeply in love with Nan and although we don't know what she wrote to him, it sounds like she loved him too. How come we never knew about it? I can see where she wouldn't want to discuss it in front of Pops and the rest of the family, but don't you think she might have at least mentioned the man in passing?"

"Your grandmother was a beautiful woman and I'm sure there were many men in her past. And remember, it was during the sixties, the time of free love and all that. Maybe Abby was into all that stuff."

"Nope, I just can't believe that. Nan believed in being in love. And you have to remember, that was back when she was just starting with the restaurant. Pops always said she spent twelve hours or more a day at the restaurant. Between that and taking care of the family she probably didn't have time for an affair.

"You're probably right. I have a hard time picturing Abby as a player even back then. So who drove away when I drove up? It looked like a rental car."

"That's the other strange thing that happened today. The man was looking for Nan. Said he was an old friend and he hadn't heard she passed and when I told him he was devastated."

"What was his name?"

"James. No wait a minute that wasn't right. It was Theodore. Theodore James."

"That sounds familiar. Was he from around here originally?"

"I never asked him, but you're right. There is something familiar about that name."

"Oh my God, of course. That's it!" Alex said excitedly.

"That's what?" Krista asked.

"Think about it silly. His name is Theodore."

"So?"

"Krista, think about it. All the letters were signed with a T. It's probably him."

"Lots of people have names starting with T. It's just a coincidence," Krista insisted refusing to believe that the puzzle could be solved so easily.

"Maybe, but maybe not. Why else would the man be here?" he asked.

"He was pretty upset when he found out she had died. Maybe I need to pay Mr. James a visit tomorrow and find out more."

"And this time, let me know what you discover okay? No more ignoring my calls?"

"I promise."

Chapter Seven

Only one bed and breakfast operated within thirty miles and Krista headed there first thing in the morning. As it turned out, she almost missed him.

"Mr. James?" Krista said as she walked up to the rental car where the man was loading a small satchel in the back seat.

Turning slowly at the sound of his name, he offered a slow smile as he recognized Krista.

"Miss Ward," he said offering his hand to her.

"Actually it's Miss Thomas, but please call me Krista," she said as she shook his hand. "I was wondering if I could talk to you, about my Nan."

"I'm sorry, but you've actually just caught me on my way home, but it was lovely meeting you my dear." Releasing Krista's hand, he opened the driver's door.

"Please, don't go yet. You've come a very long way to see Nan and well, I was hoping you can help me with something. In fact, I have a feeling you might be the only one that can provide the answers I need."

"I don't see how that's possible and I'm sorry, but I have a plane to catch. You're a lovely young woman and I know Abby was so very proud of you, but I really must go. It was wonderful meeting you."

Krista could only stand by as he got into the car and began to back away. Suddenly she blurted out what she wanted praying her and Alex's suspicions weren't wrong.

"I know about the letters," she said loudly as the car came to a sudden stop and his head whipped around to look at her. "I know about the letters between you and Nan."

Lowering his head to the steering wheel, he didn't move for the longest time. When he looked back at her, there were tears streaming down his face.

"Please don't go until we've had a chance to talk. I have so many questions and with Nan gone you're the only person who can answer them. Can I just buy you a cup of coffee before you go? If you miss your flight I'll buy you another ticket. Just please don't go yet."

"All right," he said finally. "I owe Abby at least that much."

Finally expelling the breath she had been holding in anticipation of his answer, Krista suggested he follow her back to Abby's house. "Unless you'd be more comfortable somewhere else? There's a coffee shop nearby. We could go there."

"No, I think for this story you might prefer somewhere more private," he said.

"Of course, then please follow me."

Krista hurried to her car keeping a close eye in the rear view mirror to make sure he wouldn't disappear before she placed a quick call to Alex.

"Hey Krista what's up?"

"I'm on my way to Nan's and Mr. James is right behind me. He's agreed to talk to me and you're right. He's the man from the letters. You should have seen his reaction when I mentioned them. Can you meet us there?"

"Wow, I'd love to, but I'm on duty. About the best I can do is stop by after work. Do you think he'll still be there?"

"I don't know. He said he had a plane to catch, but I offered to buy him a new ticket if he'd stay. Honestly I don't know how long he'll be here. Come over though when you can because you'll ask things I probably won't even think of."

"I'll do my best, but remember, if he still had feelings for your Nan he's grieving. Don't push him too hard."

"I'll try, but this is our best shot at figuring out what went on between them. I don't want to lose this opportunity. See you later."

Soon they were back at Abby's house where Krista helped Mr. James up the porch stairs and into a comfortable chair in the living room before making coffee for them both. When she came back with the refreshments, he was walking around the room looking at the photos that were still on display.

"Here we go," she said placing the tray on the coffee table.

"I always wondered what Abby's family looked like," he said as he placed a family picture back on the mantle.

"That was taken the Christmas before my grandfather died and I haven't had the heart to pack it away yet," Krista told him. It was the last photo they had of the entire family and she remembered how difficult it had been to gather the whole clan together that year. The only thing that had brought them all together had been knowing Pops didn't have long to live.

"She never showed me pictures of all of you. She said that it wasn't fair to the family to share that part of her life with me. But it was the most important part. We had more than a few disagreements about it actually."

Turning to look at Krista with a sad smile, he joined her on the couch and accepted a cup of coffee from her.

"So how did you find out about us?" he finally asked.

Unsure where to start with so many questions flying through her head, Krista decided to start at the beginning.

"Nan's will had a contingency in it that I had to go through the house. She said I would find the story of her life and the love she shared somewhere in the house. It didn't make any sense to us at the time, but then I found the box of letters and discovered there was a whole other side to Nan. Then I met you and it all made sense. You're the 'T' who wrote the letters aren't you?"

"I am," he said softly. "Although I'm not surprised she kept them, after all, she was always the sentimental type, but I am surprised she wanted you to find them. More than anything she didn't want to disrespect your grandfather. So you've read them all have you?"

"No, but I've read enough to know you were deeply in love with Nan. It seemed like an invasion of Nan's privacy to read further."

"While I appreciate that, you should know I have no problem with your reading them. Abby always told me you were especially close and it seems pretty obvious she wanted you to know everything."

"If you don't mind Mr. James, I think I'd rather hear the story from you."

"Mr. James......it's hard to look at you when you call me that."

"I'm sorry?" Krista asked in confusion.

"It's just that you look just like Abby the day we met and hearing you say my name takes me back to that very day."

A look of love passed over his face as he stared once more at the picture of Nan that was front and center on the mantle.

"The year was 1960," he began, "I was broke and hungry and out of options until an angel of mercy took pity on me ... "

Chapter Eight

THE YEAR 1960

"John I need two eggs over easy and a side of dry toast," Abby said to her cook as she handed the order slip to him.

"You got it boss," John said with a smile knowing exactly who the order was for. Mr. Simpson came in every Sunday morning after church and ordered the exact same thing. A widower on a pension that didn't quite cover his basic expenses, they both knew he came in not so much for the food as the company.

"And why don't you throw in a slice of that ham we just got while you're at it?" Abby suggested.

John raised an eyebrow at the statement. "Abby you know that meat's expensive. Can he afford it?"

"It's on me and I can afford it," she assured him. "He's wasting away to nothing."

"Abby you can't keep giving food away," John cautioned. "The restaurant is barely making money the way it is."

"Ah, but it is making money and as the boss it's my decision right?" she teased.

Like the other employees John was worried about keeping the only job he had been able to get in months. If the boss kept giving things away, the small profit margin she enjoyed might disappear all-together along with their jobs.

"That it is," John finally admitted before completing the order and placing the hot plate in the pass through window to be delivered to Mr. Simpson at his usual table by the window.

"There you go Mr. Simpson," Abby said placing the plate on the table with one hand and refilling his coffee with the other.

"I think there's been some mistake Abby. I didn't order ham," he told her. The hungry way he was looking at the meat told her she was right in her assessment. The weight loss was due to his lack of finances and nothing else.

"Darn it. That's my mistake," she told him with a friendly smile. "But why don't you eat it anyway – no charge? I'd just have to throw it out if I take it back and ham like that shouldn't go to waste."

"Thank you my dear," he told her with a hand to his heart. "And God bless you."

Giving his bony shoulder a quick squeeze she walked back behind the counter to see John watching the exchange.

"You're a good girl Abby," he told her with a smile.

Unlike the rest of the week, the restaurant was mostly empty on Sunday as families headed home after church for their traditional Sunday dinners. It didn't make much business sense to be open when she spent more on John's wages than she collected in revenue, but it was a good opportunity for the two of them to bake and prep for the upcoming week while waiting on the occasional customer.

Keeping an eye on Mr. Simpson, Abby headed back to the kitchen to start work on baking for the upcoming week while John prepped a large turkey that would be roasted for Monday's turkey commercial special. Concentrating on getting the lattice crust of her blueberry pie perfectly aligned, she didn't notice the sound of the bell above the front door at first. But the man who took a seat at the counter before placing a large duffle bag on the floor next to him caught her eye.

"I'll be right with you," she said with a smile before reaching for a towel to wipe her hands; watching him as she did so.

The man appeared to be middle-aged, but he carried a look about him that suggested life had already beaten him down. Dark brown hair worn long like so many young men favored these days framed his face and he looked like he hadn't slept in a bed for days. The jacket he wore was wrinkled and well-worn, hanging loosely from his slight frame. Sunken cheeks, a sure sign the man hadn't eaten much recently, were barely camouflaged by his beard.

Located close to the highway, the restaurant had had its' fair share of hitchhikers stop in and Abby suspected he was another. She grabbed a glass of water and placed it in front of him before taking out her menu pad. Without looking at her, he immediately downed the glass and asked for another.

"Welcome to Abigail's," she said as she placed more water in front of him.

He downed it again, but this time much more slowly.

"What can I get for you?" she asked pleasantly.

"Just coffee please," he said without looking up.

Placing a cup in front of him, she turned to grab the coffee pot. When she turned back, he had spilled a few coins onto the counter in front of him and was counting it out. Right away she suspected it was all the money he had and her heart immediately went out to the man.

"Coffee's always on the house for new customers," she told him before hearing John's surprised grunt behind her at the made up story.

"Thanks," the man said wrapping his hands around the cup and blowing on the hot coffee before taking a tentative sip.

Abby couldn't help but notice his long slender hands and it wasn't because of the dirt under his nails. The man had the hands of an artist.

"Would you like something to eat? We have a great ham platter on special today."

"Just the coffee please."

There was no doubt in Abby's mind that the man couldn't afford to feed himself and with a quick nod at John she knew she had to help, but the man still wouldn't look at her and she didn't want to embarrass him.

"Well let me know if you change your mind," she said before walking to the till where Mr. Simpson stood waiting to pay his bill.

"Lunch was excellent as always Abby. See you next Sunday."

"Take care now Mr. Simpson," she told him as he walked slowly out the door leaving the stranger the only customer in the place. For a minute she thought about trying to engage him in conversation but with his head still down he didn't look like he was in the mood and she headed back to the kitchen.

"I know what you're thinking Abby, but don't do it," John told her softly. "You have that look again, but you can't save everybody."

"I know that, but look at that guy. Have you ever seen someone who appeared more in need of help? He can't even look at us."

"Maybe there's a reason for that," John cautioned. "Don't get involved with him."

"John, I love you and you might be right, but I have to try. Can you put together a ham platter please?"

"Do I have a choice?" he asked as he wrapped the now prepped turkey and put it in the walk-in cooler for the next day before filling a plate with creamy mashed potatoes and gravy, a side of fresh picked green beans and a thick slice of honey baked ham.

"How about adding a piece of that cornbread you made this morning?" Abby suggested.

"Anything else?" John snapped as he added the bread to the plate.

"Maybe a smile?" Abby teased before being rewarded with a sarcastic smile from her cook.

"See that wasn't so hard," she said before backing through the kitchen door with the overly full plate of food in her hand.

"I know you told me no, but you look like you could use a good meal," she told him as she placed the food in front of the man.

"I can't," he said before pushing the plate away. "I don't have any money."

"It's all right," she told him before moving the plate back. "It's on me. I own the place. I'm Abby."

For the first time he raised his head to look at her and their eyes met causing Abby to gasp in surprise. Looking back at her were a pair of the most startling ice blue eyes in the face of a much younger man than she had suspected. In reality he was probably no older than she.

"You're the owner?" he said in surprise. "You don't look more than 25."

"I don't know if I should be offended by that or not," she replied with a laugh. "Actually I'm 20 and yes, I am the owner. My folks left me some money when they died and I always wanted to own a restaurant so here I am. We've been open about a year. Now eat before your food gets cold."

"I don't need your charity," he told her boldly even though everything about him said he did. His eyes had barely looked up as he hungrily eyed the plate of food before him.

"I understand that and it doesn't have to be charity. There's a few things that need doing around here. Maybe you can give me an hour or so of your time in exchange for the meal."

Staring back at her with those gorgeous eyes, he considered the offer before finally saying, "I can do that."

"It's a deal then," Abby told him. "Now eat."

He didn't require further prompting and quickly began to shovel the food into his mouth before noticing her watching and slowing down. It wasn't long before he had finished every crumb on the plate.

"How about a piece of pie for dessert?" she offered.

"That sounds great, but maybe I should fulfill my end of the bargain first. What can I help you with?"

When Abby had purchased the restaurant it had been falling apart. Little had changed since that time and her to-do list was as long as her arm, but she didn't want to overwhelm the man.

"Do you have any carpentry skills?" she asked.

"I know my way around a hammer and saw," he said.

"My back screen door hasn't closed properly in forever. Do you think you could take a look at it for me?"

"Shouldn't be a problem. Do you have any tools?"

"Tools I have. It's the ability to use them that's missing," she told him with a laugh. "Follow me."

Taking off his jacket, she could see her earlier assessment of the man was a bit off. His lean body was well toned and muscular.

"See how it sticks instead of closing securely," she told him after setting the tool box on the floor and swinging the door back and forth. "Maybe the wood is warped or something, but it didn't use to be that way."

"That's an easy fix," he assured her. Within minutes of looking at the door, he had reset the sagging hinges allowing the door to open and close freely.

"I can't believe I've put up with the door for months and it was such an easy thing to solve. How'd you know what to do?"

"My dad was pretty handy around the house and I picked up a few things from him," he told her.

"So your Dad has passed on?" she asked.

"Oh no, nothing like that, but I haven't seen him for a long time. Now what else can I do for you?"

Watching him work with the door an idea occurred to Abby, but she hesitated to bring it up knowing that she could barely afford the staff she already had. Ultimately she couldn't help herself.

"Maybe I shouldn't say this, but from the looks of you, I'd say you've had some hard luck lately. Would you be interested in working for me? It wouldn't be a forever job and it wouldn't pay much more than room and board, but I could sure use the help of someone as handy as you are around here."

At the offer, he turned to look at her.

"You're not just making this up because you feel sorry for me are you?"

She couldn't help but laugh at the suggestion. "Just look around this place! The food is great here, but people would enjoy it more if they didn't have to worry about the ceiling falling in on them. I could really use your help if you're willing."

"You mentioned board?"

"It's not much, but there's a back storage room with a cot and it's all yours if you want it. And you'd get three square meals a day. It's just for a couple of months or until you get tired of it. What do you say?"

"I'd say you have a deal," he said as he offered his hand to her with a wide smile that instantly transformed his face as Abby tried hard not to stare.

"There is just one thing though," Abby said hesitantly causing his smile to disappear.

"What's that?"

"What's your name?"

"It's Theodore. Theodore James but you can call me Theo."

"Nice to meet you Theo."

John took his role as Abby's protector seriously and he was less than pleased by the new turn of events. Watching from the kitchen while Theo finished the previously promised pie, he shook his head at Abby.

"What it is about you that makes you take in every stray that comes this way?" he asked in frustration. "You know nothing about this guy and you're going to let him sleep here?"

"What do I need to know?" she snapped. She was equally frustrated by his hesitation to accept her decision. "He needs help and I need work done."

"I already told you my brother-in-law could make those repairs for you," John said.

"And I thank you for trying to arrange that, but you know I can't afford it. Theo is going to do it for free."

"Theo! What kind of name is that for a man?" he said with a snort. "And it's not for free. You're going to be feeding him and seeing how he downed that pie, something tells me you're getting the short end of this deal."

"John, I appreciate that you want to look out for me, really I do. But you're not my father and I can do what I want."

The words were no sooner out of her mouth than she realized how hurtful they had been. At sixty some years of age, John was almost like a father to her.

"I'm sorry John. That came out wrong. You know I love and respect you, but it's important to me to be able to help people and there's just something about this guy. If I let him walk out of here without at least trying I think I'm going to regret it. If he robs me blind in the middle of the night, I'll admit you were right, but I don't think that's going to happen."

"You're the boss," he finally said. "I just hope you're right."

•   •   •

It didn't take long for Theo to start working on the lengthy list of repairs Abby had requested and as the afternoon passed, Abby didn't see much of the man. Towards the end of the day she found him out back sawing wood to replace a broken step on the back porch as sweat glistened on his skin in the hot weather. She wasn't surprised to see he had removed his shirt as he worked, but what was surprising was her reaction to seeing his bare chest. A warm feeling started to build in the pit of her stomach and she quickly looked away.

"You know I didn't expect you to get the whole list done in one afternoon," Abby said. "We're just about to close up for the day and I thought I should show you where you'll be staying before we go."

Putting the saw down, he used his shirt to wipe the sweat from his face.

"I thought you were open for supper," he said in surprise.

"Not on Sundays. There's no money in it and I can't afford to be open without any customers."

Turning as one to return to the restaurant, he looked at her shyly before quickly putting his shirt back on.

"Are you sure you're okay with my staying here all alone?"

John had spent most of the afternoon asking that same question, with ever more ominous thoughts about what Theo might do unsupervised.

"Is there some reason I shouldn't trust you?" Abby asked.

"Well no, but you hardly know me. Common sense would say it's a risky move."

"Look, I've always believed that no matter what troubles befall us, there is good in everyone. I choose to believe that you are a good person until you do something that tells me otherwise."

"Are you for real?" he asked with wide eyes. "I suppose you leave your doors unlocked too!"

"Of course. I don't know anyone who doesn't leave their doors unlocked in town. Where exactly are you from anyway?"

"Los Angeles most recently," he told her.

"Well things are different here," she told him as they reached the storage area. "Okay, here's where you'll sleep. I know it's not much, but it's private and quiet and more importantly there's a roof over your head."

Stealing a look at the grime that covered his jeans and the jacket he had worn that morning, he didn't even bother to argue.

"About the only thing it doesn't have is a bathtub, but you can shower at my house. I thought you could get settled in while I close up the place and we can walk over to my house together. You can take a shower while I make you supper and I can throw your clothes in the wash while we eat."

"Supper?" he asked in surprise.

"The deal was three meals a day and since the restaurant is closed for the night, you'll have to eat at my house, but don't worry. I'm an even better cook than John!" she said with a wink. "Meet me out front when you're ready and we'll head to the house."

While Theo put away his meager belongings, Abby turned off lights and made sure the back door was securely locked before joining him at the front door. It didn't escape her notice that he had changed clothes. Although wrinkled, they were cleaner than what he had been wearing.

"Here's a key for you to use while you're staying here. It will open both doors, but you probably should use the front door because the light's better out here. Ready to go?"

Nodding at her, the pair started the walk home.

"So you live around here too?" he asked as they walked side by side.

"I do. When my folks died, I inherited their house along with all the junk in it. It's old, it's drafty and it's falling apart very much like the restaurant, but it's paid for and it's one less bill to worry about. It's that big old Victorian at the end of the block. Not much to look at, but I like it. Someday, if the restaurant does really well, I would like to restore it. Dad always said it had good bones and I guess that means it's well built."

"Your folks, when did they die?"

"About three years ago. I was a junior in high school when the accident happened."

"Wow that must have been rough."

"More than you know. Ours was a very small family . . . just my folks and me. All my other relatives, most whom I had never met, live on the east coast. Then my folks died and suddenly all these strangers are making plans for my life and no one was even consulting me. They wanted me to go live with an aunt and uncle I barely knew in New Hampshire."

"How did that go?"

Talking to Theo Krista realized something. He actually said very little about himself and always found a way to turn the discussion back to her.

"Actually it didn't. When I rebelled at the thought of being uprooted to go live with people I didn't even know, friends of my parents, John and Malinda . . . you know John the cook from the restaurant? Anyway, they stepped in and said I could live with them until everything got settled. With a family of six kids already in the house it was a real sacrifice for them to take in another and I will forever be in their debt for it. I got to graduate high school with my friends and when the inheritance came through I moved out and, well, you know the rest. So," she said having arrived at the front door, "this is it. Welcome."

Far from being the rundown heap of a house she had described, the large home was more of a museum of a bygone era and would have been a great location site for movies of the Victorian age. All it needed was women in long dresses and mustachioed men in waist coats.

"Pretty horrible right?" she said as she watched him.

"Well . . . "

"Come on, if we're going to get along, we need to be honest with each other," she prompted. "I personally think the décor is hideous. It's nothing but clutter and I know I should get rid of most of what's sitting around, but I just haven't had the time."

"Okay, to be honest, it's not exactly my style," he admitted sheepishly.

"Whew! Thank goodness. If you had said you liked it, I don't know if we could be friends," she said with a laugh. "Now that we have that out of the way, you should get cleaned up while I put supper on the table and get those clothes of yours in the wash. I've had a roast cooking low and slow all day and it should be falling apart tender by now. Bathroom is at the top of the stairs first door on the right and there are plenty of clean towels in the hallway cupboard."

Abby turned towards the kitchen without waiting for him to respond. Still not quite believing his good luck, Theo made his way upstairs intending to go straight into the bathroom, before being distracted for a moment by the open door to a bedroom that was so unlike the rest of the house, he couldn't help but go in. Treading lightly in case the old hardwood floors creaked beneath his feet and Abby discover he was snooping, he pushed the door open even further to a beautifully appointed bedroom. Unlike the rest of the house, this room was sparsely furnished and free of clutter. Surrounded on two sides by large windows, the cross breeze created a cooling sensation that was a welcome relief from the heat of the day. Having seen this one room gave him a world of insight into his hostess, but resisting the temptation to snoop further, he finally turned back to the bathroom, closing the door firmly behind him.

Removing his clothes he stood naked in front of the mirror, disappointed to realize he looked even worse than he had imagined. With unwashed and unkempt long hair and a beard that had gone weeks without seeing a razor, he looked and felt like a bum. No wonder everyone he encountered had crossed the street to avoid contact with him. He would have done the same thing.

But yet this woman was different. Always with a smile, she hadn't once turned up her nose at the obvious stench that enveloped him after well over a week without a bath and more importantly, she had treated him as a man. There was no pity for the situation he was in. She had asked no questions and made no accusations about how he found himself in such dire straits. She seemed too good to be true and yet there must be some angle for her offer of help; he just couldn't figure out what it could be. She might own a house and a restaurant, but it wasn't hard to figure out she didn't have cash to waste on someone like him, so just what was she after?

Stepping into the shower, the scalding hot water beating away the dirt that had imbedded itself in his skin, he thought about his benefactor. Young and beautiful, with a quick smile for everyone, her face should have been in the movies but instead she was stuck in a small town working twelve hour days, but she seemed happy and those around her obviously adored her. She might not have noticed him watching, but Theo noticed everything and he had seen the way the old man in the restaurant glowed when she spoke to him and the cook, the man who had apparently taken her in with his family after her parents died, treated her like something to be cherished. Still it's easy to be kind when you have a full belly and a roof over your head he thought. It's another thing to have been without a job for months and too poor to afford the clean clothes necessary to even get a job.

His self-disappointment had been building ever since he made the decision to take the biggest risk of his life and head to Los Angeles hoping to find his big break. A big fish in what turned out to be a very little pond in his home town, he ended up being the exact opposite in Los Angeles leaving him so far out of his element it only took weeks before he was sleeping in his rundown car with not even a dime to his name. Audition after audition had ended badly and in a city flooded with the self-proclaimed "next big stars", he couldn't even find a job waiting tables. Eventually he was forced to sell his car for a few hundred bucks and by the time that money was gone, so was his ambition. Too proud to call home for help, he started thumbing for a ride back east, picking up odd jobs when he could. It was never enough for a regular meal and far from the cost of a motel room leaving him to sleep on park benches or in doorways like a common wino.

This very morning, after being dropped in front of the restaurant by the only truck driver willing to pick up someone like him, he had given up on the idea of going home, too ashamed by what he had become to face those who expected him to come back a star. He was a broken man and he saw no way out as tears of frustration and disappointment mixed with the hot water. Only the sound of the shower muffled his sobs.

•　　•　　•

So much time had passed since Theo went up to shower Abby began to wonder if something had happened to him. Standing at the bottom of the stairs she was about to head up when she heard the water being turned off and she turned back to the kitchen. Within minutes her freshly washed guest appeared at the door, dressed in the same clothes, but smelling so much better.

"Better?" she asked.

"Yes, thanks," he said as he hungrily eyed the food she was spooning into serving dishes.

"Why don't you put these dishes on the table and take a seat."

Without a word he accepted the dishes from her, placed them on the table before taking a seat and watched her every move as she brought the remaining dishes over before taking her own seat.

"Please help yourself."

He didn't need a second invitation and quickly filled his plate with pot roast, potatoes, carrots and thick slices of homemade bread.

At first Abby just watched him eat, wondering if his appetite was because the food was so good or more likely because he was still unsure if there would be another meal in his future. Finally she could stand the silence no longer.

"I think you'll like it around here," she started. "It's a small town, but people are friendly and I have a really nice staff at the restaurant. John you've already met and we have two waitresses, Doris and Susan, who you'll meet tomorrow. They've all been with me from the beginning."

Thinking that would prompt him to respond she waited, but he barely looked up from his food. She'd encountered that type of behavior before from people she had helped. Many were reluctant to talk; too embarrassed over their situation or too wary of her.

"So Theo?" she said. "That's a rather unusual name. Were you named after a family member?"

"No. My mother was British and she named me after an actor. She often called me Teddy, but I prefer Theo."

"Oh, that's interesting. You don't have an accent so I would guess your father was American."

"Yeah."

"Why don't you tell me a little about your family?" she asked. For a millisecond it appeared he would answer, but instead he said nothing.

"You know you don't have to answer my questions if you don't want. I don't mean to pry but I thought maybe I could get to know you better."

Putting down his fork he leaned back in his chair and looked at her.

"I'm sorry and I really do thank you for all this, but I'm just trying to figure you out."

"What do you mean?"

"Well take this for instance. You invite me back to your place, where you obviously live alone, and yet you know nothing about me. There's nothing sensible about any of it."

"Look, I might be from a small town where people don't lock their doors, but I'm not stupid. I know it's a risk and I know you could murder me right here and now and help yourself to whatever you want and take off, but you won't. Don't ask me how I know that but I do. It's all in the eyes and when I can get past the fact that you have the most beautiful eyes I've ever seen on a man, your eyes tell me you're a good person. True, you appear to have had some struggles lately but that doesn't mean you're going to turn to a life of crime now does it?"

His reaction to her sermon was subdued but she could tell she had made her point by the slight upward curve of his lips.

"My folks met at the end of World War II. Mom was an army bride."

"How romantic. There used to be a couple here in town that met during the war. She was French and I loved listening to her talk, but she had a really hard time adjusting to life here and they moved away shortly after they arrived. Was it difficult for your mom?"

"I don't think so."

"Where did you grow up?"

"Philly."

"I've never been there. Actually, I've never been anywhere really but I'd love to see Paris and London and Italy someday."

"What's stopping you?" he asked unexpectedly.

"I guess I don't know. I probably should have done it when I got my inheritance, but all I could think of at that time was opening the restaurant. Now I have neither the time nor the money to travel. Why did you leave Philadelphia?"

"You're going to think I'm stupid, but I left for the bright lights of Hollywood. I wanted to be an actor."

"And it didn't work out so well?"

"That's putting it mildly. It took every dime I had and within months I was broke. No one would hire me. I couldn't even find a job waiting tables. Finally I had to sell my car and was left with nothing. I've been hitchhiking trying to get back home."

"Won't your folks help you out?" she suggested.

"I didn't ask," he admitted as he hung his head. "My dad was against the whole idea from the start. Kept telling me to get a real job and be a man. Having to admit I failed and then ask him for money . . . well it's just not going to happen."

"And your mother?"

"She was wonderful," he said as he raised his head for the first time to actually look at Abby. "She had always wanted to be an actress before the war and she encouraged me each time I tried out for local theater at home, but neither one of us realized how hard it was going to be to get a real acting job. In LA I was just another guy. There was nothing special about me that made me stand out from the hundreds of other guys all trying to land a single role."

Having seen his startling eyes, Abby knew that wasn't true. His eyes alone would make her do a double take.

"So what now? You're not going to give up are you?"

"What choice do I have?" he asked as he threw down his napkin and got up to stare out the window.

"I'm no expert on the acting business but it seems to me if it's important enough to you, you shouldn't give up."

"Look, I tried and look at how I ended up," he spat out. "Not a penny to my name and taking charity from a woman. You know what that's called right? Can you imagine how it feels to be a man and have to accept charity from you?"

"Everyone needs a helping hand now and then but what I offered you isn't charity," she reminded him. "You're going to work hard for a bit of food and a crappy bed and don't you forget it. Let's face it, I probably should feel guilty for taking advantage of you."

For the first time since they met Theo actually smiled and as she smiled back at him, Abby knew that something had changed between them.

"I'm sorry," he said finally. "You don't deserve me unloading on you like that."

"It's okay, we all need a friend to dump on every once in a while."

"Is that what we are now . . . friends?" he asked.

"I think so."

Chapter Nine

THE YEAR 2019

"And that was the start of a beautiful friendship," Theo told Krista.

He had been talking for hours and even though he was a complete stranger, Krista recognized the love in his voice as he spoke about her Nan. At first his words had been hesitant, as if retelling the story compounded his grief at her passing, but eventually his voice was strong and confident and somewhere along the line as she watched him carefully she finally realized who he was.

"Forgive me for not recognizing you when we met, but now I remember watching your old movies with Nan."

A quick smile crossed his face at her words.

"It's been years since someone has recognized me and I thank you for that. So you've seen some of my work?"

"Not just some, but I think I've seen every movie you ever made. Nan and I spent hours watching your films on the classic movie channel. I always thought you were her movie crush but knowing what I know now it was obviously much more than that. Watching the movies was probably her way of being able to see your face and staying connected to you once you got rich and famous."

"We actors are a vain lot and I can't help but wonder what you thought of the movies?" he asked without a hint of embarrassment.

"Truth be told I had a bit of a crush on you myself!" she said with a laugh as his smile got wider. "There must be more of Nan in me than I thought."

Their discussion was interrupted by the ringing of the doorbell and Krista looked up to see Alex through the window.

"I hope you don't mind but I invited a friend to join us. He's been helping me here at the house and he was with me when we discovered the letters."

Without waiting for a reply she went to the door and let Alex in watching as his eyes went immediately to Mr. James.

"Hi," Krista said warmly. "How was your day?"

"Busy," Alex told her before placing a quick kiss on her forehead.

"Alex, this is Mr. James…Nan's friend."

As Theo started to get up from his chair Alex hurried over.

"Please don't get up sir. Alex McMillan. It's a pleasure to meet you," he said before offering a strong handshake.

"It's a pleasure meeting you as well young man. So you are young Krista's beau?" he asked with a smile. "That would have made Abby so happy. She always insisted the two of you were meant for each other."

"Abby told you about that?" Alex asked before shooting a look of surprise at Krista and taking a seat on the sofa next to her.

"Abby was always a romantic at heart and she told me there wasn't a couple better suited for each other than the pair of you even if you didn't realize it. She always said you reminded her of us."

"I'm sure you must realize sir that news of your relationship with Abby is going to be hard for some members of the family to hear. As far as we can tell she never mentioned you to anyone, including her husband."

"I'm aware of that," he told Alex. "It was something we spent many hours discussing and I don't mean to cause any problems by my appearance here. With that I think I've kept Krista here long enough and must be going."

"Please don't go," Krista asked hurriedly. "There's so much more I want to ask."

"Unfortunately, I don't have the stamina I once had my dear and I've grown quite tired. But if you like I would be happy to stop by tomorrow and tell you more. I think Abby would like that. For now though I must find a hotel seeing as I checked out of mine this morning."

"That would be wonderful," Krista said, her face lighting up with excitement. "But why don't you stay at my house? I have a small guest bedroom and I could cook supper for all of us tonight."

"It sounds like the offer your grandmother made to me the day we met," he said with a smile.

"And like her I hope you'll take me up on it."

"I wouldn't have it any other way."

•   •   •

"Abby would be proud of your cooking skills my dear," Theo said as the trio sat down to dinner once he was settled in. "She always hoped you would grow up and have interest in taking over the restaurant."

"Krista has always been a great cook," Alex interjected.

Beaming from ear to ear Krista thanked them both. "I enjoy cooking, but unfortunately for Nan, I enjoy teaching children more. But that didn't stop us from spending hours in the kitchen together and I learned a lot from her."

"It definitely shows," Theo told her. "You know, as good a cook as she was it didn't prevent her from having a mishap every now and again. I remember a kitchen filled with smoke after one particular evening when she tried a new recipe she had badgered a woman for. The dessert she was trying to make burned to a crisp. Waves of acrid smoke billowed out of the oven by the time she finally realized it. She was mortified of course but eventually we could laugh about it. That was the thing about Abby, nothing got her down for long."

"She was an amazing woman," Alex said.

"No one realizes that more than I," Theo told him shaking his head slowly. "Tell me about your family. I've already told you Abby chose to keep that to herself. She was terribly worried about disrespecting your grandfather but I feel close to them nonetheless."

"She and Pop's were married after he came home from the Army in early 1961 I think it was. He worked as a welder in one of the local factories and they both put in really long hours. So much so that when my aunts and uncles started to arrive Nan would take the kids to the restaurant with her. They would do their homework in one of the corner booths and as they got older she would have them do chores around the restaurant for pocket money."

"If you don't mind I would love to see the restaurant when I'm here. I drove around town a bit when I arrived but must have gotten my directions mixed up after all these years. I couldn't find it."

"Did you notice the new office building at the corner of Elm and Washington? That's where the restaurant used to be," Alex told him.

Krista quickly interjected. "When Nan decided to retire she couldn't find a buyer and it turned out the real estate was what was so valuable in the end. There were lots of tears from all of us on the day the place was bulldozed to the ground but Nan kept a smile on her face. I remember her telling me that it had served its' purpose."

"It sounds just like her to say something like that," Theo said. "But tell me more about your family."

For the next two hours Krista and Alex relayed stories about Abby's children and grandchildren that had all three of them rolling with laughter before they were done.

"Abby was a lucky woman," Theo said finally as he put down the cup of tea he had been drinking. "Your family sounds wonderful."

"Do you have children?" Krista asked.

"Unfortunately I never married. Your grandmother was the only woman for me and, well, you know."

"I'm sorry," Krista told him.

"Don't be. Life can be a trade-off. I fell in love with a woman who married someone else and I suppose my penance is to be alone now. But now, if you don't mind, I am a bit tired and think I will turn in but I will continue Abby's story in the morning. Alex, it was a pleasure meeting you and Krista thank you for your hospitality. Good night my dear."

Once again struggling to get up from the sofa he brushed off their offers to help and got slowly to his feet. As he straightened his eye caught the picture of Abby placed prominently in the center of the mantle and he blew a kiss towards it before shuffling off to the guest room.

"Have you asked him about the Oscar yet?" Alex asked when they heard the bedroom door close as Krista got up and began to collect their dishes.

"Not yet," Krista admitted as she walked into the kitchen followed closely behind by Alex. "Since he did win an Oscar that year it's a pretty safe bet the one we found was his, but why would Nan have it?"

"There's a simple way to find out . . . just ask him," Alex said logically.

"I will eventually, but I want to find out more. Sure they were friends, but those letters made it sound like a love affair. Something happened between where he left off with his story and when the letters started. Why don't you read them and see what you think?"

"Actually I've been thinking about that and I have decided not to read them. It's too personal and not my place."

"That's not what you said when you encouraged me to read them," she said in surprise. "Now I feel like a fool."

"Wait. You don't understand what I'm saying," he said as he took her into his arms. "Abby loved you more than anything and she chose you to discover this secret for a reason. But that was you and not me. I am happy to support you and would love to hear more of what Theo has to say but reading her letters should be left to you."

Looking into his eyes, Krista felt a wave of emotion run through her. Before she even had time to process it, Alex leaned in for a soft gentle kiss on her lips. When he pulled back she continued to stare into his eyes as a smile appeared on her face.

"I'm so glad you're part of this," she told him. "I couldn't imagine sharing it with anyone else."

"We've wasted an awful lot of time," he told her as he smiled back at her. "Guess we should have listened to Abby."

"If I know Nan, she's watching over us from above with a big smile on her face," she said. "Want to come over for dinner tomorrow after work?"

"That sounds great. There was something I wanted to mention too but I don't know how long Mr. James will be in town. It's classic movie week at the theater in Lakeville and guess what's playing a few days from now?"

"No . . . are you serious?" she asked with a laugh.

"I checked it on my phone when Theo was talking and it's one of his movies. Something called 'A Diamond Is Forever' which if I'm right is the first movie he won the Oscar for."

"Nan loved that movie!"

"I remember. So what do you say I take us all out to dinner and then we see the film? Can you imagine telling people you watched an Academy Award performance with the actual winner?"

"I'll check with Mr. James tomorrow when he gets up but even if he doesn't want to go, you've got yourself a date!"

•   •   •

Opening her eyes the next morning, Krista felt guilt over neglecting Nan's house for another day. She was so close to finishing and knew that the entire family was waiting for the work to be done so the estate could be settled but having Theo in the house she knew it would have to wait. Learning the details of their decades old love story was too enticing to pass up and she hopped out of bed, took a quick shower and made her way down to the kitchen intending to make a full breakfast for her guest. Instead she was surprised to see him, already dressed in another suit, sitting at the kitchen table with a cup of coffee in front of him.

"Good morning Krista", he said pleasantly as she walked in.

"Good morning Mr. James."

"Come now, I think we're past the formalities. Please call me Theo," he told her.

"Theo then. Did you sleep well? I'm sorry I wasn't up before you."

"No worries, I'm not enough of a gentleman to wait for my hostess and thought you wouldn't mind if I made coffee. It's the one thing I can do on my own in a kitchen."

"Let me get you some breakfast at least," Krista said as she began to pull eggs and bacon out of the refrigerator.

"Please don't bother. When you get to be my age toast and coffee is about all I want in the morning, but don't let me stop you."

With a smile, she straightened to look at him. "You are a man after my own heart," she said before she put the food back in the fridge and pulled out a jar of jam and popped bread into the toaster. "I've always skipped breakfast myself but that was sacrilege to Nan. Half of her revenue came from breakfast service."

"Back when I was young and strong I ate a full breakfast every morning but as we age, well that much food is just a waste."

"I should have asked you this last night. I am very much looking forward to hearing more stories about you and Nan, but I'm not keeping you from anything am I? If you have to get back home, please don't let me hold you up."

"Nonsense. There's nothing pressing calling me home and I am enjoying getting to know Abby's granddaughter. However, I was wondering something last evening."

"What's that?" she asked before refilling his coffee cup and placing the toasted bread on the table.

"What about your family? Have you shared with them anything about me?"

It took a moment for her to answer because she had been wrestling with that very question.

"Not yet," she said hesitantly. "To be perfectly honest I don't know how they would react...not so much about your friendship with Nan, but let's face it, the few letters I've read make it pretty clear there was more between you than just friendship. That together with the fact that Nan told no one in the family about you makes you both look pretty guilty of going behind Pops' back. I'm not positive about the rest of the family but I know my mom will come unglued when she finds that out. So, no, right now they know nothing about you."

"I can see I've put you in a difficult position my dear. Maybe it's better if I just be on my way."

The thought of him leaving before Krista heard the whole story was unbearable and she reached her hand across the table to touch his arm.

"No. I mean, please don't go. Alex and I agree Nan wanted me to find all this out. It would be a slap in the face to her to not go through with it no matter how painful it could be for some in the family. Once I've heard the whole story I'll decide what, if anything, to tell them. I owe it to Nan."

"If you're sure?" he said hesitantly. At her strong affirmative nod, he wrapped his hands around his coffee cup and started his story once more. "That night everything in my life changed although I didn't know it at the time ... "

Chapter Ten

THE YEAR 1960

Sending Theo back that night to the uncomfortable cot in the storage room was hard for Abby, but as safe as she might have felt with him in the house, having a strange man spend the night would have started all of her neighbors talking. The idea of 'free love' hadn't made its way to this part of the country yet and Theo's appearance alone was enough to set tongues wagging in town. When she had suggested he come and go through the front entrance of the restaurant it wasn't merely for the better light as she had led him to believe; it was also to let those who might be watching his comings and goings from her house understand where he was spending his nights. She needed information about Theo to get out in the most positive way and a few carefully placed bits of information about her new handyman shared with a few customers should be enough to spread the word without creating unneeded gossip.

"Good morning everyone," Abby said as she entered the restaurant the next morning. It was still dark out but the doors would soon be opened to the usual flood of early morning regulars. Trying not to be obvious about it she looked for Theo, but saw no sign of him.

"Morning Abby," Susan and Doris said in tandem as they busied themselves marrying ketchup bottles and filling salt and pepper shakers. Each in their mid-fifties, they were dependable, hard-working, and the customers loved them.

"Morning ladies. Hope you had a nice day off," she told them as she passed by on the way to her tiny office. Early morning was the one time she had to pay bills and get her books in order; a task she hated more each day. Stopping by the kitchen pass-through window she greeted John. "And how was your evening John?"

"Quiet," he said. Abby knew he had most likely found his favorite spot in a recliner in front of the TV and drifted off well before the evening news. He was a hard worker during the day, but liked nothing more than to relax in front of the tube during his evenings.

"That's nice" Abby told him without really listening. Her head swiveled back and forth looking for Theo.

"Is he...?" She started to ask.

"If you're asking about your latest charity case," he said without a smile, "he's out back fixing shelves in the garage. He's been out there since I opened up this morning. I'll say one thing for that boy, he's a hard worker."

Seeing the satisfied smile on his boss' face he admitted he might be wrong. "Fine, he didn't steal anything, at least from what I can tell, but that doesn't mean I won't be keeping my eye on him," he said as he waved a spatula at Abby.

"I wouldn't have it any other way," Abby said with a grin. "I'm going to take some coffee out to him. I'll be right back."

Grabbing a couple of coffee cups and a full pot, Abby made her way out to the back garage where the sound of hand sawing could be heard. His back to her he didn't hear her approach at first and she watched the muscles in his back work as he pulled the saw back and forth. The same warmth she had felt deep within her the day before was back and for the first time she realized her growing attraction to the man might be more to worry about than whether he would steal from her.

"You're up early," she finally said to stop her thoughts from going where they shouldn't. "I brought you some coffee."

Turning towards her she was taken once again by the blue of his eyes and for a moment she had trouble breathing.

"Thank you," he said as he accepted the coffee and wiped sawdust off a nearby bench so she could sit. "And thank you again for last night. It was really nice."

Each sipping their own coffee neither one said much until Theo rolled his shoulder with a grimace.

"Is something wrong?" Abby asked. "You didn't hurt yourself did you?"

"No. I just slept on it wrong I guess. It'll work itself out eventually."

"Sleeping on a cot doesn't help much I'm sure. If it doesn't get better in a little while I can rub some of my mother's homemade liniment on it for you. It smells to high heaven but I swear just a little rubbed into the skin and you'll feel worlds better."

"It should be okay but I'll let you know."

"Why don't you come back to the restaurant and have some breakfast before we get too busy," Abby suggested. "After all breakfast is part of the deal and you can meet Susan and Doris...that is if John hasn't already told them about you."

"You mean warned them about me don't you?" he asked with a wry smile.

"Did he say something to you?" Abby asked quickly.

"He didn't have to. I can see the way he watches whatever I'm doing. He doesn't trust me and I don't blame him. I wouldn't trust someone who looks like me either."

"I'll admit that first impressions mean a lot but I've always believed that actions speak louder than words. He'll come around and see what I see. Just give him time."

At her statement, he suddenly stopped what he was doing and looked deep into her eyes. "And just what exactly do you see?" he asked softly.

If she hadn't been raised to be a lady, Abby might have responded in another way, but that wasn't her. "I see a man with more strength in him than he can see himself. A man who has dreams he's not ready to let go of and a man who someday will become the man he is meant to be."

Her unexpected response left both of them unable to speak...he with tears in his eyes and she holding her breath knowing that she wanted to say so much more and more than anything she wanted him to kiss her. Instead she chose to let the moment pass.

"Now let's get you some breakfast."

Without another word, or waiting to see if he would follow her, she turned and went back inside to the frantic beating of her heart.

●   ●   ●

As the day progressed more and more customers commented about Abby's new helper. At first many eyed him with suspicion much the same way John had but Abby's careful comments about Theo soon changed all that.

"I can't believe I'm getting such quality work in exchange for room and board," she told one customer as they watched Theo repair the fence lining the parking lot. "I've never seen such craftsmanship."

"Do you think he would help me paint my house?" the customer asked. "My wife keeps badgering me about it and by the time I get home from work I'm just too tired to tackle such a big job."

"Well, I don't know. He's awfully busy working for me," Abby said with a smile, "But if you ask him he'll probably say yes. He's the type that wants to help where he can."

"I don't know," a woman a few stools down at the counter said. "He doesn't look very trustworthy to me. Does the man even bathe?"

Feeling protective of Theo Abby took great offense at the woman's statement and tried to silence her with a death stare but the woman just kept talking apparently oblivious to Abby's anger.

"And Abby, I'm surprised at you. How does it look for you, a beautiful young woman, taking in a strange man, especially one who looks like a drug addict?"

The last phrase was whispered in hushed tones.

"Donna, you know as well as I do that looks aren't everything. He's a good man and I won't hear another word against him. As far as what I do or don't do, that's none of your business."

"You tell her Abby," the man next to her said with a laugh. "I have some things that need fixing around my house too. If you say he's a good guy I believe you. What did you say his name was again?"

"Theo," Abby said with a smile. "Theo James. Remember that name because some day he's going to be famous."

Little did any of them know Theo's dreams of being an actor, but that was his story to tell and when they looked back at her with raised eyebrows Abby just smiled at them sweetly. It wasn't long before she saw two or three of the men talking with Theo in the parking lot. By the end of the day her customers had already taken him into the fold.

•   •   •

"Abby I locked the front doors and put up the closed sign," John told her at the end of a very busy day. "I also have three lasagna's in the fridge for tomorrow's special and I'm calling it a night."

"Thanks John. See you tomorrow," Abby said without looking up from her paperwork. As usual she hadn't quite gotten to it before the morning rush began.

"Don't stay too late," he told her.

"Nope. I'll be right behind you," she said absentmindedly before suddenly remembering Theo and turning around in her chair but John was already gone.

Putting everything away she turned off the light above her desk, stretched her aching shoulders and went in search of Theo to find him sitting on the edge of the cot, deep into the pages of a well-worn book.

"Are you hungry?" she asked quietly from the doorway so as not to startle him. "What are you reading?"

"It's nothing," he said before quickly stuffing the book into his duffle bag.

"I'm not judging you," she said thinking that he was embarrassed by what he had been reading. "If you look at some of the titles in my library you might be surprised by what I read. Please may I see the book?"

With a shrug of his shoulders he handed it to her.

"e.e. cummings?" she asked in surprise. "That's poetry right?"

"Yeah. I stumbled on this book when I first got to LA and it sounds stupid, but it spoke to me."

"*I carry your heart...*" She recited before he finished.

" . . . *I carry it in my heart.* You know Cummings?" he asked excitedly.

"Poetry isn't really my thing, but I do like his work. But you Theo James, you are a mystery to me. You're an actor, a lover of poetry and you're handy with a tool box. That's an unusual combination."

"Yeah, well, poetry is just another thing my father would find fault with," he admitted, but there was a smile on his face knowing that she accepted his love of poetry. "Maybe you would like to hear more of his work?" he suggested.

"I'd like that," she said warmly. "But for now let's get home and see what I can find for supper."

•   •   •

They had known each other for only two short days but as each were soon to discover, they were well suited together. Once Theo loosened up and accepted that their arrangement was not charity Abby discovered he possessed a sharp wit softened by a quick sense of humor that often left her laughing so hard her sides hurt. Dinner over and the kitchen put back in order Abby suddenly wished he didn't have to go back to the storage room but didn't know how to say it.

Theo beat her to it. "It's a nice night out," he told her. "Do you feel like going for a walk?"

Abby's warm smile provided his answer. "Let me get a sweater and I'll be right back down."

As they strolled side by side each were at first deep within their own thoughts and surprisingly, neither seemed to mind. It was a comfortable silence allowing them to enjoy the night after a long day and Abby found herself wondering if every day with Theo would be the same. His recent troubles aside she was finding him to be easy going and personable and definitely someone she would welcome as a friend.

"So you grew up here?" he finally said. "This whole town is kind of like a Norman Rockwell painting."

"The way you phrased that I'm not sure if that's a good thing," she said with a laugh. "But for me it was wonderful. In a small town you know everyone and they know you and everyone looks out for each other . . . sometimes too much so, but it's nice to know if you need help it's there."

Turning to look at her in the moonlight he asked, "Is that why you helped me?"

"I suppose that's part of it, but there was more to it. When you dumped out your change on the counter and it didn't look like you were even going to have enough money to pay for the coffee something in me wanted to reach out to you."

"Are you telling me that new customers don't really get free coffee?" he asked with a laugh.

"Not really," she admitted. "But it's not a bad idea now that I think about it."

"Aren't you worried that people are going to take advantage of you?"

"I don't really spend my time worrying about it and even if they did, it would probably be because they need something more than me. I have a roof over my head, food on my table, great friends and employees and enough money to pay my bills. There's a lot of people worse off than me and if I can help some of them then why not?"

"There's one thing you didn't mention when you were listing off your blessings."

"What's that?" she asked.

"Love. Is there a special man in your life?"

The question raised Abby's heartbeat a notch.

"No, but when would I have time for romance? I spend all day at the restaurant where most of my customers are married. Even if I had time to date the dating pool around here is pretty limited."

"Have you ever had a boyfriend?"

The line of questioning was making her uncomfortable but not because it was too personal. Her attraction to Theo was growing exponentialy and she didn't want him to know.

"Of course I have. Then he went to college and I never heard from him again."

"And no one since then?"

"There is one guy, his name is Robert and we went out a couple of times, but then he got drafted and I haven't seen him since he left. We've exchanged a couple of letters but that's it."

"And when he comes home . . . ?"

With the tables now turned making her the recipient of his questions, Abby became defensive. "Why are you asking all these questions?" She didn't want to talk about Robert or her bland love life anymore. "Why don't you tell me about growing up in Philadelphia?"

"There's not much to tell. It was a lot like your childhood but in a bigger city."

"Do you have any brothers and sisters?"

"Two older brothers and a sister still living at home."

"Are you close to them?"

"We used to be, especially my brothers, but when I left for LA they make it clear they felt the same way about acting as my dad. Both of them went to work in construction right out of school and, honestly, I think my wanting to be an actor embarrasses them."

"Why do you say it that way?"

"Say what?"

"Why do you say you want to be an actor? Seems to me you either are or you aren't. Maybe you're not really committed to it yourself. Maybe that's why no one will hire you...because they think you don't really want it."

"Damn. I never thought about it that way."

"Then say it."

"I am an actor," he said without much conviction.

"Is that how actors project?" Abby teased. "Say it with conviction!"

"I AM AN ACTOR!" Theo shouted into the night. "I AM AN ACTOR!"

Grabbing Abby he pulled her up into his arms and spun her around as he repeatedly shouted the statement into the darkness of the night. Lights began to come on in the otherwise dark street before a voice shouted, "Pipe down. People are trying to sleep!"

Like a couple of teenagers, they began to laugh before he put her down and they ran hand in hand down the block. Finally stopping to catch their breath, laughing still, they turned to look at each other as something changed in Theo's eyes catching Abby off guard.

Without another word he pulled her to him and gently kissed her lips before she pulled back and looked quickly around to see if anyone was watching.

"I'm sorry . . . I couldn't help myself," Theo told her. "You look so beautiful in the moonlight and I . . . "

"It's okay" she said, suddenly shy and unsure of herself. If she had been bolder she would have told him it was what she wanted too, but girls in small towns in the Midwest didn't go around kissing complete strangers in the moonlight; at least she didn't think they did. "I've got to be up early again tomorrow. Maybe it's time we call it a night."

The disappointment in his eyes didn't go unnoticed by Abby but she was frightened by her attraction to the man. Still a virgin, she wasn't naïve about relations between men and women and she even knew some girls who had already had sex, but she had always thought she would wait for marriage before giving herself to a man. With Theo she wasn't so sure of that anymore. As scruffy looking as he was, something deep inside her said he was a man that would change her life and she wasn't sure she was ready for it.

"I guess you're right," he finally said. "Do you want me to walk you home?"

"That's okay. I'm not far from home now and it doesn't make sense for you to go back there and then go back to the restaurant. I'll see you tomorrow okay?"

"Abby, I didn't mean to . . . " he started to say before she cut him off.

"It's fine really. See you tomorrow." Turning for home, her steps quicker than normal, she knew without a doubt that he was watching her walk away before she heard his slow footsteps fading into the night.

Chapter Eleven

"Doris do you know where Theo is?" Abby asked the next afternoon.

Since the awkward conclusion to their evening together he had kept his distance from her all day, even skipping lunch claiming he was too busy to eat. At first Abby had been relieved to have space between them. Their shared kiss the evening before had left her confused and confounded by what she was feeling for the man. As much as she enjoyed his company she knew his time with her was limited and getting involved with the man was sure to lead to heartbreak. John had been so sure Theo would steal from her but the only thing Theo could steal that mattered was her heart and she wasn't about to let that happen.

"Susan said something about him going to do some work at the Piggly Wiggly for Mrs. Anderson. Did you need him for something? Maybe I could help?"

"Thanks for the offer but I was just wondering since I haven't seen him all day."

"Weren't you the one to suggest he could hire out for other jobs?" she asked. "You're not a little jealous are you?"

"Of course not," Abby insisted as she turned the lightest shade of red. "It's good that he is earning some actual money. It will help him get home when he's done working here." Her entire staff had been told Theo was hitchhiking back to the east coast but unless he had told them more, Abby hadn't shared anything else. She had no desire to embarrass him by filling them in on the details.

"Maybe he'll stay," Doris suggested.

Truth be told, the thought had also crossed Abby's mind but she knew better. He may have faced nothing but rejection in Los Angeles but deep down Theo was destined to be an actor and his dream wouldn't come true in this little town. At some point he would be moving on and that's what kept Abby from letting her feelings for him get out of hand.

"I think he's set on getting back home," Abby finally said turning her head away in an effort to hide the tears that suddenly welled up at the thought. "You know, I'm beat today. Unless you guys object I'm going to knock off early."

At her suggestion all three staff members turned to look at her in surprise. None of them had ever known Abby to take time off during a work day.

"Are you all right?" John asked quickly. "You're not coming down with something are you?"

"Mrs. Miller told me that half her class was out sick today with the stomach bug," Susan offered.

"I'm fine," Abby assured them. "I'm just tired is all. An early night is all I need but I'll be here first thing in the morning. John can you make sure Theo gets something for supper?"

"Are you sure you're all right?" he asked again.

"Stop fussing. I'm perfectly fine. Besides I'm the boss and if I want to take a few hours off I will."

"See you tomorrow then?" Doris asked.

"5:30 sharp," Abby said before grabbing her pocketbook and sweater and heading out the door.

Walking home she realized leaving John to deal with Theo was a cop out, but her thoughts about the man were all a jumble and she just couldn't face him tonight. A night off was what she needed to get a better perspective and she knew just what she should do.

After a quick supper, Abby grabbed some stationery and a pen and walked out to the swing in the backyard. It had been months since she had written Robert and she felt guilty for neglecting him when he was so far from home. The two dates they had been on before he was drafted were pleasant enough, but not exactly memorable and she hoped he might meet someone else and save her the unhappy task of breaking things off with him when he returned. But then the letters started. He had only been gone a few short weeks when the first letter arrived and with it his declaration of admiration for her that somewhere along the line turned into so much more. At first she had willingly written to him as a friend, but when his letters turned to love and a future together, she chalked it up to his being all alone in a foreign country. Choosing her words carefully she had done everything in her power to let him know she considered him as only a friend but he just didn't seem to get it. Eventually she stopped writing all together rather than lead him down the wrong path. With most men that would have been the end of it but he had continued to write every few weeks with the most recent one having arrived just before meeting Theo.

Her decision to return Robert's letter was sure to send the wrong message but it was the best way she could think of to get Theo out of her mind and she put pen to paper, being careful to stick to the facts and say nothing that would give him any hope of there being more than friendship between them. Finished, she re-read the letter just to be sure she wasn't sending the wrong message before sealing it up and walking back into the house, placing the envelope on the hall table so she would remember to mail it the next day.

Heading up the stairs she was stopped midway by the sound of the doorbell. The porch light had already been turned out but she could see a shadow at the door. Hurrying back down she was surprised to see Theo when she opened the door.

"What are you doing here?" she asked by way of greeting. "Didn't John get you supper before he left?"

"No, he did, but he said you weren't feeling well and I came over to see if there was anything I could do for you."

"I'm fine," she told him quickly. "I'm just tired is all. I was going to make it an early night."

"Oh, well don't let me stop you. I just wanted to make sure you were okay."

He looked like a boy who had just lost his best friend and even though she was playing with fire, she realized she didn't want him to go.

"Since you walked all the way over here, why don't you come in for a bit?" she suggested.

"Are you sure? If you want to go to bed, I can find something else to do."

"I'm sure. Please come in."

Stepping aside as she opened the door fully, Theo walked by her into the house and she caught the faint whiff of cologne realizing at the same time that his hair had been smoothed back into some sort of order. Knowing that he had made an effort with his appearance on her behalf put a smile on her face.

"Would you like something to drink? I have Coca-Cola."

"That would be great," he said as she turned towards the kitchen and left him standing in the hallway.

While she got the drinks, his eyes landed on the letter waiting to be mailed.

"Robert?" he said gesturing towards the letter as she handed him the soda. "Isn't that your boyfriend? The one that's in the army?"

"He's not my boyfriend," Abby told him turning the envelope face down before moving into the living room. "He's a friend who's far away and I thought I'd write him is all. It's nothing."

"I'm sure he would disagree. Getting a letter from the girl back home probably means a whole lot more than nothing to a guy in the service."

"So you're saying I shouldn't be writing him?" she asked angrily. "Since when do you tell me what I should and shouldn't do?"

At her sudden and unexpected reaction, Theo held up his arms in surrender.

"I'm sorry. It's none of my business who you write to and I didn't mean to come over here and start a fight with you."

"We're not fighting."

"Sure seemed like it to me," he told her with a smile. "And after everything you're doing for me I sure don't want to fight."

Hoping to change a sensitive subject, she quickly asked, "Is it true you worked over at the grocery story today? I hope they paid you. The Anderson's are one of the wealthiest families in town but the wife is also the stingiest person I know."

"I'm not done yet, have to go back tomorrow and paint the shelving I put up today, but we agreed on a cash payment."

"Must be nice to have some money in your pocket again."

"It won't be much but you're right. It will be nice and thanks to you I have even more work lined up for some of your customers. What did you say to them anyway? When I first got here they looked like they were scared of me and now all these people want to hire me."

"I just told the truth, that you're good with your hands and you work cheap."

"That's another debt I owe you," he said as he moved closer on the sofa.

"You don't owe me at all," Abby reminded him as her cheeks flushed with the nearness of him. The smell of his cologne was making it hard to concentrate on what he was saying and before she could back away he leaned in and kissed her. This time she kissed him back and before she knew what was happening they were locked together in the most passionate embrace she had ever experienced.

The taste of his lips was a combination of the sweetness of the soda and mouthwash and when his tongue pushed its way inside her mouth a whole new sensation threatened to overwhelm her as butterflies erupted within. His beard scratched at the sensitive skin of her face and for a fleeting moment she wondered at the sensation before the feel of his hands at her breast caused her to gasp in surprise. He quickly pulled back looking at her with heavy lids and swollen lips.

"Abby you make me crazy with desire," he said softly before his lips covered hers once more and his hands slipped under her shirt to feel the warm skin of her back before she pushed him away.

"Theo," she said breathlessly. "I...I mean . . . I've never . . . "

"Okay," he said suddenly and angrily. "I get it. You don't want to be with someone like me. I guess I made an assumption but I was wrong."

Getting to his feet, he smoothed back his hair and began to pace around the room as he tucked his shirt back into his jeans.

"Damn it Abby. I thought you wanted me as much as I wanted you and I'm so sorry. I better go."

Jumping to her feet as he turned towards the door she grabbed his arm.

"Wait. Please don't go. You don't understand. It's not that I don't want you. It's just that . . . well, I've never done this before."

"You've never kissed a man before?" he said in confusion.

"No, I've never . . . I've never . . ."

"You're a virgin? Is that what you're telling me?" he said in surprise. "Oh my God Abby I'm so sorry. But how could that be?"

"Don't make fun of me," Abby said angrily. "Not every girl hops into bed with guys they barely know."

"I'm not making fun," he assured her. "You're so beautiful I just assumed you would have . . . it doesn't matter. I think it's wonderful."

"Sure you do," she said sadly.

"I'm not kidding and if you'll just look at me for a minute I can tell you that I am too."

Raising her eyes to meet his she seemed as surprised as he was moments before. "So you've never . . . ?"

"No I haven't, although it's not exactly something a guy like me likes to admit, but I had this old fashioned idea that I wanted to wait until I was married before making love to a woman. Then I met you and ever since all I can think about is what it would be like to be with you."

"So do you want to . . . ?" Abby asked as she looked up towards her bedroom in trepidation before her voice trailed off. She couldn't bring herself to say the actual words.

"Oh I want to, more than you know actually, but now I think we both need to think about it some more first. I don't want you to have any regrets. I think I'll head back to my cot now before you become too big a temptation."

Surprisingly disappointed by his decision they said a lingering goodbye at the front door before he headed into the darkness.

Chapter Twelve

The days following their near intimacy were filled with sexual tension and furtive glances shared between them. Theo found himself unable to forget his desire for Abby and each time she was near the smell of her perfume nearly drove him wild. The decision to delay anything further between them was the right one but that didn't make it any easier to be around her and not want more.

He wasn't the only one filled with desire and for the first time in her young life Abby was nearly consumed with thoughts of the man. Having him so close was torture and the suddenly confident and strong young woman was replaced by a giddy school girl who couldn't keep a smile off her face or her mind on her work. John was the first to notice the change and seeing the two of them together he wrongly assumed more had happened between his boss and her charity case. Not brave enough to confront Abby with his suspicions he went straight to Theo; cornering him in the garage that was becoming his workshop.

"I ought to throttle you," John said angrily as he took a swing at Theo. As unexpected as the attack was Theo easily sidestepped the blow angering John even more.

"What the hell is wrong with you man?" Theo asked as he moved away, unwilling to get into a fight with the older man.

John, hand's up like a boxer, glared back at Theo in fury.

"What have you done to Abby?" he spat. "I swear to God if you have done something inappropriate with her I'm going to kill you."

"What are you talking about?" Theo asked in confusion. "Nothing inappropriate has gone on between us and even so, what is it to you? She's a grown woman."

"She's like a daughter to me and if you touched her you better pack your bags and get the hell out of town before I show you what we think of men like you around here," John threatened.

"John, calm down. Nothing happened."

"Well something happened. You only have to look at her to see the change in her. Since you two have been thick as thieves, well it can only be one thing. And if you dishonored her you're going to pay for it."

If John's concern for Abby's welfare hadn't been so obvious Theo would have laughed in his face, but he knew the man cared for her even more than he was beginning to and he couldn't fault him for his assumption. He and Abby had spent every night together since they met even if John had no way of knowing that nothing had happened between them other than a few innocent kisses.

"Look John, I might not be the kind of man you would hope for Abby but I'll be honest. I have real feelings for that girl. Even so, nothing inappropriate has happened between us. I wouldn't do that to her."

"On the level?" John asked as he slowly lowered his fists.

"Yeah man. I'm telling you the truth."

"Well okay then. But you should know something about Abby. There's something special about her and when she gives her love she doesn't go halfway. The man she falls in love with is going to be the man she spends the rest of her life loving . . . there won't be any turning back for her. I can tell right now you aren't that man so don't start something with her that will only break her heart or you'll have me to deal with."

The conviction of John's words touched Theo's heart. He had already come to the same conclusion and as much as he wanted all of Abby he was afraid of hurting her if he allowed more between them.

"I understand."

Neither man seemed willing to back down, but at least they had reached common ground and they both went back to work.

Days spent together at the restaurant with each tending to their own separate responsibilities were topped off by evenings spent together at her home where their relationship blossomed even as Abby slowly counted down the days until Theo would move on. Her lengthy list of repairs had quickly been completed and even adding chores around the house was no longer enough to keep him busy each day, freeing him up to earn some real money from customers who were desperate for his skills with a hammer. Having money in his pocket seemed to transform Theo from a desperate man to one with a new found confidence that Abby couldn't help but comment on.

"Something's different about you lately," she said as they sat across from each other late one evening.

Unlike the beginning stages of their friendship when after supper Theo had helped finish dishes and almost immediately returned to his cot at the restaurant, these days he lingered as the pair enjoyed time together reading, sharing poetry, talking a walk, or just talking. Tonight was no different and after their shared meal they had found their way out to the back yard to enjoy the mild evening.

Turning to her he asked what she meant.

"I'm not sure I can describe it. It's like there's a new sense of purpose about you but I know that doesn't make sense. You seem . . . I don't know......more self-assured somehow."

"Not quite the loser I was when we first met is that what you're saying?" he said with a cynical grin.

"That's not what I was saying and you know that. Whatever the change is it makes me wonder something else."

"I can't wait to hear this," he teased. "What exactly do you want to know now?"

The pair had teased each other incessantly over the number of questions Abby asked when she was first getting to know him. Now that he was more open she didn't have to ask so often; these days he was actually volunteering information.

"Will you keep trying?" she asked softly.

"Trying? Oh . . . you mean acting?"

"Yeah. I know that the whole experience in LA was horrible and all but you just have to look at your eyes to know you'd make a brilliant leading man. Woman will swoon over you up on the big screen."

"Abby, you have to realize that good looks alone don't make a successful actor right? We've all seen those beautiful people on the screen who can't act a lick and those careers fizzle out pretty soon. Acting meant everything to me but to be repeatedly told that I'm not good enough . . . well it takes something out of you. Even if you know you're a good actor, and I used to think that of myself, when professionals tell you you're not good enough it gets in your head and at some point I have to be honest with myself and admit that I was wrong."

"Don't you think Clark Gable and Rock Hudson and Marlon Brando were ever turned down for a role? Of course they were. Maybe not as often as you have been," she said with a chuckle hoping that he would see the humor in it and relieved when he smiled back at her, "but I'll bet every actor has gone through low times. The ones who gave up are the ones that are driving taxis or working in a bank now. Those men will live with regret the rest of their lives. I guess what I'm trying to tell you Theo is that doesn't have to be you. I believe in you and I don't think you should give up."

Her unexpected yet impassioned declaration left her breathless and he could only look at her in awe. No one, his mother included, had ever seemed to believe in him quite so much and he didn't know what to say.

Moving in front of him she cupped his face in her hands. "I believe in you and it's time for you to believe in yourself again."

"Abby, I . . . " The words caught in his throat and without hesitation he leaned in and kissed her gently on the lips. When she offered no resistance the kiss deepened as they clung desperately to each other before finally pulling away.

"I'm sorry," he started to say as he traced her lips with his finger.

"Don't be sorry," she told him.

"Abby please don't make me sleep alone tonight," he whispered into her ear as he pulled her close to him again.

It had become more and more difficult at the end of each evening to send him back to the restaurant and the only thing that stopped her from inviting him to stay at her home was nosey neighbors who were sure to gossip if Theo moved in. It had been weeks since they admitted their inexperience to each other and Abby had begun to doubt Theo would be her first. At the whispered words she no longer had any doubt and without another word she took his hand in her own and together they went upstairs.

·　　·　　·

Abby hadn't moved with a fast crowd in high school, but she had heard stories about first time experiences. A quick grope in the backseat of a run-down car or a stolen moment in a twin bed while someone's parents were away for the weekend were whispered about in hushed tones that left her confused. Rather than being a romantic experience, it all seemed rather sordid. She wasn't expecting much, especially for her first time which she had been told would be painful, but the reality of it all turned out to be very different.

As inexperienced as they both were their first attempt was awkward and at times somewhat embarrassing. Neither one of them knew where to put their hands or legs and their attempts to remove the other's clothing proved frustrating until Theo suggested they just slow down and talk to each other. Still by the time they were both undressed, laying naked next to each other, nature ran its course and they lost themselves in an explosion of sensations that left them breathless. Snuggled together afterwards, the perspiration on their skin cooling the build-up of heat, neither one of them could talk until Theo noticed the tears on Abby's cheeks.

"Did I hurt you?" he asked as he turned on his side and gently wiped the tears away. "I've heard it's painful for the woman the first time."

"Maybe a little at first but then it was . . . I don't know how to describe it. It was like my whole body exploded from the inside out. Was it the same for you? Is it supposed to be that way?"

Laughing he admitted he didn't know. "I think it's different for everybody but the way my brother's tell it women don't always feel that way but guys do. Maybe I didn't do it right?"

"Well if you didn't know what you were doing, trust me . . . you shouldn't change a thing," Abby said with a smile before kissing him again as her hands moved of their own volition to wantonly explore his body.

Having given in to their temptations there no longer seemed a reason to be coy about what they wanted and they spent the rest of a very long night learning how to bring pleasure to each other, stopping just long enough for Theo to recover in between.

"Oh my God Abby, I think you're going to kill me," he exclaimed after one particularly inspired bout.

"I'm sorry," she said with just the briefest hint of embarrassment. "Is doing it over and over again wrong? I don't know how anyone could stop something that feels this good."

"You wanton woman!" he said with a laugh. "If the way my brothers talk is any indication married couples have sex all the time . . . although maybe not so many times in a row."

"And do you trust their description?"

He couldn't contain his laughter. "Not one bit. It's a guy thing. We talk about sex all the time and you can only believe maybe half of what we say."

"So I'm not really killing you?" she said as she slowly trailed her finger down the center of his chest.

Somewhere between yesterday and this very moment she had become quite comfortable with touching him and laying together with him, with only moonlight illuminating her bedroom, and she didn't question the morality of what they were doing. All she knew was it had never felt more right.

"Of course not," he admitted before he pulled her to him again. "But I don't know how I'm going to get through tomorrow without being able to touch you every time I see you."

"In case you haven't figured it out tomorrow is actually today," she told him with a quick nod at the alarm clock. "And I have to be at the restaurant in an hour."

"Which means," he said throwing off his side of the covers and reaching for his jeans, "that I need to go if I'm to get there before John. I already had one run-in with him over you and I'm not looking forward to a second."

Clutching the covers to her chest, Abby sat up in bed. "What are you talking about?"

"It was nothing," he assured her as he continued to dress. "He confronted me about being inappropriate with you and took a swing at me."

"What? Why didn't you tell me before now?" she cried.

Turning to look at her as he buttoned his shirt, he could see the concern on her face even in the dim light and he quickly went to her side and took her hand in his.

"I'm sorry, but at the time I didn't think it was that big of a deal. Now though, it might be."

"What do you mean? What did he say? It's so unlike John to be violent."

"I'm not really sure what triggered it but he made what at the time was a wrong assumption and he wanted me gone. He never said the words directly but he said because we were spending so much time together and you were so happy all of a sudden he assumed we were having sex and he wanted me to leave town so I wouldn't break your heart. He said when you fell in love it would be a forever thing and that it wouldn't be with me."

"And what did you say?"

"I told him the truth . . . that we weren't sleeping together . . . although now obviously that's not the truth . . . but that I had real feelings for you and I wouldn't hurt you."

So softly he almost didn't hear her at first, Abby asked, "Will you?"

"Will I leave town? Hell no."

"No. I mean will you hurt me?"

Taking her face in his hands he stared deep into Abby's dark eyes. "I could never hurt you," he said gently. "Abby what we shared tonight was so much more than just sex. I've never met anyone quite like you before and think I'm falling in love with you."

"But you're going to leave soon," she said sadly as the first tear rolled down her face.

A feeling of dread over his imminent departure had been building in her for weeks and until now she hadn't considered how much sleeping together had magnified that feeling. Deep down she knew that some strange and powerful force had brought them together and being torn apart would be gut wrenching for both of them.

"I don't have to go," he told her quickly. "I could stay here and find work so we could be together. People seem to like me now and I could do odd jobs for people."

"No, you can't."

"You don't want me to stay?" he asked, shocked by her denial.

"More than anything I do but that's not your destiny. You need to be in front of people doing what you love...acting. Sure we need handymen too, but that's not your calling and you would be miserable."

"No I wouldn't because I would be with you," he insisted before she put a finger to his lips to silence him."

"Maybe not at first but eventually. We can't deny what we're destined to do with our lives without there being consequences and I won't be the cause of your unhappiness."

"Maybe you're right but then why don't you come with me? Obviously I don't have a dime to my name but you could open up a restaurant in Philly or even go to work in one of the fancy restaurants in New York and we could be together."

The desperation in his voice was so profound it almost swayed her but remembering what she had told him about destiny she just couldn't.

"Theo I would love to spend the rest of my life with you but I'm a small town girl. The thought of being in a big city like New York terrifies me. I need to be here, where I'm doing what I love, surrounded by people who love me and depend on me."

"But I need you," he blurted out.

"And I need you too but I don't think either one of us is in love. How could we be? We barely know each other."

"Don't tell me what I feel Abigail," he said suddenly as he got off the bed and paced around the room. "You of all people don't do that."

"I'm sorry. You're right. I shouldn't have spoken for you. Never in my wildest dreams did I think that the man who walked in my restaurant just a few weeks ago would come to mean so much to me on so many different levels and honestly, I don't know what to do with those feelings. I know you're going to leave soon and just thinking of it, even with you standing right there, I can't breathe at the thought."

"Then don't let me go," he said desperately as he pulled her into his arms and crushed her to his chest.

"I have to," she said simply before pulling away from him.

Chapter Thirteen

PRESENT DAY

"I'm never going to forget the look on her face when she said that to me," Theo told Krista as his eyes once more went to the photo of Abby. "She probably should have been an actress because she hid what she was feeling so well. It was much later when I discovered how hard that moment was for her. We had just spent the best night of our lives together and she was pushing me away. At the time I remember wondering how such a wonderful woman could be so cold after what we had shared and it wasn't until I was gone that I learned the truth."

"She loved you didn't she?" Krista asked even though she already knew the answer.

"We loved each other, but your grandmother was the most selfless person I've ever met and she knew that we each had our own lives to lead. She was willing to give up what she wanted most…"

"True love," Krista interjected.

"Yes, true love…she was willing to give it up so that I could have a chance at my dream."

"Were you happy in the end?

"Oh my dear, we are such a long way from the end of our story that I can't possibly answer that question with just a yes or no," he said shaking his head sadly.

"So tell me more," Krista asked even though Theo had been talking all day long.

114

His words were bringing their love story to life for Krista and she wanted to know it all.

"It's hard to admit but remembering it all is proving to be quite emotional for me. Can we take a break until tomorrow?"

Realizing she may have been asking more of her guest than he was physically capable of providing Krista quickly agreed.

"Is there anything I can do for you? I can put supper on the table in fifteen minutes."

"If you don't mind, I'm just going to take a cup of tea to my room and turn in early," he told her as he struggled to get out of the chair. By now she had learned not to insult him by trying to help and he slowly straightened.

"Are you sure you don't want something to eat?" she asked.

"If I'm hungry later I hope you'll allow me to raid your refrigerator but tea will be fine."

"I'll bring it right in," she assured him. "And Mr. James?"

At the quick look of censure on his face, she corrected herself, "I'm sorry . . . Theo…thank you for all of this. I know it's difficult to relive it all again but it means the world to me."

"I should be thanking you my dear," he said as he reached out to take her hand in his own. "Being able to spend time with you makes me feel closer to her and that's something I never thought I would feel again."

Bringing her hand to his lips he bestowed a gentle kiss before walking slowly to the guestroom.

While Krista prepared the tea she placed a quick call to Alex.

"Hey," he said by way of greeting. "I was just going to call you."

"Is something wrong?"

"Nothing more than usual. Wouldn't you know with just five minutes left in my shift, I picked up a drunk and now I'll be tied up here for hours doing paperwork. I'm afraid I won't make it over tonight."

"That's disappointing," Krista told him. She had been looking forward to updating him on the most recent development in the story. "Would you like me to drop off something at the station for supper? It's just leftovers but you're probably hungry."

"That's really nice of you but Paul's wife already dropped food off. Besides, could you imagine the ribbing I'd get if you showed up here?"

"Why? Don't they know about us?"

Their relationship was still in its infancy and neither had considered how to share the news with others in their lives.

"I did mention it to Paul and he told me that everyone has always known," he told her.

"What's that?" Krista asked in surprise.

"According to my partner, apparently everyone in town knew we had feelings for each other and were just waiting for us to admit it which makes me wonder what else people in town might know."

"Are you saying they might know about Nan and Theo?"

"Not at all," he said with a chuckle. "If there was even a hint of that story floating around your family would definitely know by now, but there is talk in town that he's staying with you although surprisingly no one has figured out who he is yet. With the number of old ladies in town I would think someone would have recognized him by now."

"I'm surprised by that too but then again we haven't left the house much. Will you be able to join us tomorrow night?"

"Heck ya. That's our movie date remember? Have you mentioned it to Theo yet?"

So caught up in the retelling of the story Krista had indeed forgotten about seeing one of Theo's old films.

"Not yet, but I will first thing in the morning. He's turned in for the night already and I feel guilty about it."

"Why?"

"Alex, he's almost eighty-five years old and I have kept him talking all day long! At his age it's got to be hard to deal with not only physically but emotionally as well. There were a couple of times today when he had tears in his eyes and could barely say the words. I have to try and remember how hard this whole thing is for him. He shows up and hears the woman he loves is dead and I didn't even give him a chance to grieve before I started badgering him with questions."

"Sweetheart I think you're looking at this wrong."

"What do you mean?"

"He's getting a second chance to remember what she meant to him and being able to tell the story to you, a woman who looks so much like Abby, probably brings her back to life for him."

"I never thought of it that way but now that you say it I can see that in him. Sometimes when he's talking it seems like he's so far away."

"Just let him do it at his own pace and he'll be fine. I think he realizes that going through this is important to both of you."

"You're such a nice man…makes me wonder why I didn't realize it before."

"If we've learned anything from your Nan and Theo it's not to waste time on regrets," he told her. "I better go but I'll pick you both up after work tomorrow night."

●　　　●　　　●

The next morning Theo had once again beaten Krista to the kitchen and she joined him at the table for a cup of coffee relieved to see he appeared recovered from the previous days' marathon.

"Did you sleep well?" she asked.

"Yes thank you but I'm sorry to have been such an old fuddy-duddy last night. I realized too late that talking about the moment I realized I was in love with your grandmother was going to be hard."

"I think I understand and it's me who owes you an apology. As much as I want to know everything, what happened between you and Nan is intensely personal and I'm not sure if the tables were turned I would be able to so willingly share the story."

"It's not that," he said quietly before looking directly into her eyes. "It's important to me to be able to find the right words to explain that even though what happened between us was wrong in many ways, it was incredibly important to both of us. Unless you've fallen in love with a person that you can't be with it's hard to understand why we let it happen even when we knew we shouldn't."

"Actually I'm beginning to understand how you feel. Until Alex came along I didn't have a clue what it meant to be in love with someone."

"So you love him is that it?" he asked with a smile. "Abby would be so pleased."

"I think she would but I haven't actually told Alex yet."

"What's stopping you?" he asked.

It was a valid question and one Krista had been thinking about herself.

"Nothing I suppose but I want to be sure what I'm feeling is actually love and I'm not sure what it's supposed to feel like. How was it for you and Nan?"

"I'm not sure our experience will be the same as yours. That was decades ago and people had different thoughts about love back then."

"You mean hippies and free love and all that?"

"Not exactly. The world was different then. We were more connected . . . not like today when everyone has their nose in an electronic device and people are losing the ability to interact with each other. Back then life, especially for small towns like this, had an innocence about it. I'm not saying that affairs didn't happen then, obviously they did, but there wasn't the willingness young people have to jump into bed with each other that seems to be so prevalent now. When I was young falling in love with someone took time . . . you got to know each other first and became friends. Falling in love came after that. Abby and I were the exception rather than the rule. We had limited time together and we couldn't wait to admit how we felt about each other."

"Alex and I have known each other since we were children."

"And did you think of him as a friend?" Theo asked with a smile.

"I did."

"But now it's more than that?" The whimsical smile on Krista's face told him what he wanted to know. "I think you know the answer to your question already. If you can't imagine your life without him in it you're probably in love. I can already see Alex feels that way about you so maybe it's time you tell him."

"You may be right but how did you get so smart? You seem to have an uncanny ability to read people," she said.

"That's part of being an actor," he told her. "I've spent a lifetime watching people and their reactions to various situations which has allowed me to create my characters. Sometimes I wonder if the people whose characteristics I have borrowed for a film recognize themselves on the screen."

"Oh I almost forgot," Krista said excitedly. "Alex wants to take us both out tonight for dinner and a movie."

"That's lovely but don't you think your date should be just the two of you?" he suggested.

"It's not a date; at least not the way you're thinking. It's classic movie night at the theater and you'll never guess what's showing! It's 'A Diamond Is Forever'".

"Oh my. That does bring back memories. It was one of my favorite films," he told her.

"It was Nan's also but surprisingly she always cried at the end of it. I could never understand why since it wasn't a sad ending but for some reason it struck an emotion in her. Anyway, what do you say? Would you like to go?"

"Of course. Now, if you're ready, let's continue the story."

Chapter Fourteen

1960

With just days left before Theo was scheduled to catch a train back east the time he and Abby shared became more precious than ever. Under John's watchful eye and in an effort to maintain Abby's reputation in the community, they kept their distance during the day making sure any conversation between them was as detached as possible. Even so John continued to keep an eye on them but there was no repeat of the confrontation in the garage.

Nights however were a different story. Barely in the front door of the house, they rushed into each other's arms trying desperately to fulfill their need for each other as the countdown clock in their heads slowly ticked off the precious minutes they had left together. More often than not they went straight to the bedroom, not wanting to waste one single moment they could share.

They had each promised the time they had left would be as full of love and laughter as possible and all talk of what was to come would be set aside, but with just a few days to go they were finding it increasingly difficult to keep that promise.

"When I'm gone you should hire John's brother-in-law to help out with repairs," Theo told her as they snuggled together in the dark. "I've seen some of his work and he's really good."

"But he won't be you," she said softly as she reached for his hand and pulled it close to her chest.

"Come on, Abby, don't go there," he encouraged with a kiss on her shoulder.

"I'm sorry. I know we agreed to stay positive but sometimes I can't help myself."

"It's okay, I understand, but it's not like we're never going to see each other again. We'll write often and you can come out and visit me wherever I end up and I'll come back and visit you."

"Of course we will," she said sadly knowing it was the same promise lovers had made throughout time and yet somewhere along the line their correspondence would dwindle to nothing and the promised visits would never quite materialize as their separate lives would get in the way.

"Please don't make this harder than it already is," he begged.

"I don't mean to and I know I'm the one who said you need to go back and try again, but that doesn't mean I have to like it."

The maudlin turn their discussion had taken was interrupted by the ringing of the phone. Wrapping a sheet around her Abby went to the hallway to answer it while Theo stretched out in bed, arms folded behind his head trying to think of a way to make his departure easier for her.

"Bobby, hello," he heard Abby say. The excitement in her voice as she spoke to the man caused a flare of jealousy to erupt in him. "Seriously? That's wonderful and I'm writing down the date. Yes, one o'clock. I'm sure that will work. Thank you so much. Please make sure you stop in and say hello next time you come home. Good-bye."

Theo didn't miss the spring in her step as Abby returned to bed and he found himself uncharacteristically angry that a two minute conversation with another man could elicit such happiness.

"Bobby? Who's that? Another boyfriend?" he snapped.

At the unexpected angry tone Abby looked at him in confusion. "Of course not. Why would you think that?"

"You sure perked up when you answered the phone. What was I supposed to think?"

"Stop it. I have wonderful news and you're ruining it," she said with a touch of anger of her own that made him realize how stupid he was being.

"I'm sorry. You're right. So what did wonderful Bobby say?"

Choosing to ignore his last snide remark Abby looked at him with pride.

"You have an audition."

Stunned into silence, the corner of his mouth slowly started to curl into a smile.

"What are you talking about?"

"That man you appear to be so jealous of was a childhood friend of my parents. He happens to be a rather successful theater producer and he wants to offer you an audition for his newest play. I can't remember what it's called but it's on Broadway!"

The last bit of news caused Theo to sit straight up in bed and the smile on his face was electric.

"Say that again?"

"He's offering you an audition for a Broadway play! Don't get me wrong, it's not a job offer obviously but . . . "

"But how did this happen? How does he even know about me? Damn it Abby if this is a joke . . . "

"It's not a joke I promise. A few weeks ago I read something in the paper about Bobby and his success in New York...actually I had forgotten all about him, but anyway I saw this article and I figured what could it hurt so I sent him a letter with one of the photos from your bag and told him a little bit about you and asked if he could just meet you. It was so long ago I kind of forgot about it and I didn't want to mention it in case he said no, but this could be the break you needed."

"When? Where?"

"In two weeks. I wrote all the details down for you and Bobby said when you get to New York to give him a call at his office and he'll have a script delivered to you."

"Jesus Mary and Joseph" he exclaimed as he got to his feet and began jumping all over the bed tossing Abby every which way before dropping to his knees and taking her in his arms.

"How can I ever thank you for this? You are the best thing that ever happened to me," he said before kissing her deeply and holding her tight.

His excitement should have been contagious but instead Abby found herself fighting back tears. His happiness meant nothing but despair for her if he got the job. Ashamed to admit it even to herself, deep down she hoped he would move back with her if acting didn't pan out for him.

"You know a lot of great actors got their start in the theater," he said excitedly. "But not many of them can say they started on Broadway. Course I don't have the job yet but I have a good feeling about this and it's all thanks to you."

His desire for her growing by the minute, Theo pulled her onto his lap and soon they lost themselves in a whole other world of excitement.

Afterwards, as Theo slept deeply at her side, Abby lay awake struggling with her competing emotions. She was too good a person to begrudge him this opportunity, after all she had arranged it, but that didn't make it hurt any less to see how excited he suddenly was to leave. Whatever her feelings were she would set them aside and show nothing but happiness and support for the man she now realized she loved more than anything.

●　　　●　　　●

The next day Theo couldn't contain his excitement and after weeks of the community thinking he was a drifter, he finally came clean with what brought him to town and, more importantly, what his future held. Abby stood silently by, a desperate smile forced onto her face, as Theo repeated the story while giving credit for his good fortune where it was due and answering question after question from Abby's customers. Most having never met an actor, listened in awe, but John was quick to realize there was more to the story.

"Good news right?" he asked as he and Abby stood side-by-side in the kitchen watching while Theo held court in the dining room.

"The best."

"Why don't I believe you?" he asked causing her to give him a funny look.

"What are you talking about?"

"Abby I know you're my boss and all but I've known you far too long to be fooled. You've fallen in love with him haven't you?"

She could only nod her head before her gaze went once more to Theo.

"I knew it. Oh Abby why did you let it happen? You had to know he would leave eventually."

"Do you really think I set out to fall for him?" she asked "It just happened."

"And he loves you." It wasn't a question. John had obviously figured it out for himself. "So what happens now?"

"Nothing. He leaves and I stay here and in all likelihood we will never see each other again."

"But couldn't you......"

"Don't say it. We've already talked about every possible option and it brings us right back to the same horrible conclusion. Nothing is going to change that. I'm just trying to make the next two days as pleasant as possible for him. I owe him that."

"Something tells me he'd think it was the other way around. If you wouldn't have taken him in, who knows what would have happened to him."

"It doesn't matter anymore so let's just drop it okay? I was thinking of having a good-bye party for him at my house. Do you think people would come?"

"Are you kidding? No matter what I thought of him when he first arrived that boy has become part of the community. You won't be able to keep them away. Want me to spread the word?"

"Please, but I'll do everything else."

"Are you sure?"

"Yes. And John?"

"Yeah?"

"Thanks for not saying I told you so."

Giving her hand a quick squeeze John turned his attention back to the orders waiting to be filled as Abby walked slowly to the privacy of her office. She hadn't yet discussed the party with Theo but she knew he would be pleased. By the end of the day not only did everyone finally know the man they had come to think of as a handyman was really an actor, but news of the party had made its way to every corner of town. That night back at Abby's house Theo sat at the table with pen and paper while Abby got an early start on desserts for the party.

"Whatever are you working on?" she asked as she put an apple pie in the oven.

"I'm making a list of everything every casting director ever told me I did wrong so that I don't repeat the mistakes in New York," he told her.

"That sounds backwards to me," she said as she took a break and sat opposite him.

"What do you mean?"

"If you start out this chance by focusing on the negative where do you think that will lead? Why not focus on everything positive those people have told you and go from there instead?"

"I never thought about it that way and besides the positive list is a lot shorter than the other," he said with sudden doubt in his eyes. "What makes you think this is going to turn out any different than LA?"

"Just a feeling, but do you know something? I just realized I've never seen you act. Why don't you do a scene for me?"

"You mean right now?"

"Why not? My kitchen can be your stage."

"What scene should I do?"

"Do you remember any of the auditions you did? Can you do something from one of those?"

"There was this one movie role I tried for, it wasn't the lead, but it was a good solid part and the scene they had me read was about a man whose wife had just died. He comes home from work and the Police greet him at the door to tell him she's dead."

"How horrible! Give it a try."

Standing from the table Theo walked around the kitchen for a few minutes; head down, arms gesturing wildly, before he stopped and looked back at Abby.

"What do you mean she's dead? She can't be. We had plans together she and I. Kids, a house, a lifetime of growing old together. You're wrong. You have to be. She can't be dead. I'd know it if she was...I'd feel it inside right? We have this incredible connection and I'd feel it if she

125

was gone. Why would you lie about something like this? For God sakes it can't be true. Tell me it's not true . . . "

Dropping to his knees, head buried in his hands, sobs began to pour from Theo and Abby burst into tears herself before he quickly went to her side.

"Abby why are you crying?"

"It was so sad and my heart was breaking for you," she told him, unable to stop crying but realizing finally that his tears had been part of the act.

"Sweetheart, it wasn't real remember? I was just acting."

Pulling her into his arms he tried to console her even as he wondered why her reaction had been so extreme.

"I'm sorry, but that was wonderful," she said as her cries subsided and she dabbed at the corner of her eyes. "Theo you're a fantastic actor and you're going to be so famous someday."

"I think you're a little prejudiced but I'll dedicate my first Tony award to you anyway," he said with a satisfied smile. "If you were my only critic this business would be a whole lot easier."

Although the scene had been wonderfully acted it wasn't the only reason for Abby's tears; her own fears of losing Theo had overwhelmed her and the rest of the evening was spent trying to ignore her feelings as Theo's growing excitement about the audition blinded him to her quiet demeanor.

Each getting undressed on their own side of the bed as Theo kept up a steady stream of conversation, Abby stopped what she was doing to watch him knowing that she would never find a man who excited her more. Long hair and heavy beard aside, the man's physique was stunning even to a novice such as herself and in moments she felt her body warm with desire for him. They had become as comfortable with each other as an old married couple and more than anything she knew the intimacy they shared each evening would be what she missed most.

Turning to find her watching him Theo grinned at her in all his naked glory before crawling across the bed and pulling her closer to him.

"Are you too tired for me to make love to you tonight?" he asked softly as he moved a stray strand of hair from her face. "It's okay if you are."

"Never," she whispered into his ear before her hands began to roam his body causing him to moan in response. "But tonight, I am going to make love to you."

His eyes opened wide at her declaration but he offered no resistance as she pushed him back onto the bed and quickly removed the remainder of her clothing. His eyes never left her.

"When did you become such a wanton woman?" he asked with a smile.

"Shhh," she said putting her finger on his lips to silence him. "Don't let the neighbors know but I intend to make this the most memorable night of your life."

Surprising even herself Abby set her conservative upbringing aside and when she was done pleasuring him they climaxed together in an explosion of ecstasy that left them both gasping for breath.

"Do I even want to ask where you learned to do all that?" Theo said as he gasped for air.

"Was it too much?" Abby asked in sudden embarrassment; although the pleasure she got from their romp was far too enjoyable to want to change a thing.

Pulling her to him Theo could only laugh. "You are such a surprising woman Abigail Peterson. I don't know how I'm ever going to get on that train."

Everything in her was screaming at him to stay but she said nothing and simply nestled closer to him. It wasn't long before she heard the soft rhythmic sounds of his breathing indicating he was asleep before she also drifted off.

Chapter Fifteen

Theo slipped out of the house around five the next morning looking around carefully as he always did to make sure none of the neighbors saw him leaving. He had taken to leaving even earlier after too many close calls where he just barely beat John to the restaurant but this morning, after such an eventful evening, he had overslept. Making quick work of the walk from the house he couldn't help but whistle with happiness as he walked. For the first time in years his life was going well and he knew without a doubt that the audition would land him his first real job and he had Abby to thank for all of it.

Whatever she had seen in him that first day in the restaurant would remain a mystery to him but he was grateful she had taken a chance on him. Getting to know her had been an unexpected bonus and within days of meeting her he found he was falling in love. It seemed everyone in town loved Abby, but the love he felt for her was accompanied by an unshakable feeling that she was the one person he was meant to spend his life with. Even he didn't know why he knew that but with every upturn of her lips, every caring gesture towards someone less fortunate, and every laugh erupting from deep within her, he had fallen deeper in love with the woman. Leaving her tomorrow was going to be pure torture.

Complicating matters further was knowing that she was beginning to have feelings for him also. Neither of them had professed love for the other but he suspected she felt it too and he struggled with the desire to tell her how he felt even as he walked out of her life. In the end he had made the decision to not say the words to her; a decision that was put to the test last night when Abby had turned the aggressor in the bedroom and rocked his world.

Holding her in his arms last night he couldn't imagine a better companion for his life's journey and it took all of his willpower to not drop to one knee and offer to make her his wife. Instead, he had pretended to be asleep as she lay in his arms. Long after she had drifted off he thought about the words he would say to her when it was finally time to leave and could think of nothing that would convey the depths of his feelings and his gratitude for what she had done for his life. He needed the words of another to express what was in his heart and slipping out of bed, he had put pen to paper. Finished, he folded it carefully and slipped the note into his pocket until he could give it to her. Placing a gentle kiss on Abby's cheek he had slipped quietly down the stairs and headed back to his cot at the restaurant.

Fishing his key out of his jeans he noticed a light on in the restaurant kitchen. Suddenly on alert he quietly opened the door while listening for sounds of a possible intruder. Ready to call out John suddenly came into view in the kitchen and the two of them locked eyes. For a long time neither man said a thing before John finally broke the silence.

"Out for an early morning walk were ya?" John asked.

The look on his face was impossible to decipher and Theo didn't know how to proceed. He was tired of lying to the man about his relationship with Abby but still wanted to protect her from scandal.

"Not exactly," was the best he could come up with.

"Don't bother lying to me," John finally said as he looked away and continued with his prep work. "I know you've been spending your nights with her."

"John, it's not what you think."

"It's exactly what I think and we both know it," he said angrily while waving the knife in his hand at Theo. "The only reason I don't kill you right now is that right or wrong Abby's in love with you."

Theo's eyes grew wide at his words. How John could know that was beyond him but how he knew didn't matter. Finally someone else had confirmed what he had suspected. She loved him.

"I told you before that you better not hurt her and by this time tomorrow when you step foot on that train she's going to be destroyed and I don't know if she'll ever recover from it. I want you to think about that the next time you waltz into a young woman's life and fill her full of promises."

The anger behind John's words was tempered by the worry in his eyes and Theo found himself in awe of the man and how much he cared for Abby.

"John, you're right." The simple admission caught John off guard and he stopped what he was doing to stare at Theo. "But I love her too and I'd give anything if she would come with me. I've asked her many times but she won't leave here. I'm not going to give up trying though. Someday we will be together and I will spend the rest of my life trying to make this up to her. She's a strong woman, stronger than anyone I've ever met before, but I'm eternally grateful she will have you to help her through this. I know I don't have any right to ask this of you especially after what I've done, but if she ever needs anything will you please call me? I don't know where I'll end up but call my folks. They'll always know where to find me."

Taking an order pad Theo wrote down his parent's phone number and handed it to John who looked at it carefully before folding it and putting it in his pocket. Expecting John to have more to say on his shortcomings Theo couldn't have been more surprised when the older man reached out his hand to him. Grasping it firmly Theo nodded his appreciation and the moment was over. By the time Doris and Susan showed up, followed closely behind by Abby, the two men had regained their normal stoic demeanor towards each other.

"Morning everyone", Abby said without her usual cheerfulness. "It's such a busy day with the party and all that I am only going to work until the breakfast rush is over and then I'm heading home to finish getting ready for the party. We're closing early today so that you guys can get ready yourselves. There will be plenty of food and drinks so make sure you come early okay?"

"You shouldn't have to get ready for the party on your own," John said. "Why don't you let one of us come and help?"

"I can help," Theo told her with a warm smile.

"Thank you both but John I need you here to keep things running smoothly through lunch and Theo, you're the guest of honor. Besides, weren't you going to help Mr. Simpson replace a broken window on his house? He doesn't have any money so I already paid for the materials at the hardware store and there is an envelope of money sitting on my desk for your labor. You'll need that for your trip I'm sure. Anyway, it's going to be a busy day so let's get to work everyone."

Busy was an understatement. Before any of them knew what hit them the restaurant was packed with customers and Abby wasn't able to get away as quickly as she had hoped. Fortunately for her she had done a lot the night before and when she finally got away she spent the afternoon finishing up the food and icing down the beer and soda. With only minutes to spare she raced upstairs for a quick shower finishing just as the first guests arrived. The unexpected number of guests was overwhelming and Doris and Susan quickly pitched in to get food on the table.

It wasn't until she saw Mr. Simpson that Abby realized she had yet to see Theo. As the guest of honor she had expected him to be the first to arrive but there had been no sign of him. Making her way through the crowd of people to Mr. Simpson's side she asked if he had seen Theo.

"Not since late this afternoon," he said as she knelt down next to him. In the throng of people he was having trouble hearing her.

"Did he say where he was going?" she asked with concern. It wasn't like Theo to just disappear, especially today.

"Something about going to get ready for the party," he told her. "Isn't he here?"

"No, and to tell the truth I'm a little bit worried," she admitted.

"Oh there he is," Mr. Simpson said as he pointed a shaky finger towards the front door.

"Where..?" Abby started to ask before her jaw dropped and she couldn't speak.

Standing before her was a man with the bluest of eyes and a smile that lit up the room; a face that she had seen hundreds of times before but yet had never truly seen. It was Theo. His beard was gone, his hair freshly cut in a much shorter style, and he was dressed in a brand new suit. The transformation was so dramatic it could only be described as epic.

Rising to her feet she stared at the handsome man who stood across from her. In the crowded room, some also realizing for the first time that the stranger was none other than Theo, Abby's heart threatened to beat out of her chest as he smiled back at her. Before she could say a word he was surrounded by others and swallowed up in the crowd.

Hands shaking, face flushed, Abby made her way out of the room to the relative quiet of the kitchen and tried to collect herself. More than anything she had wanted to throw herself into his arms and cover his newly discovered face with her kisses and she might have done so if everyone else hadn't beaten her to him. This new Theo was James Dean, Paul Newman, and Tony Curtis all rolled up in one and he was the man she was in love with.

"Abby are you okay?" Doris asked as she walked into the kitchen with an empty plate.

"I'm fine" Abby told her quickly before finding something to do with her hands that might hide the shaking.

"Did you get a look at Theo? I never would have guessed there was such a handsome man under all that hair. He sure cleans up nicely."

Talk about an understatement Abby thought to herself trying not to let her desire for the man get away from her. Caught up in her own thoughts she didn't realize Doris was still talking.

"I'm sorry," she finally said. "I was miles away. What did you say?"

"I just asked if you wanted me to put out more plates. People just keep showing up."

"Oh yeah, right. There are more plates back in the pantry. I'll get them."

Using the busy work as an excuse to escape from Doris' prying eyes, Abby hurried back to the pantry before standing at the window, wrapping her arms around herself and staring at nothing. Lost in her own thoughts she jumped at the feel of Theo's arms wrapping around her waist as he placed a soft kiss at her neck. Used to the feel of his beard on her skin the bare skin of his cheek was a new sensation to her and she melted into his touch for just a moment before trying to pull away.

"Don't worry," he told her as he pulled her back. "I closed the door when I came in. Why are you hiding in here?"

"I'm not hiding," she lied.

"Why don't I believe you?" he said as he continued to snuggle her neck. "Did I surprise you with my new look?"

"I think you surprised everyone. Who would have thought a shave and haircut would make a whole new man out of you? What made you decide to do it?"

"I couldn't exactly go to the audition the way I was and I thought it was about time you saw the real me."

"And this is the real you?" Abby asked as she turned to face him. "The women in New York are going to love you."

"I didn't do it for them."

"It doesn't matter. You're going to have girls falling over themselves in no time and pretty soon you won't even remember us back here."

"There's only one woman I want to remember and that's you," he said huskily.

Even in the short time they had shared the same bed Abby knew exactly what that look meant as he lowered his lips to hers in a hungry kiss she didn't hesitate to return until the jiggling of the door knob startled them both as they pulled away from each other.

"Abby are you in there? Susan do you know where Abby keeps the plates?" Doris said from the other side of the door. Trying hard not to laugh they covered their mouths before they heard her footsteps fading away.

"How soon do you think we can send the guests home?" he asked as he pulled Abby back to him. She could feel his need between them and felt her own desire growing once more.

"As much as I want to be alone with you, this is your fault," Abby said with a smile. "If you weren't so incredibly charming and friendly you never would have made so many friends in your short time here.

Now we better get back before someone figures out what we're doing in here. I'll go first with the plates and then you can follow me a few minutes later."

"You've gotten awfully good at this cloak and dagger stuff," he teased before Abby shut him up with a simple brush of her hand at his zipper that caused his body to jerk.

"One of us has to be," she told him before turning with a smile and walking out of the room knowing full well that his excited state would force him to wait to come out of the room.

•   •   •

By the time the night was over dozens of townsfolk had stopped by to say their farewells to Theo as Abby watched over it all with a mixture of happiness for him and sadness at what was to come. Most who knew her left that night with yet another story of Abby's kindness towards others, never knowing that the shared experience between her and Theo had resulted in so much more than a helping hand. While his short time as part of the community was longer than most of those Abby had taken in it was only a blip in their lives and he would soon be forgotten by those who had come to say their good-byes.

Only John knew how bittersweet the moment truly was for Abby. He was the last to leave the party and with surprising charity after butting heads with Theo for weeks, he wished him the best of luck in his future. Knowing both men the way she did Abby was quick to see the look they shared as they shook hands before John and his wife headed for home.

"What was that?" she asked as they turned as one and headed back into the house turning off the porch light as they did.

"It was nothing," he said innocently before pulling her into his arms for a kiss.

Not willing to be dissuaded by the handsome face and strong jaw line she still hadn't gotten used to looking at, she wouldn't be put off.

"Did you and John have words again?" she asked.

"Really, it was nothing," he insisted. "This morning he caught me coming in. He knows I didn't spend the night on the cot."

"So he . . . ?"

"Yes, he figured it out and he lectured me on leading you astray."

"But you didn't."

"That's not how he sees it and if your father was alive I doubt he would either. I'm sorry if I hurt you Abby. You have to know that was never my intention."

Unwilling to admit the depth of her despair over losing him Abby worked hard to keep a stoic smile on her face knowing that the moment he stepped on the train she would feel the full force of losing him.

"I know you would never hurt me just as I know that leaving tomorrow is the right thing for you. This is the start of an awesome life for you and I'm just grateful I could play a small part in it. Do I wish things had turned out different? I probably wouldn't be a woman if I didn't, but I wouldn't change knowing you for anything in my life and I can't wait to see what you do with this opportunity."

His gaze never wavered from her eyes and she had to bite her lip to keep from dissolving into tears. Finally, he lifted her from her feet and slowly carried her up to bed. As they made love that evening it was with a tenderness they had never shown before; slow and unhurried as if tomorrow would never come. For one final evening they were together the way the world had intended.

• • •

Abby's insistence on seeing Theo to the train the next morning was met by his equally strong resistance to it.

"Of course I'm going to the train station with you," she said yet again. "I want to spend every minute with you I can."

"I appreciate that, I really do, but it's going to be hard enough to say good-bye to you and the last time I see you I want to be holding you in my arms for a kiss. Please, you've done so much for me already but do this one more thing," he begged.

If she hadn't been laying naked in bed next to the man she might have had more willpower but eventually she couldn't resist the sad look in his eyes and she grudgingly agreed.

"Besides, it's not going to be the last time we see each other. You promised," she reminded him.

"Of course," he corrected himself, "but it will be the last time for a while."

Their promises of writing and frequent visits sounded wonderful but each separately wondered if that would indeed be the case.

"I better get going or I'll miss my train," Theo said finally. His meager belongings had long since been brought over from the restaurant. Clothes freshly washed and ironed, he hadn't seen the small package Abby had snuck in with his belongings as she packed his things.

"I guess so," she said quietly. As both of them got up and dressed a heavy pall fell over the room. Finally, grabbing his bag in one hand, Abby's hand in the other, they made their way down to the front door and turned to each other for their good-byes.

"Damn it. I forgot something," Theo said suddenly before racing upstairs as Abby gripped her hands into fists trying hard not to cry.

Back in the bedroom Theo once more took out the hastily penned note to Abby, read it yet again before placing a soft kiss on her name, folding it up and placing it under her pillow. With one final look around the room he went back downstairs to find tears flowing steadily down her beautiful face.

"Please don't cry," he whispered as he pulled her into his strong arms. "God this is so much harder than I thought it would be. You mean everything to me and I'm never going to be able to repay you for your kindness. No matter how this audition turns out I will never be able to thank you enough."

"How could they say no to this handsome face?" she cried as she cupped his face in her delicate hands to see tears welling in his eyes. "You were born to be on the stage and someday I'll be able to say I knew you before you were famous."

"Come with me," he asked desperately. "I don't want to do this without you."

"I love that you want me there Theo, but this is your journey not mine. Remember that I believe in you and will never stop, but you have to believe in yourself and remember you are an actor. Nothing will change that."

Remembering her pleas to shout it out one of those first evenings together, he said loudly, "I AM AN ACTOR!" before smiling back at her through his tears.

"Now go break a leg," she told him as his lips lowered to her own and they clung together in a last desperate attempt to forestall the inevitable before she pushed him away and watched him walk out the door into the early morning light.

With a final wave he disappeared from her sight.

Chapter Sixteen

PRESENT DAY

If the tears rolling down Theo's cheeks were any indication, saying good-bye to Abby again after sixty some years was no easier than it had been back then and Krista stepped out of the room to give him time to compose himself while she dried her own tears. It might have been another time and another place, but Theo's words brought the story to life for her and each time he finished telling another part of their journey together the feelings she experienced during the retelling lingered as if she had actually experienced them. As the story came to the point of their inevitable separation a deep sadness had taken root in the depth of her soul that was magnified as Theo had begun to cry. Trying to put herself in Nan's place she could never have made such a difficult decision to let him walk away and yet, if she hadn't, none of her family would exist today.

Regaining a bit of self-control she headed back to the living room to find Theo sitting in the same spot, but with a well weathered black and white photo in his hand he couldn't take his eyes off.

"I found Abby's farewell gift the next day," he said without looking up from the photo. "She had buried it deep in my duffle bag, I suppose so I wouldn't find it right away and come rushing back."

"Was that photo her gift?" Krista asked gently before taking a seat at the other end of the sofa.

"Among other things and I've looked at it every day since I left. It's seen better days and I probably should have had a copy made before now, but it wouldn't be the same."

"You mentioned there were other things?"

"Yes although if you were expecting a grand romantic gesture it was much more sensible yet equally unexpected. It was an envelope full of cash. Hundreds of dollars along with a note that said she knew I would need more money than I had earned at the Piggly Wiggly to make my new start. I knew it was all the savings she had in the world and yet she had sent the money away with me. That's why I would have turned back if I had found it earlier and she knew it. She had already given me so much I couldn't possibly take that too, but there was no way to return it and in the end it did help."

"Nan told me once that the most charitable thing she could do for others was to spend her last dime trying to help. She said no one ever got into heaven with money in their pockets."

"How very much that sounds like her," he said with a soft smile as he fingered the photograph once more. "She had so many of those sayings, all seemed designed to justify what she did for others when in reality she had no need to justify anything. Everything she did was from the heart and I think that's what I'll miss so much about her."

A sudden buzzing of her cell phone on the coffee table interrupted their discussion and Krista picked it up to find a text from Alex.

"Alex said he hasn't left work yet and asks if we'll pick him up at the station to save some time before dinner tonight."

"Whatever works for you children," he told her. "And again if you'd rather it be just the two of you I can certainly bow out."

"Absolutely not," Krista said with a smile. "I'm growing quite fond of you if you hadn't noticed and Alex and I are both looking forward to seeing the movie with you."

"Well then, if you'll excuse me, I'll go get ready for our adventure."

•   •   •

The more time Krista spent with Theo the more she was beginning to understand Nan's attraction to the man. Quick witted, with a surefire memory belying his age, he kept them entertained throughout dinner with stories of Hollywood's back lots. Theo may have sensed it within her, but after such a trying few days Krista was grateful for a break from the emotions the story had brought forth in her.

"How that party didn't end up splashed across the front page of Variety the next day is still a mystery to me," he said as Alex and Krista struggled to contain their laughter at the antics of the unnamed A-listers Theo was referring to.

"Come on tell us who it was," Alex implored when he stopped laughing.

"One thing you need to know about Hollywood my young friend. It's like Vegas. What happens at parties in the hills stays there. It's an unwritten code that we all abided by...that is at least until another actor got a role you really coveted. Then all the claws come out. It's not quite that cut throat in the theater though."

"Then why did you switch to films?" Krista asked.

"Sad to say I was seduced by the money and fame. Those in the theater rarely if ever get the kind of stardom those in film experience. I wanted that and I was one of the lucky ones."

"And the film we're going to see tonight, it was your first right? That's what Nan told me."

"It was, although in some respects I wished it had come later in my career."

"Why is that?" Alex asked as he pushed his empty plate away.

"The film ended up being the highlight of my career and it happened much too early on. Critics lauded the film and my performance in it, but many in the business didn't hesitate to say I hadn't paid my dues like so many others had. I had more than a measure of success with later works but a lot of people, myself included, couldn't get past such great success with my very first picture."

"What did Nan think?"

"Abby would never say anything negative, especially about my career. She always was my staunchest supporter and she had a knack for being able to turn my doubts to something more positive. I have to say I'm quite looking forward to seeing the film tonight. The last time

I saw it was on premiere night and I'm anxious to see if it still resonates with me today."

"Speaking of that, the theater is just a few doors down but we better hurry if we're going to make it on time," Krista told them.

•   •   •

Alex had never seen the movie and as the house lights came up at the end of the film Krista and Theo both turned towards him to gauge his reaction as the sparse crowd around them exited the theater.

"Theo you were fantastic," he finally told them. "That's the way movies should be written."

Giving them both a formal bow Theo thanked him for his compliment before they exited the theater. No one in the theater had seemed to recognize Theo and for some reason that saddened Krista but she waited until they were back at her house to mention it.

"I was sure someone would recognize you," she said as she settled onto the sofa with a cup of tea while Theo and Alex enjoyed a beer.

"I'm afraid unless you are a diehard classic movie fan those days are well behind me," Theo admitted. "My last picture was almost thirty years ago and while I did a lot of theater after that, not many these days would recognize the handsome young man that won your grandmother's heart."

"I think you're still handsome," Krista said before rising to place a quick kiss on his cheek.

"Hey now," Alex said with a smile. "Theo you're not trying to steal my girl are you?"

"You never know," he replied with a wink. "You've already seen I can be quite fond of the Peterson women."

Krista started to say something but closed her mouth before casting a quick look at Alex that did not go unnoticed by Theo.

"What is it my dear?" he asked.

"Well, we were waiting for the right moment to ask you this but . . ."

"Certainly by now you realize you can ask me anything. What is it?"

"When we were cleaning out Nan's house we found something up in the attic and now that I know about your relationship with Nan I'm pretty sure it belongs to you."

"What is it?"

"Alex would you get it from my closet please?" Krista asked before he leapt out of his chair and hurried to the bedroom.

When he returned, they both watched for a reaction from Theo and they weren't disappointed.

"It's been over five decades since I've been that box but I know just what's in it," he said excitedly.

"So, it's......"

"It's my Oscar and how appropriate you should show it to me after seeing the film this evening."

Krista and Alex looked excitedly at each other now that they had the answer to one of the biggest mysteries they had discovered in the house.

"We suspected but tell us about it if you would," Krista asked as Theo raised the lid of the box and pulled out the Oscar as if it was the most precious thing in the world.

"Well let's start where we left off earlier...with my leaving Abby behind . . . "

Chapter Seventeen

Almost a month had passed since Theo had packed his bags and headed back east but for Abby it was still as fresh a wound as it was that morning. Her heart was indeed broken and although time had already passed she didn't know if she would ever get past the heartache of missing him even if he wasn't entirely out of her life. They had started to correspond on a regular basis and each day she raced to her new post office box hoping for a letter from him; sometimes finding nothing but empty space and others discovering several letters at once that she quickly stuffed in her pocket to read when she was alone just as she had with his parting gift to her.

Devastated by Theo's departure, she had rushed back upstairs that morning and thrown herself on the bed, pulling his pillow close to catch the last faint scent of his aftershave as she cried her eyes out only to feel something unusual under the pillow; a single sheet of paper in a strong masculine handwriting. Wiping her tears away she read the words he had penned to her that had become the mantra they shared:

"I carry your heart with me
I carry it in my heart"

The words of e.e. cummings, so familiar to her after the nights the pair had spent reciting his poetry to each other, had made her cry even harder before she carefully folded the paper and clutched it to her chest. Since then she had tucked the poem safely in her pocketbook to read whenever loneliness for Theo threatened to overwhelm her.

Abby spent the lonely nights without him writing long letters filled with words of her loneliness and details of her everyday life; missing him so much yet being cautious to say nothing that would cause him to change the course of his life and return to her, but in the end it didn't matter. His most recent letter brought with it the exciting news of his new job. The audition he had been so nervous about was now behind him and it wasn't a surprise to Abby that for the first time in Theo's life, he was now a professional actor having landed a small part in the Broadway production. His letters were crammed with details about what he was experiencing - the beautiful and ornate theater, the excitement of rehearsals and running lines with his fellow actors, and even the quirkiness of the director all came to life for her through his words. Abby tried to be happy for him but each letter seemed to take him even further away, dashing all her unspoken hopes that they might someday be together again.

John watched her carefully as the days went on. The only one who knew what Theo had meant to Abby, he more so than any of the others knew the true cause of the sadness in her eyes each morning after yet another sleepless night missing Theo. Worried for her he had tried several times to talk to her about it only to be brushed off when questioned. Insisting she was fine he knew she was anything but. If Abby had contact with Theo she never mentioned it. To those in the restaurant he had become only a memory; another of Abby's charity cases that had moved on to another life. John however, knew it was much, much more.

"Abby, why don't you come over to the house for dinner Sunday night?" John asked after one particularly trying day. The entire staff had been rushed off their feet all day and he hadn't seen Abby eat a single morsel. The girl was wasting away in front of his eyes. "Malinda was just saying how much she missed having you in the house. What do you say?"

"John, I'm fine," Abby told him having seen through his ruse. "You don't have to worry about me."

"Stop lying to me girl," he said forcefully. "You may have everyone else around here fooled, but you're anything but fine. Have you eaten anything at all today? Do you sleep at all?"

"John, please stop," she implored.

"I can't. I care about you too much to let you do this to yourself. If Theo hasn't even had the courtesy to let you know how he's doing then . . . "

"You don't know what you're talking about and I won't let you say anything bad about him."

"Abby he broke your heart and left you here to pick up the pieces. He doesn't deserve your protection anymore."

"I don't want it spread around but I have heard from him. Actually more than once. He got the job. Can you believe it?"

"Well that's wonderful isn't it?"

"It is but it means he won't be back. Not any time soon anyway." Tears welled up in her eyes and she quickly looked around to make sure no one else had seen.

"Come here and sit down," John said as he took her hand and they sat together at the prep table. "Did you really think he was going to come back here?" he asked gently as she stared at her lap, her hands clasped tightly together.

"Yes, no, I don't know. I want him to succeed but I don't think I realized it meant I would never see him again. "

"It doesn't have to you know."

"Of course it will. He's thousands of miles away and he's going to become a big star. He'll never come back here and we both know it."

"Abby I think you underestimate the man. He's in love with you."

At his surprising words Abby's head snapped up and the corner of her mouth curled into the smallest smile.

"He told me so himself," John assured her. "If you love him too why don't you go to him?"

"I can't," she said. "What would I do in New York City? And besides, there are too many people here depending on me. I can't just up and leave."

"You're right. I can't really see you living there either but why don't you at least go out and see him for a visit? I know you have money tucked away and the restaurant is doing okay. Take a week and go be with Theo. See what his life is like for yourself and remind him of what you feel for each other."

For the first time since Theo had left John saw a true smile on her face at the possibility of seeing her young man again.

"I'll write him today," she said excitedly.

"Abby?"

The soft voice behind her was familiar yet not and Abby slowly turned around to see a soldier home from the war. Standing before her wasn't the boy she remembered seeing off but a man who had seen the worst horrors humanity had to offer. The eyes that looked back at her with such desperation were empty and bereft of the joy she remembered him having. Whatever he had experienced had changed him.

"Robert...welcome home," Abby said with as much excitement as she could muster before moving forward to offer a hug.

Since she had mailed her last letter, the one Theo had seen on the hall table, she had heard nothing from Robert and she was grateful that whatever he had been hoping to rekindle between them seemed to have disappeared. But if that was the case why was he standing in front of her?

"I got in late last night and knew I would find you here," he said as they walked to a nearby table and took a seat in the nearly empty dining room. "How have you been?"

"I'm fine but I'm shocked to see you," Abby said stumbling over her words. Shocked was the least of what she was feeling. Knowing Robert would never have made his way to the restaurant upon his return if he didn't think there was something between them, suddenly there was a whole lot of guilt eating at her.

"Why would you be? You have to know you would be the first person I wanted to see when I got out." Reaching across the table he took her hand in his. "I've been dreaming about seeing you again ever since your last letter. For a while there I was beginning to think you had found another guy while I was gone."

"Robert, I . . . " Abby said gently as she tried to disengage their hands. "I think maybe you've got the wrong idea."

"I know. Seeing the look on your face when you turned around I know there's no one else and I'm so relieved. I don't have much time - I really should get to my folks and say hello - but let's go out tonight. We can drive up to Lakeville to that really nice restaurant and have a nice meal and a long talk."

"Robert, I would love to but . . . "

"Great! It's settled. I'll pick you up at your house at nineteen hundred hours then."

Without giving her a chance to say no he turned crisply on his heel and walked out as she stood looking after him with her mouth hanging wide open.

"Hum . . . " John said as he sidled up to her. "Didn't expect to see him come around here again. Didn't you break things off with him before he left for the Army?"

"There was nothing to break off," Abby said sharply. "We only went out twice and that was it and that was months before he was drafted."

"Then why was he here? I wasn't eavesdropping but everyone in the place could hear what he was saying to you. Even as old and slow as I am I could tell he thinks you're his girlfriend. Why would he act that way if he hasn't seen you in two years?"

"I made the mistake of answering his letters," she admitted with a shake of her head. "But it was just as a friend."

"Oh Abby, how could you?" he exclaimed disappointedly. "Even if you didn't mean to, getting letters from a girl back home means something to a guy in the service. No wonder he talked to you like that. He thinks you're his girl!"

"Of course he doesn't," she insisted. "There was nothing in any of the letters that would have given him that thought. I was very careful not to lead him on."

"It doesn't matter now," John insisted. "What are you going to do about it? You're not going out with him tonight are you?"

"It doesn't appear I have much choice now do I?"

"What about Theo? Will you tell Robert about him?"

"There's no reason to and I don't want you telling him either."

"I thought there was nothing to tell?" John teased. "Unless you count the letters the pair of you have been exchanging."

At Abby's surprised look, John couldn't help but laugh.

"Yeah, you're not as sneaky as you think. I know what you do every Wednesday when you disappear in your office and then have to go out for a walk."

"Does everyone else know too?" she asked with a sigh.

"No. Just me and truth be told I am happy for you," he said as she threw him a surprised glance. "As much as I disliked Theo at the beginning he turned into a good guy and I'm glad he didn't just dump you and move on. There might be some hope for that man yet…that is if he makes an honest woman of you."

At John's implication of their inappropriate relationship, Abby's face turned crimson.

"If you're suggesting he come back and marry me, that's not going to happen. His life is different now and I'm happy for him."

"How many times will you tell yourself that?" he asked her as he shook his head in disbelief.

"I know you're trying to help John but please, for me, let it go. Maybe in a perfect world things between Theo and I would have turned out differently but it's not going to happen. That doesn't mean I won't cherish what we shared while he was here and it's not going to stop us from being friends in the future and yes . . . we will continue to exchange letters."

"But you're not going to tell anyone about it right?"

"There's no need. What's between us is just that . . . between us. No one else needs to know," she said with a pointed look his direction.

"Message received loud and clear. But let me say one more thing about it and then you'll never hear me mention it again. If the two of you are so stubborn you couldn't admit even to each other how you feel then maybe you don't deserve to live happily ever after. You let the man you should be spending the rest of your life with walk out that door. At some point you'll realize that and even I won't be able to comfort you when that day comes."

Giving him a quick peck on the cheek, Abby noticed the tears in his eyes as he placed his arm around her shoulder and gave it a squeeze. He was probably right, but if his prediction did come true, there wouldn't be another soul on the planet she would turn to for comfort.

"You look wonderful tonight Abby," Robert said as he looked at her over his menu. "Just as I remembered."

"Thank you," Abby replied before turning her eyes back to the menu in front of her. Unable to find a polite way to back out of the date she had made an extra effort to look nice and was determined to make it a pleasurable evening.

He had taken her to the same restaurant they had dined at on their previous two dates and she wasn't surprised. He had always been predictable. Still his apparent belief that they were a couple was unexpected as she thought she had made it painfully clear to him that she had no romantic interest in him before he left for the Army. She clearly remembered the tears in his eyes when she told him she thought they were better suited to other people.

It wasn't that he wasn't a nice man; if anything he was too nice and it was hard to be around that kind of syrupy sweetness all the time. Robert was the kind of man who wouldn't hurt a fly which was all well and good but there was nothing about him that excited her. He was plain vanilla; good, but nothing special. But how do you tell a man that? She had tried her best to let him down gently and although she knew she had caused him pain there had been no scene, no angry words . . . just a grudging acceptance that they would not date again and yet here they were, sitting across from each other at the same restaurant years later.

Still, the army had changed him. While difficult to put into words, there was something haunted about his face now. The eyes that had shone in excitement each time he had looked at her before were now empty and dull. The angles of the baby faced boy were now harder and sharper as if being a soldier had turned him into a man. It added just enough of an edge that he had become a bit more interesting.

Whether he realized it or not he wasn't the only one who had changed during their time apart. Abby too had grown up although Robert had no way of knowing that she was now a woman in every sense of the word, and while still caring and loving towards others, she also knew what she wanted in a man and Robert wasn't it.

"Tell me about the army," she encouraged after the waitress left with their orders.

"I'd much rather hear about you," he suggested quickly, making her wonder if he was one of those men who came home from war unable to talk about it.

"Honestly, there isn't much to tell," she started as she toyed with her wine glass. "Still at the restaurant obviously . . . "

"And business is going well?" he asked.

"It took a while but I'm making a profit even if I have to put in long hours to do so."

"I see you finally fixed up the place. That must have cost a pretty penny. It's too bad because I could have done it for you now that I'm home."

"What are you going to do now that you're back?" she asked in an effort to get him off a subject so closely tied to Theo.

"Probably go to work in the factory. Welders make pretty good money and I need to save what I can. I've got my eye on one of those new craftsman houses on the outskirts of town. It's a big house; perfect for a large family."

The implication was right there in front of her and she knew she should have taken the opportunity to shut down his belief that there was something between them but how could she? He looked back at her with more hope in his eyes than she had seen from him all evening and she just couldn't break his heart. Instead she kept her mouth shut and tried to keep a smile on her face as he began to open up about his Army stint and what he told her made her cringe.

"Everything over there is dense jungle making it hard to see the enemy before they were right on top of us so the Air Force began a campaign to drop chemicals over the jungle to kill the vegetation and destroy the crops. You should have seen it. Big clouds of whatever it was covering roads, rivers, canals, rice paddies and farmland and even us at times. Within days all the vegetation was withered leaving no place for the enemy troops to hide. We even used it on the ground around our bases so they couldn't sneak up on us but we had to be careful; if we got doused we'd cough and choke on it for days."

"How horrible."

"That was nothing in the bigger scheme of things. War is an awful enough thing but what I didn't expect was to become so hardened to it. Once you've seen a few dead bodies it didn't seem to bother me so much anymore. In fact, after a while I hardly noticed them at all, especially when they were Vietnamese."

As he had been speaking, his gaze had left her face and he ended up being unable to look her in the eye again as a tear started to roll down his cheek before he brushed it away with the back of his hand. She couldn't imagine the toll it all must have taken on him.

"It's understandable don't you think?" Abby suggested gently. "I mean as horrible as it is, you have to be able to get through each day and do your job somehow. Maybe your reaction is the only way your mind could deal with what you were witnessing."

"The docs and the chaplains all said kind of the same thing but that doesn't make it any less difficult to accept. I never thought I would be one of those men - being callous to that kind of suffering - but I guess I am."

"That doesn't make you a bad person Robert. It just makes you human."

Hardly realizing it the pain he seemed to be in had touched Abby's heart and before she knew what was happening she felt something for him. He was a wounded bird and suddenly the need to mother him and help his wounds heal erupted within her and she just knew she couldn't push him away. Reaching across the table, she covered his shaking hand with her own without saying a word until eventually he looked up at her again with just the beginnings of a smile.

"I've really missed you," he told her.

Unable to say the same to him she simply nodded her head and smiled back.

•   •   •

That night turned into the beginning of a friendship Abby thought they would never share but there was no doubt in her mind Robert thought it was much more. Always the gentleman, he kept his physical distance from her, seemingly content to be nothing more than companions while sometimes dropping a comment about deeper feelings. There was nothing flashy about the time they spent together

-an occasional movie or bowling, a walk in the neighborhood, grilling steaks for dinner. Everything seemed platonic leading her to believe Robert now understood her desire to be nothing more than friends. At least that's what she told herself.

The funny thing was, with Theo so far away from her living a life she knew only through his letters, Robert's presence helped alleviate some of her loneliness. Always busy with work, home and helping others, the loneliness without Theo had snuck up on her to the point where she dreaded going home to her empty house. With Robert's friendship even that was lessening.

She should have realized things weren't quite that simple for Robert however. He had secured a job as a welder at the local manufacturing plant and was beginning to build the nest egg that would allow him to purchase the house he had set his heart on. It wasn't long into his return before he asked Abby to tour the property with him.

"This is beautiful," she told him as they wandered from room to room of the large home. "But why would you want something so large?"

"So each kid can have their own room of course," he said happily. "When I was growing up that was a luxury we didn't have and I spent my entire childhood sharing with my younger brother. Kids need privacy don't you think?"

"The two of you make a nice looking couple and I think your family would be very happy here," the realtor said.

"Oh, we're not a couple," Abby quickly assured the man.

"Not yet," Robert said just as quickly before he put his arm around her. "But I'm hoping."

Flustered by the predicament she found herself in Abby ducked away from his touch and moved into the kitchen as the two men talked building construction. Staring into the backyard she too could picture a happy family with children playing on a swing set or starting a pickup game of baseball, but it wasn't Robert she pictured as father to those children. Why couldn't he just accept she only wanted to be friends? As much as it would hurt him she simply had to break off their friendship.

"Robert, if you don't mind," she said walking back into the living room, "I really must get back to work."

"Of course Abby. I'll meet you out at the car," he told her before she hurried out of the house leaving him to say their goodbyes to the realtor.

Joining her in the car he couldn't contain his excitement as they pulled away from the curb. "That's definitely the house for us," he said leaving no ambiguity about his intention.

"You mean for you right?"

"Don't you like it?" he asked turning his head to look at her in surprise.

"It's lovely but Robert, we aren't a couple. We're just friends," she said softly but firmly. "I thought you understood that."

"It's okay, I know you aren't quite there yet, but Abby you have to know I'm in love with you. I've always been in love with you. It might take a few more months but we'll get married and buy the house and raise a large family. That's all I want. That's all I've ever wanted. Besides all the best marriages start out with friendship. Please don't tell me all this has been for nothing."

The pain in his voice was palpable and Abby's heart was breaking as he pleaded with her for a future together. How could she dash it all? Trying to be nice in the face of his obvious adoration she didn't know what to say.

"It's not for nothing. You've become a cherished friend and I don't want to lose you."

He jumped at the opening she had provided and like a flip of a switch the smile was back on his face by the time they pulled up to the restaurant.

"Thanks for coming with today. I'll call you tonight," he said as she got out of the car.

Walking back into the restaurant, her slow steps mirroring her despair over her inability to say no to the man, Abby went straight to her office to start a letter to Theo. Pen in hand she tapped the paper trying to decide if she should tell him about the situation with Robert. She didn't want Theo to think she was trying to make him jealous, but he was the one person she shared everything with and as a man he might be able to help her out of the mess.

"Abby," Doris said as she knocked before popping her head in the door. "Phone call."

"Thanks," Abby said. "I'll take it in here."

So caught up in the situation with Robert she hadn't even noticed the ringing phone and she quickly picked it up before hearing the other extension being hung up.

"This is Abby."

"There's the beautiful voice I've missed so much," Theo said in the deep rich voice she had also missed.

"Oh my god Theo is that really you?" she exclaimed in excitement before lowering her voice. "I've missed you so much! How are you?"

"I'm fine, better than fine actually, but I miss you so much it hurts. And you?"

"So much better now," she admitted.

"What's wrong?"

"Nothing really. I'm fine, work is fine, and the restaurant is doing well. Everything's fine, but it's not the same without you. How's the play going? Do you like your new agent? Do you like the rest of the cast? Oh there is so much I want to ask you."

"Slow down, slow down!" he exclaimed. "Most of it you already know from the letters but there is so much more I want to share with you."

"Then tell me."

"First I want to ask you something. You can say no if you want, but I have an unexpected week off next week."

"You're coming back?" she asked excitedly.

"No, but would you come meet me? I know you don't like to be away from the restaurant but would you meet me so we could spend the week together?"

"In New York?"

"No, I understand you aren't a fan of big cities but my cousin owns a couple of cabins on a lake about a half day's drive from you. At this time of the year no one else rents them and he said I could use one for the week. The other one will be empty so we'd have total privacy and you won't have to do a thing; just pack a suitcase and show up. What do you say?"

"What time should I be there?" Abby asked with a nervous laugh.

"Oh my God I was so afraid you were going to turn me down!" he said with his own laughter.

"Are you kidding? The last few months have been the longest of my life without you. Of course I'll be there. So where am I going?"

Spending the last few minutes of the call sorting out the details, she was disappointed when someone came into the room on his end and he had to end the call abruptly. After so much time apart, the idea of spending a whole week together in such solitude was both thrilling and daunting. What if Theo had changed now that he was a successful actor? What if he no longer found her desirable?

Doubts aside, the excitement at seeing him again began to build within her and her face flushed with desire for him. In just four days they would be together again and she would know if what they had started was still there between them. But for now the only thing standing between her and Theo was finding a plausible excuse for her sudden and extended absence.

Abby had never missed a day of work and her staff, especially John, was certain to question this unexpected vacation. It seemed the simplest reason she could provide, without lying, the better. Straightening her dress and taking a deep breath she walked out of the office, relieved to see an empty dining room as she gathered the staff together.

"I know this is short notice everyone, but I have decided to take a vacation. But to make it work I need your help."

"Of course Abby. You can count on us," Susan told her.

"It's about time," Doris said with a smile. "When was the last time you took a day off anyway?"

John didn't say a thing, choosing instead to cross his arms in front of him and stare at her.

"I know it's short notice, but I'm going to be gone all next week. Doris and Susan if you could please come in on Sunday and help John out, I'd really appreciate it."

"Of course," they said in tandem.

John remained silent as Abby turned her attention to him.

"Aren't you going to say something?" she asked with what she hoped was a charming smile.

"You wouldn't by any chance be heading to New York would you?" he asked finally.

Thankful for being able to be truthful, Abby shook her head. "Of course not. I'm going to spend the week relaxing at the lake reading a few good books, maybe dipping a line in to fish, and not waiting on a single person or cooking a single thing."

It was the truth, even if it was leaving out the fact that she wouldn't be doing it alone.

Having known him so long Abby knew he was suspicious of her answer, but he wisely said nothing in front of the others.

"We'll get on just fine without you," he said grudgingly. "Now I have some work to do in the kitchen."

As the staff went back to work Abby stepped back into her office and released a long sigh. It had gone better than she expected but she knew John too well to believe he would let her walk out the door without more questions and she only had to wait until the end of the day when the two of them were alone and locking up for the night for the questions to start.

"It's not like you to go off on your own," he said quietly. "What's really going on?"

She had spent the afternoon deciding how to answer his inevitable questions and had finally settled on the truth. As the one person who knew about her relationship with Theo she owed him that much.

"Theo called this afternoon and we're going to spend the week together."

"So you lied to me. You are going to New York," he said angrily.

"No, so stop being angry. I told you the truth. We're meeting at a place a few hours away. It will be nice to catch up on his life."

"Why can't he come here?" he asked. "Why all the sneaking around?"

"You know why or do you want me to say it's because we're sleeping together and we don't want anyone to know?" Abby said with her own touch of anger. "I'm sorry I'm not the good girl you wanted me to be but I can't change it now. Do you have any inkling how hard it has been for me since he left? I'm miserable without him and now I have a chance to see him again. If you were in my place would you turn it down?"

"Of course not, but I don't want you to get hurt all over again," he said gently before walking over to take her hands in his. "Abby you're like a daughter to me and I can't stand to see you unhappy."

"Then you have to know, seeing Theo again is going to make me happy."

"Until he leaves again."

"Right...until he leaves again," she whispered to herself.

•   •   •

The days before leaving to meet Theo flew by and Abby was beside herself with excitement spending even longer hours at the restaurant in an attempt to get as much done as possible only to go home and stay up half the night packing and unpacking and packing again. The last lake vacation she had was as a child when the family would take yearly fishing trips to her father's favorite honey hole. The car had been packed tightly with everything possible they might need on those vacations and even though Theo had told her he would bring everything they needed himself, it felt odd to only put one small suitcase in the car.

Half expecting Theo to call again before she left she had heard nothing from him and had a brief flash of doubt. What if she arrived and he was nowhere to be found? Chalking her doubt up to a bad case of nerves she locked the house up tight, checked her purse again for directions to the lake and got behind the wheel for the long drive, her excitement growing with each passing mile.

Chapter Eighteen

"At the time neither one of us realized that week would become such an important part of our lives. It was the one time we could be together without being judged for what we were doing," Theo told Krista. "By the end of that week together we had hatched a plan to meet back at the cabin each year during the first week of April."

"That certainly explains Nan's disappearances," Krista said as she remembered the baffling solo trips her aging grandmother had taken much to the concern of her family. "My mother always complained that Nan would never change her plans no matter what she missed that week. Uncle Matt said it was Nan's sanity week -you know- to get away from all the kids and stress from the restaurant."

"Obviously that was one of the benefits of it but for us at least, it was much more important. It was the only time we could love each other unconditionally without worry of who we were hurting. At least that's what we told ourselves after your grandparents got married. We knew what was between us was wrong and your grandmother lived with tremendous guilt over it. One of her rules after her marriage was that she wouldn't discuss Robert or her marriage or eventually even her children with me. They were the single biggest part of her life, even more than what we shared, and she never talked to me about any of them. She felt it would be disrespectful to bring them into it and said the only way she could live with her guilt about our affair was to separate the two parts of her life. Still she became quite adept at spinning tales of her life at home without actually providing any details. We talked of the restaurant and church and all her efforts to help people. We even talked about travels she eventually took, including I later found out, a trip to Paris with her daughters. Her letters were full of thoughts and feelings and emotions and experiences, but nothing about the love of her family until after your grandfather was gone."

"But weren't we already part of it? I mean, we were part of Nan so we should have been part of what you shared," Krista said in confusion. Having an affair was one thing; pretending your family didn't exist in the middle of that affair was another. Could her grandmother really have been that callous?

"Please don't judge Abby my dear," he cautioned at the look on her face. "You still don't know the whole story and honestly it took me years to get it myself. Your grandmother was not the heartless person you now think. It's all in the letters so I'm sure you've read about it."

"Actually I haven't gotten to that point yet. Hearing you talk is bringing this all to life for me better than the letters have. I've actually only been reading to the point where you are in the story each night."

"Letters can only tell so much. You have to remember Krista that my telling the story of Abby's life back here is me putting my own spin on what she was going through and what I learned from her. We were so in love, but more than that we were best friends."

"I understand. That's why the two parts together...you and the letters...paint a better picture. So tell me what happened that first time at the lake."

"It was probably understandable that after so much time apart from each other we were both nervous. I was no longer the out of work and desperate man I was when I walked into the restaurant and Abby was no longer a girl. What we had shared together during those first few weeks here had changed both of us but now that I didn't need her financial help anymore and she didn't need to save me I worried that her feelings for me might have changed. On the other hand she told me she worried that after a short time in New York I wouldn't find her desirable anymore. How silly we were to worry about that. The minute

I saw her step out of the car all the feelings for her came flooding back and we flew into each other's arms.........."

"You're late," Theo jokingly told her as he peppered Abby's face with kisses.

"You're early," she teased back wrapping her arms around his lean waist before his lips landed on her own and they were lost in a kiss that reignited their desires and made her knees go weak.

"God but you're beautiful," he told her as he gazed down into the liquid chocolate of her eyes and her hand caressed the side of his face, memorizing each feature and the barely there lines and wrinkles.

She had almost forgotten the handsome face beneath the scruffy beard but she could never forget the ice blue of his eyes that sparkled brighter than the calm lake behind him. Her fingers gently outlined his full lips and the sharp angles of his jawline before he covered her hand with his own and pulled it to his chest.

"Say something will you?" he asked with a smile.

"I love you," Abby said quietly as she smiled up at him. "I should have said it before you left but Theo I love you and I didn't want another moment to go by without letting you know it."

"And I love you...more than you'll ever know. I think I loved you the moment you put that plate of food down in front of me."

She laughed. "That wasn't love, it was hunger!" she reminded him.

"That's only partly true," he insisted as they wrapped their arms around each other and walked into the cabin. "When you smiled at me I fell hard. You hadn't judged me because of how I looked and then when you opened up your heart to a stranger it touched my heart like nothing I had ever experienced before."

"And look at us now. You're a big shot actor and we're here in this beautiful place........."

Her voice drifting off leaving tears in her eyes, he gently wiped them away before finishing her sentence, " . . . together. We're here together. That's all we need right? So no more tears okay? Now let me show you around."

The grand tour of the cabin took less than five minutes and she was instantly charmed by the rustic feel of the place. The first floor consisted of a basic kitchen, a sitting room attached to a stone patio overlooking the lake, and small bathroom, but it wasn't until they climbed the stairs to the single bedroom that the true beauty of the place was revealed. The room encompassed the entire top floor of the cabin with a queen size bed dominating the space causing a tingle of desire to flow through her before she caught the view from the balcony. Theo noticed the look of surprise on her face and quickly slid back the glass doors so they could step outside and experience the magnificent scenery first hand.

The sun was high in the sky and the lake surface as calm as glass. It couldn't have been any more serene until a strange animal call pierced the air.

"That my dear is the haunting call of a loon, or so I'm told," he said at her questioning look. "I heard it yesterday too and the cabin caretaker told me what it was. He said it's kind of like a duck, but not quite…black with white spots, and if we are careful and quiet out on the lake we might see a pair."

"I would love that," she told him excitedly as she scanned the lake for the bird.

"He also told me," Theo said as he stood behind her and nuzzled at her neck, "that loons mate for life."

"Then I am definitely a fan," Abby said trying not to let Theo's actions get carried away. "Can we go out on the lake now?"

Pulling away from her, he looked at her in surprise. "Now? I thought maybe . . . " His words trailed off as he cast a meaningful look at the bed behind them.

"Please," she begged as she pulled him towards the staircase. "I promise I'll make it up to you."

"Does anyone ever say no to you?" he teased. "Let's go then."

Running down to the dock, Theo turned to look at her. "Canoe or boat?" Both were readily available and without giving it a thought, she chose the canoe which elicited a scared look from him.

"Why are you looking at me like that?" Abby asked with a smile as she kicked off her shoes and reached for a life jacket. "You do know how to canoe don't you?"

"Actually no, but I think the more important question is how do you know? You are one of the most capable women I know, but seriously? You know how to row a canoe?"

"It's paddle. You row a boat and paddle a canoe and yes I do. As a matter of fact I learned in summer camp and I quite enjoyed it. We can stay in the shallow water at first until you're comfortable but you're going to love it. It's the most serene way to get out on the lake."

"Just remember if I drown it's going to be your fault," he said giving her a quick kiss. "Okay, show me what to do."

Summer camp training aside it took them a bit of doing to get the canoe in the water, suited up with life jackets and Theo seated carefully in the front before Abby also stepped into the back of the canoe. It began to rock gently in the water causing Theo to hold on for dear life and left Abby unable to contain her laughter as he turned his head to look back at her in terror.

"It's fine, it's supposed to do that," she assured him before using her paddle to push gently away from the dock.

As the canoe slowly glided across the still, shallow water, Abby provided patient instructions to Theo who quickly seemed to get the hang of it all before his excitement at mastering the activity got the best of him and he turned just a little too quickly to look at her. The unexpected shift in his balance rocked the canoe violently before they were both pitched into the cold, but thankfully shallow, lake water as the canoe bobbed gently away from them into the shoreline.

"Shit, shit, shit," Theo cried as he erupted from beneath the water and reached for Abby. Struggling towards the shore Abby started to laugh so hard she could hardly stand. "What in God's name are you laughing about? We could have drowned!" he said in bewilderment.

"Oh come on, you have to see the humor in what just happened! The look on your face as the canoe started to rock was priceless!"

"Me? You should have seen your face! I guess we both looked pretty stupid didn't we?"

"I think you look like an adorable drowned little puppy," Abby told him as she moved the wet strands of hair out of his eyes.

"A freezing one at that. Come on, let's get up to the cabin and get into some dry clothes before we catch our deaths."

Stopping only to drag the canoe securely up onto the shoreline, they raced each other into the cabin where Theo knelt on the floor trying to start a fire in the fireplace. Shivering so hard his hands could hardly strike the match, Abby draped a bath towel over his shoulders and rubbed his back in an attempt to warm him. It took some time but finally the April chill that had kept tourists away from the lake was forgotten as the warmth of the now roaring fire permeated the small space and they climbed the stairs to the bedroom for a change of clothing.

Peeling off her wet clothes she caught their reflections in the full length mirror near the dresser and realized Theo hadn't moved as he watched her undress. Suddenly self-conscious in the face of his gaze she held the towel in front of her nakedness as she turned to him.

"Do you even realize the effect you have on me?" he asked huskily before slowly crossing the room to stop mere inches from her.

Reaching up to take the towel from her, he let it drop to the floor between them before slowly pulling his shirt over his head and leaning ever so slightly to place a soft kiss on her lips.

"I've missed you and I together," he whispered into her ear before raining butterfly kisses across her collarbone. "And when I close my eyes at night this is what I dream of."

A gasp escaped from him as Abby's cold hands found their way onto his waist and up his chest onto skin that was already warming from the desire building in him before they moved back again to unzip his jeans and together they struggled to remove the cold, wet denim.

Theo reached down to pick her up as she entwined her legs around his body and he carried her to the bed, placing her down gently as if she was the most precious thing in the world. Saying nothing, her eyes followed his every movement even as her hands renewed their familiarity with his body. Covering her body with his own, flesh pressed upon flesh, they finally gave in to their long denied desire for each other.

●   ●   ●

Later as they lay snuggled beneath the covers, the fireplace warmth having long since gone out, they watched the sun slowly set over the lake and heard the haunting call of the loon yet again.

"Do they really mate for life?" Abby asked as she burrowed even closer into his arms. Her body felt fluid and totally satisfied and she never wanted to leave the bed.

"Sounds like it," Theo said as he stroked her shoulder. "Do you believe that humans have one person they are destined to be with their entire lives?"

"If you would have asked me that question before we met I would have said no, but the way I feel about you I have to believe it," Abby told him.

"I feel that way about you too but life has a funny way of changing things doesn't it?"

"What do you mean?"

"Well, I can't imagine spending my life with anyone but you but a lot would have to change for that to happen at least with one of us."

"Like I'd have to move to New York or LA or some other big city."

"Or I'd have to give up my career."

"Not an option," Abby said quickly.

"I appreciate that, but if you won't come with me where the work is what other options would we have? After the last few months without you I'm not sure I'm willing to do it again."

"I understand what you're saying. It's been hard on me also but I won't let you give up your career."

"Would you ever consider coming to New York?" he asked.

"I wouldn't rule it out completely but right now you don't even know that's where you will end up. You could be on either coast depending on how your career goes. So for right now, and as hard as it is when we're apart, we'll have to remember that someday we'll be together and everything we have been through will be worth it. For now let's just enjoy this week and not think about what happens on Sunday."

What had originally seemed like a luxury to have seven whole days together flew by; their days filled with fishing, hiking, enjoying an early morning sunrise on the deck or a late night campfire. Abby was also able to coax Theo into a much more successful attempt at canoeing that found them paddling the entire circumference of the lake one evening just before sunset. They were almost back at the cabin when they spotted a loon gliding slowly along the water surface.

"Isn't it beautiful?" Abby whispered as she slowly angled the canoe parallel to the bird, being careful to stay back a respectful distance.

In the waning moments of the sunset it was difficult to see the ebony colored bird on the dark water, but as the loon changed direction Abby gasped in surprise causing Theo to turn towards her. Afraid to speak lest she scare the bird away, Abby pointed at two tiny loon chicks resting on the back of the adult.

"Wow," Theo mouthed back at her before they both heard the haunting call of another loon echoing across the water and the loon quickly swam off out of their eyesight.

"I wonder if that was the Dad calling for Mom and the babies," Abby asked.

"Maybe," Theo said as the canoe kissed the shoreline and they both got out to pull it safely up on shore. "The day I got up here the caretaker said loon pairs come back to the same lake every year to have their babies."

"We should do that," Abby suggested looking earnestly at him.

"Babies?" he asked in surprise. "You're kidding right? No way I'm ready for babies and I'm not sure I will ever be. I've seen too many marriages fall apart when the babies arrive."

Theo would be a wonderful father someday and his comment was surprising and more than a little disappointing but Abby was quick to clarify.

"Sorry, I didn't mean that. It's so wonderful up here we should come back every year. Just you and me - before all the tourists arrive for the summer."

"That's not a bad idea," he said as they walked hand in hand up to the cabin. "Let's make a promise that the first week in April, no matter where we are or what's going on in our lives, we'll meet back here and spend a week together. What do you say?"

"I promise."

"So do I," he told her with a kiss.

●   ●   ●

The cool weather of April was what kept others from the lake and Abby and Theo took full advantage of their solitude and a shared love of the outdoors. Fishing, canoeing, and one unfortunate instance of skinny dipping when they discovered that the day's sunshine did little to warm the lake water, were all on the agenda. But Abby's favorite time was when they walked together on one of the many trails surrounding the large lake. There, in the still confines of the deep forest, she felt most connected to Theo and it was there where they had one of their most important conversations.

"You didn't really mean what you said the other day did you?" she asked as they walked hand in hand.

"About what?"

"A family. Don't you want a family some day?"

"What? Oh, yeah that," he said as he helped Abby over one of the many fallen logs blocking the path. "Someday I suppose, but that day would be well into the future. I think it's important when a couple has children that the kids get all the love and attention a parent can give. With my career that would be almost impossible."

"Oh," she said dejectedly.

"Hey, what's wrong?" he said as he stopped walking and turned her towards him. "I'm not saying I never want kids. Our children would be amazing don't you think? But definitely not right now. One play does not make a stable career. I want to be able to afford to give my children the very best life has to offer. I don't want to be a struggling out of work actor who has to count on his wife to put food on the table. Maybe five or six years down the road when my career is on track we can talk about marriage and children, but not now. Surely you understand that?"

"I do, but I always wanted a large family. I guess it will just come a little later than I thought," she said with a weak smile.

Continuing their walk Abby was overwhelmed by a feeling of sadness she tried to hide from him. She and Theo were so compatible in most every way, but knowing he didn't want children in the foreseeable future was a blow to her. Obviously they weren't getting married anytime soon, but in the back of her mind she was hoping for a lifetime together and that life included a house full of kids. Would she have to pray that Theo was an overnight success for him to consider their future together? It appeared so.

That night, their last together at the lake, the couple slept little. After spending the entire week catching up on each other's lives there seemed little that was left unsaid but then again, neither one knew when they would have time together again.

"Bobby is already casting his next play," Theo told her, his fingers playing absentmindedly in her long curls. "He asked the playwright to rewrite a role just for me."

"That must mean he really likes your acting," Abby said excitedly. "Why didn't you tell me before now?"

"Because I might not be able to take it."

"Why in God's name would you turn it down?" Abby said incredulously as she sat up in bed and turned to look at him. "It's everything you hoped for."

"Well I don't want to jinx it and I was saving this as a surprise for you but . . . I might have a role in a movie."

"Oh Theo, that's terrific! But how?"

"Opening night of the play there was a studio executive from MGM in the audience. He came backstage and asked to meet me."

"That's so exciting!"

"Yeah, it was, but that's all it was. He just met me and left. That is until I got a phone call just before I left for the lake. The studio wants to fly me out to LA for a screen test. Again, it's not a job offer but it's a lot further than I got the last time I was in LA."

"Oh sweetheart I'm so excited for you!" Abby cried before straddling his body with her own and peppering his face with kisses. "You're going to be a movie star!"

Her excitement was infectious and soon they were both laughing until Theo suddenly wrapped his arms around her and rolled over pinning her beneath him.

"Thank you," he told her, his eyes heavy with desire as he kissed her deeply. "None of this would be happening without you and your kind heart. I love you."

Without giving her a chance to echo his sentiments he covered her lips once more with his own before their insatiable desire for each other made them forget everything else.

Packing their respective vehicles the next morning each said little; exchanging only sad looks of encouragement as they both tried to salvage the few moments they had left together.

"I wish you could come with me to LA," he said in her ear as they held each other close. "You're my good luck charm."

"You don't need me," she insisted as she tried hard to choke back the tears that threatened to overwhelm her. "You make your own luck."

The melancholy call of a loon interrupted their embrace to echo their sadness.

"Let me know if you get the job," she asked before pulling back and wiping her eyes trying desperately to give him a smile.

"Of course…and Abby?"

Moved by the tears glistening in his eyes, Abby whispered, "Yes my love?"

"Remember our promise . . . no matter what we're doing, no matter where we are, we meet back here next year at the same time."

"I promise," she said crossing her chest and sticking out her finger for a pinky swear.

"I promise also," he told her with a smile as they locked fingers. "And one more thing . . . don't ever stop loving me."

"It would be impossible."

They exchanged a few more desperate kisses and a lingering hug before it was time to go with each walking slowly to their cars. Theo got behind the wheel, gave one last wave her way, and drove away leaving only the memory of a perfect week for Abby to take back home with her.

Chapter Nineteen

Back at work after the most perfect vacation Abby could have imagined, she was surprised at the number of people who commented on her appearance. The slight tan she had acquired at the lake wasn't what they noticed however.

"My gosh Abby, you look wonderful. Vacation must have agreed with you," Doris said as she walked in on Monday morning.

Susan echoed her sentiments. "You look like a changed woman. Where did you go again? Was it a spa?"

"Thank you both I think. Did I really look that bad before?" she asked with a chuckle.

During the long drive home, Abby had decided to concentrate on how wonderful the week had been rather than her sadness at being parted once more. The smile hadn't left her face but that wasn't what was fueling her happiness. It was excitement for Theo who was leaving early this morning for LA.

"Of course you didn't," Doris quickly clarified. "You're a beautiful woman but there's an extra sparkle in your eyes this morning. You must have had a good time."

"That I did, but how were things here?" Abby asked to change the subject. "Where's John?"

"I'm right here," he said as he came up behind her holding a case of eggs fresh from the farm. "Let me put these eggs away so I can give you a proper welcome."

Following him into the kitchen Abby was enveloped in a bear hug as soon as his hands were free.

"Missed you girl," he said softly.

"I missed you too," she told him before he released her.

"Was it everything you hoped for?"

Abby didn't need to ask what he was talking about.

"It couldn't have been better."

"As much as I don't like the sneaking around you two are doing, I'm happy for you. Really I am."

"But?" she asked when his voice trailed off and he couldn't look her in the eye.

"But now that you're back, I think there's a problem you're going to need to deal with."

"What's that?"

"Not what. Who. It's Robert. He's been here every day asking questions about where you were and what you were doing."

Her inability to face Robert before her departure had placed John in the unenviable position of doing her dirty work.

"I'm sorry about that," she said sadly. "I know I should have told him before I left but I just couldn't face him. So what did you tell him?"

"I told him the truth…at least the truth you told us. That you were going to spend the week relaxing and enjoying yourself. That's what you did right?"

"Thank you for that."

"Don't thank me too soon. We're not even open yet but he just walked in," John said nodding towards the front door. "Good luck."

Doris was already heading towards Robert before Abby cut her off.

"Good morning Robert! I didn't expect to see you before work."

"Where were you last week?" he asked sharply.

His tone was the only indication she had that he was unhappy with her. There was no smile, no frown; nothing on his face to indicate his displeasure and once again the phrase "plain vanilla" came to Abby's mind.

"Robert, I'm sorry," she said as she steered him to a booth in the furthest corner. "I should have told you I was taking a little vacation but it came up so suddenly and I had so much to do here before I left and I . . . well, I'm sorry."

Her apology seemed to have tempered his unhappiness somewhat. "I accept your apology but would it have been so difficult to pick up the phone before you left? I was frantic wondering what was going on. John just said you needed a week away. He wouldn't even tell me where you had gone."

"That's because he didn't know," Abby assured him. Having already put John in the middle of her deception more than a few times she didn't want to drag him into it further. "And I didn't go anywhere special. Just spent some time by a lake. My family used to do the same thing when I was growing up."

"So it was like reliving childhood memories?"

"Something like that. But I'm back now so am I forgiven?"

Having to ask forgiveness for living her life as she chose seemed silly but her respect for Robert made her ask.

"Of course. And now that you're back I hope you'll go out with me tonight. There's a new Italian place that just opened in Madison. I thought we could drive up and check it out."

For the first time since they had become friends he was actually suggesting something that, for him at least, was rather adventurous. Italian food was one of her favorites and really good Italian cuisine was difficult to find in their area. She quickly agreed.

"I'll pick you up at seven. Our reservations are for eight," he told her before getting up. "Now I have to get to work. Have a nice day."

With a quick kiss on her cheek he bolted out the door and she turned back to find all three of her staff watching from the kitchen; John with a look of concern and Susan and Doris smiling from ear to ear.

"What are you looking at?" she asked before turning the open sign on and walking back to the kitchen.

"He's very handsome Abby."

"Susan is right you know but I'm surprised you're dating him," Doris said. "I just don't picture the two of you together."

"Yeah," John interjected. "I don't see the two of you together either."

Abby knew he was teasing, but the others didn't and they quickly launched into a litany about the type of man Abby should be with while John sat back with a self-satisfied smirk on his face for having started the whole thing.

"Okay you guys, enough about my love life. Robert and I are just friends. We are not a couple, we are not dating. We're just friends and nothing more so while I appreciate all the advice I'd prefer it if we move on to another topic. Or better yet, why don't we all get back to work?"

•   •   •

Discussion about Abby's dating life was forgotten when the bell above the front door announced their first customers of the day but Abby couldn't forget. Theo was finally in LA leaving her on pins and needles waiting for an update that never came. By the time Robert arrived for their dinner date she was still in the dark.

Robert's appearance should have been her first clue that the evening would be different than all the others they had spent together. Dressed in a new black suit, hair freshly trimmed and smelling like he had just stepped out of a department store fragrance counter, he extended a bouquet of roses to her as she opened the door.

"Oh my," she exclaimed in surprise. "What did I do to deserve roses?"

"I'm just happy you're back," he said as he stepped into the foyer. "You look lovely tonight," he told her before kissing her cheek.

"Thank you. Let me put these flowers in water before we go."

Walking into the kitchen she found a vase for the flowers just as the phone rang.

"Do you want me to get that?" Robert suggested from his position in the hallway. He was right next to the phone.

Certain it was Theo calling, she hurried out to Robert.

"That's okay, I'll just let it ring. We don't want to miss our reservation," she told him before picking up her purse. "Let's go."

"Abby don't be silly. We have a few minutes. Just answer it. It might be important."

His firmly planted feet indicated he wasn't going anywhere until she answered the still ringing phone and with shaking hands, she picked up the receiver.

"Peterson residence." she said formally holding the receiver tightly to her ear.

"Abby you'll never guess," Theo shouted into the phone.

"I'm sorry, but could you possibly call back tomorrow night? I'm just about to walk out the door," she said quickly.

"What? I have big news, I . . . " he said excitedly as she tried to keep all emotion from her face.

"I'm sorry sir but I really have to go. Good night."

Placing the phone back in its cradle she turned slightly so Robert wouldn't see the tears in her eyes. From the very little Theo had spoken she knew that he got the movie role and it killed her to have to cut him off.

"Why did you ask them to call back? You could have taken the call" Robert asked. "I didn't mind."

"It was nothing," she lied as she picked up her purse once again. "Just a vacuum salesman."

"Well then let's go. I've got a big night planned."

•   •   •

The drive to Madison took almost an hour and they were nearly late for their reservation leaving Robert fussing about it the entire time while Abby sat silently staring out the car window thinking of Theo's call and the excitement in his voice. Not knowing his number in LA she would just have to wait and pray that he would indeed call her again tomorrow.

"Abby our table is reay." Robert said to break her out of her private thoughts.

So consumed with thoughts of the aborted call she had barely noticed walking into the restaurant. Following the hostess to a secluded table in the back corner she noticed candles set into old wine bottles dripping with wax and providing just the barest of illumination. A waiter appeared tableside offering Robert a small taste of what appeared to be a very expensive bottle of wine. The drama unfolding before her would have been amusing were it not for her thoughts of Theo. Robert somberly swirled the wine in his glass and took a small sip before nodding solemnly at the waiter who then poured each a full glass.

By the time they had placed their order, Abby was struggling to pay attention. Her mind was on the west coast, but it didn't matter. Robert kept up a steady stream of one-sided conversation and didn't seem to notice her lack of interest. It wasn't until their surprisingly good meal was over that she realized how nervous he seemed.

"Is something wrong?" she asked. "You seem a little jumpy tonight."

"Oh I'm fine...just a little anxious but that's to be expected."

"Whatever for? Is it the restaurant? Didn't you enjoy your meal?"

"No, the food was fine. Better than I expected actually, although it's a bit rich for my tastes."

"Then what?"

Struggling to reach into the pocket of his slacks, he suddenly eased out of his seat and dropped to one knee in front of her as she stared at him in horror; understanding finally why his behavior had been so out of character. At the scene unfolding in front of them other customers turned to watch and the restaurant quieted.

"Abby, will you marry me?"

There had been no declaration of undying love, no words of adoration or even romance. Instead, a man she barely knew and only thought of as a friend, was on his knees in front of her holding out a beautiful diamond ring while everyone in the place stared at her.

"Robert, this is really unexpected," she said as he stared up at her with a hopeful smile on his face. "Really unexpected," she told him pointedly.

"It wasn't until you left last week that I realized I don't want to be without you," he said quickly. "Let me put the ring on and see if it fits. I had to guess at what size to buy but we can always have it changed later."

He slipped the ring on her finger as the room erupted into applause. No one it seemed, including Robert who quickly took his seat at the table again after an even quicker kiss, had even realized she hadn't accepted his proposal. Abby looked down at the ring on her finger and tried desperately to think of a way out of the situation. The last thing she wanted to do was hurt Robert but she couldn't let him believe she was really going to marry him.

"I can't wait to tell everyone," he said before beginning to ramble on about the wedding and their future together.

"Robert, I don't think you and I . . . "

"I know. Weird isn't it? I mean before I left for the Army we really didn't know each other. I think it was your letters that made me realize you were the one for me and when I got home we just picked right up where we left off which just goes to show we were meant to be together. I can't wait to tell all of our family and friends what a lucky man I am!"

"Congratulations to you both," the waiter said interrupting Robert's litany. "As a special treat we'd like to offer you both tiramisu for dessert."

"Thank you but I think we'll pass," Robert answered for the both of them. "Just the check please."

Although she would have welcomed the chance to taste the popular Italian dessert, Abby just wanted to go home and figure a way out of the mess she now found herself in and she said nothing as Robert paid the bill and they started the long drive home. Once again Robert kept up a conversation with himself, barely noticing his now assumed fiancé said nothing.

Feigning a headache Abby didn't ask him in once they arrived home.

"I understand…all the excitement of the engagement and all," he said before giving her a chaste kiss on the forehead. "Get a good night's sleep because tomorrow everyone will know our good news."

"Could you please do something for me?" she finally asked. "Could we keep this between ourselves for a little while?"

"Whatever for? Don't you want everyone to know?" he asked in disappointment.

"I just want to be able to think about it."

"Well, don't think too long. I don't know how long I can keep this secret to ourselves. Good night sweetheart."

As if he didn't have a care in the world Robert walked back to his car, whistling an off-key tune as he did, before pulling away into the darkness and she went inside and collapsed onto the stairs. Tears instantly spilled from her eyes and for maybe the first time in her young life she didn't know what to do. Obviously she couldn't marry Robert, she was in love with Theo after all, but she also knew she didn't want to hurt him. Tomorrow she would have to clear up this misunderstanding. He was going to bed tonight on cloud nine but tomorrow he would be crushed.

Chapter Twenty

Having the entire day to plan what she would say to Robert should have been a benefit, but instead Abby found herself stressed to the point where the previous days' compliments had turned into questions of concern from staff and customers alike.

"Didn't you get much sleep last night my dear? You look tired this morning," Mr. Simpson said.

His Sunday only visits a thing of the past, he continued to place the same order and feign surprise at the extra food each of them included with his meal. Seeing the extra nourishment was finally beginning to put a little weight back on the man, Abby realized a moment of satisfaction before answering.

"I'm fine. Just a lot on my mind," Abby said with a brief smile as she topped off his coffee cup.

"If you ever need someone to talk to I am just a phone call away," he insisted with a smile of his own.

"Thank you for that but I'm fine," she said again before giving his arm a pat and moving on to her next customer.

It had been like that all morning. If she hadn't known everyone so well she might have taken offense at the comments about her appearance. But it wasn't just customers. John had been watching her like a hawk all day and she wasn't surprised when he followed her into her office during the mid-afternoon lull.

"So what happened last night?" he asked closing the door behind him. "You look like you were up all night."

"I know I look like crap and yes, I was up all night."

"What has Theo done?"

Looking back at John in surprise, Abby was quick to anger. "Theo has nothing to do with this," she said sharply. "It's Robert."

"That milquetoast? What could he have done to upset you so much?"

"Please don't speak badly of him. He's a very nice man."

"Sorry," he said holding his hands up in front of him. "Didn't mean to disparage your new boyfriend but what has he done?"

"John please just stop it. I thought maybe you could help but if all you're going to do is make fun of me then why don't you just go."

"Sorry Abby," he said with genuine contriteness before pulling up a chair. "I didn't realize this was something serious. Tell me."

"Robert asked me to marry him," she said softly.

Leaning back in his chair, John let out a long slow breath.

"Wow, I didn't expect those words to come out of your mouth. What did you tell him?"

"I didn't give him an answer."

"Why the hell not? You're in love with another man. That right there is your answer."

"I know, but everyone in the restaurant last night was staring at us and he was down on one knee and he put the ring on my finger and then everyone started clapping. He never even realized I didn't accept. He spent the rest of the night talking about our future and kids and I just didn't have a chance to say no."

"Well you have to fix that and you can't wait. He's probably told everyone he knows by now."

"He promised he wouldn't. I told him I had a lot to think about."

"Abby, you can't let this drag on. I'm sure you don't want to hurt him but you have to tell him."

"Don't you think I know that?" she said angrily. "He's such a nice guy and he would make a great husband for someone, but that someone is not me. Oh why did I ever let it get this far?"

"Do you want me to tell him?" John offered even though the look on his face indicated it was the last thing he wanted to do.

"I appreciate that more than you know but this is something I have to do myself. We're supposed to have dinner at my house tonight and I'll tell him then."

"Don't dance around it. Just come right out and say you aren't in love with him and you can't marry him. I know his type. If you give him even the tiniest of openings he is going to walk away thinking he still has a chance."

"You're right. I should have done that last night but I just couldn't embarrass him in front of all those people. Tonight it will be just the two of us and maybe he won't be so disappointed."

"Abby, if I was in his place I would have fallen in love with you too. He's going to be devastated."

•   •   •

Talking to John had clarified what Abby needed to do that night but it didn't make her feel any better about what was to come. With the engagement ring safely tucked away in her purse, she kept her hand in her pocket when Robert arrived but he noticed immediately.

"Hey, how come you don't have your ring on?"

"Robert, please come and sit down. I want to talk to you."

"Before you say anything I have another present for you," he said as he pulled a small box from his jacket pocket. "After last night I couldn't wait any longer."

Carefully opening the box Abby was surprised to see a key and she looked back at him in confusion.

"It's for the house. I signed the papers today. We can get married next week and move in before summer starts."

"You did what?" she asked with alarm. "You bought a house?"

"Not 'a' house. Our house. The one we looked at together. It was a bit of a stretch financially but with our two incomes we'll be able to afford it and it's got plenty of room for children when they come along. Are you surprised?"

If she had agreed to marry him she would have loved the surprise, but that wasn't the case.

"You have to undo it. Cancel the contract," she said quickly as she handed the box back to him.

"Whatever for? I thought you loved the house," he said sadly.

"But I don't love you," she blurted out suddenly as he stared at her in abject shock.

She had had enough and once the words started she couldn't stop.

"I sorry, but I am not in love with you and I can't marry you. Last night . . . "

"Last night you said yes," he cried. "What changed between last night and today?"

"I never said yes. Just think back. I never gave you an answer. You just assumed it, maybe because you wanted it so much, but I never answered your question. And then everyone was staring at us and clapping and you looked so happy and I just couldn't tell you then. Don't you see I didn't want to embarrass you?"

"But you're okay making me look like a fool now?" he shouted with more emotion than she had ever seen from him. "For gosh sakes Abby I bought a house for you!"

"I'm sorry but I didn't ask you to do that. I don't love you. You jumped to that conclusion all on your own. I barely know you but I know you're a good man. If things were different, maybe if we knew each other better, I might have different feelings for you, but I'm not in love with you Robert and I can't marry you."

Reaching for her purse she pulled out the ring and placed it gently in his hand. "I'm sorry."

The anger that had erupted from him moments before was gone; replaced by an eerie calmness as he got to his feet.

"I'm going to hold on to this until you change your mind."

"Robert, I'm sorry."

"If you don't mind, I don't seem to have much of an appetite anymore so I'll bid you good night."

Watching him stride down the sidewalk she felt only relief that it was over. A bruised ego was a small price to pay to avoid a lifetime of unhappiness in a one-sided marriage. Maybe in time he would realize that himself.

•   •   •

A few weeks later, with no phone call and not a single letter from Theo, Abby had never felt so low. For all his promises to never stop loving her, Theo's continuing silence was unnerving. Could he really be that upset over the phone call? Every wasted trip to the post office box ratcheted up the fear that she had lost him. But it wasn't just Theo she was worried about.

Robert was a continuing annoyance. He hadn't asked her out again but once a day he appeared at the restaurant or her house, sometimes with a small gift in hand. It was obvious he wasn't ready to walk away from her and all too often when the doorbell rang she hid in the shadows rather than answer the door. She felt like a prisoner in her own home and the situations with both Robert and Theo were creating stress to the point where she rarely slept, ate little to nothing each day and was physically ill. Dark circles appeared under her eyes and it was a struggle to drag herself into work each day where she found herself snapping at everyone and annoyed about every little thing that went wrong. Alternating between anger and tears all day was becoming the norm.

"Honey why don't you just go home and crawl into bed?" Susan suggested one morning after the entire staff witnessed Abby's cross words with a customer over burnt toast. "Or better yet, maybe you should see a doctor."

"I'm fine," Abby insisted as she brushed past her with the plate of toast the customer had complained about.

Susan wouldn't be so easily dismissed and she followed her into the kitchen. "You're not fine. Something is obviously wrong and we're worried about you."

Doris chimed in. "Susan's right. Something's wrong. You need to see a doctor. You haven't eaten a thing all day and you're wasting away to nothing."

"You want me to eat? Fine" she said taking an angry bite of the untouched toast. "I'm eating."

They watched her gulp down the toast unsure how to react to her extraordinary behavior.

"Abby, stop it," John said as she reached for yet another piece. "What is wrong with you? You're acting like a crazy woman. Come on now, have a seat and tell us what's going on."

"There's nothing going on and I just wish you would all mind your own business. I'm perfectly fine," she said before clasping her hand across her mouth and running for the bathroom.

Minutes later, as her staff quietly discussed Abby's strange behavior, she emerged glassy-eyed from the bathroom, her face an unhealthy shade of green.

"I think you're right. I'm not feeling well. I'm going home. I'll see you all tomorrow."

Brushing off their offers to escort her home, Abby grabbed her things and headed out the door intending to go straight home before another bout of stomach upset overtook her. She had been sick on and off for a couple of weeks now and something was obviously wrong. Changing directions she headed towards her doctor's office.

Chapter Twenty-One

Abby had been sitting in the same spot in her living room for hours; unable to move or even turn on a light as day turned into night. Alternating between fear and wonder, the doctor's words reverberated in her head. She was going to have a baby; a baby Theo had made perfectly clear he didn't want and for which she was wholly unprepared. Arms wrapped tightly around her stomach she thought about the life growing inside her; a living testament to the love she and Theo had shared. The miracle of life that in any other circumstance would have been welcomed and treasured.

She would be a mother but an unmarried one in a small town with conservative values where people judged everything about everyone. She wasn't naïve enough to believe people would accept her situation. It had already started with whispering and finger pointing from the nurses in her doctor's office. Was that the reaction she would get from everyone in town when her condition began to show?

But she was getting ahead of herself; after all there was Theo to consider. He had made it perfectly clear he didn't want children and even if he would marry her the scandal would destroy his career before it even got started. She couldn't let that happen. It seemed the only way to ensure his future was to not tell him but no matter if their relationship was over, he deserved to know even if he wouldn't marry her. She could raise the baby on her own and he could go on about his life. It was a sacrifice she was willing to make for both the child she now carried and the man she loved.

Consumed with thoughts of an uncertain future, Abby jumped at the sound of the doorbell. Peering around the corner her heart dropped when she saw Robert on the other side of the door. He was the last person she wanted to deal with at the moment and she froze in place hoping he would go away.

"Abby," I know you're in there. I saw you through the window. Please let me in."

Using her shirt sleeve to wipe away her tears she took a deep breath before going to the door.

"Robert now is not a good time." she said as she opened the door just a crack. "I'm not feeling well."

"I know and that's why I'm here. I brought you some soup from the restaurant," he told her holding up a small bag. "John said they're worried about you so I came over to see if I could help."

The last time she had heard those words it had been Theo standing on her porch.

"Please, I really just need to go to bed."

"And you can go straight up as soon as you've eaten."

Without waiting for her permission he pushed the door open further and walked past her into the kitchen leaving her no option but to follow as he pulled out a pot and began to heat the soup. He asked no questions and made no comment about her appearance while she watched him work from her seat at the table. Finally he placed a small bowl of soup in front of her.

"Now eat," he instructed.

The soup smelled wonderful, but afraid to eat too quickly lest she throw it all back up, Abby sipped slowly while Robert carried on a solo commentary about his week. Before she knew it she had drained the bowl and for the first time in days, the food appeared to be staying put.

"Would you like some more?" he asked kindly when she had finished.

"It was wonderful but I think I've had enough."

"Well then let's get you to bed."

Taking her by the elbow he led her upstairs, helped her onto the bed and spread a light blanket over her.

"I'll let John know you won't be going in to work tomorrow," he said. "A couple days off will do you good and before you know it you'll be feeling like yourself again. I'll stop over tomorrow and check in on you, but until then sleep well my dear Abby."

If she had been feeling better Abby would have protested at the liberties he was taking but for the first time in her adult life having someone take care of her was welcome. She simply nodded her head as he leaned in to place a gentle kiss on her forehead and was sound asleep before he had even closed the bedroom door.

•   •   •

She slept well into the next afternoon and after a long hot shower and a change of clothing she felt like a different woman, although one still with an enormous problem in front of her. One thing she was certain of however, was the need to tell Theo about her condition before any more time went on. But it wasn't the kind of news one put in a letter and once again the stationery in front of her sat empty as she struggled with how to break the news until the sound of mail being pushed through the slot on the front door interrupted her thoughts.

Sorting through the large stack of mostly junk mail, a New York postmark caught her eye and she eagerly ripped open the thick envelope, disappointed to find it wasn't from Theo. Instead it was a short letter from Bobby accompanied by a handful of magazine articles. Quickly reading the letter a smile broke out on her face at his kind words for her help finding Theo before going on to direct her attention to the numerous trade magazine articles about the up and coming star. Apparently Theo's success in New York was greater than he had let on and she eagerly read the articles, some of which contained photos.

After six weeks of rehearsals the play had opened to much fanfare and the critics loved them with one opening night review mentioning Theo directly. *"In an abbreviated moment in the limelight, newcomer*

Theo James may have stolen the show." How thrilled he must have been to read that.

When she came to the last article however, her excitement evaporated at the photo of Theo flanked by a beautiful blond actress. His arm wrapped tightly around the woman, he appeared to be perfectly at ease with the stranger beside him even as he leaned in to no doubt whisper words of love into her ear. Abby scanned the accompanying text before tears came to her eyes.

The photo only told part of the story. Although it didn't come right out and say it, the words implied Theo had found another woman, or indeed a series of them, to keep his bed warm at night. Combined with the lack of contact between them and this damning evidence, Abby knew that whatever they had shared at the lake was inexplicably gone. Uncontrollable sobs wracked her body and she collapsed in a heap on the floor.

How could he do this to her? Where were his promises of never ending love? Had everything they shared been an act from the start?

If she had had only herself to consider Abby might have allowed herself to wallow in her grief, but that wasn't an option any more. She had a child to consider. Getting to her feet she gathered Bobby's letter along with the magazine articles and placed them in the burn barrel out back. Lighting the match she said a silent good-bye to the only man she would ever love before watching evidence of his betrayal go up in flames. Her hands caressing her still flat belly she slowly walked back into the house just in time to hear Robert's voice.

"Abby? Abby where are you? Oh there you are," he said as she came in from the back yard. "I hope you don't mind, but I let myself in in case you were still in bed. Oh my, you still look horrible. Let's get you back to bed and then I think it's time we give the doctor a call."

"There's no need," Abby told him with a drawn out sigh.

"Of course there is. You're obviously ill and we need to get you a prescription or something."

"I'm not ill and I've already been to the doctor."

"You have? Well what did he say? Is it the flu or what?"

She hadn't intended to tell him. She hadn't intended to tell anyone until she had figured out what to do herself, but his obvious concern was more than she could handle and she needed a friend now more than ever.

"I'm pregnant," she said watching carefully to gauge his reaction. "I know it will be a shock to you, but I'm going to have a baby."

For a man so conservative, so set in his ways, she expected horror and revulsion and got none. Only a brief raise of his eyebrows indicated he had even heard her.

"Well then," he said slowly. "I wasn't expecting that but it's not the end of the world."

At his kind words, she burst into tears yet again.

"There, there now," he said as he pulled her into his arms and gently patted her on the back.

When she finally stopped crying, they sat together on the sofa.

"Why aren't you horrified?" she finally asked. "I'm about to be an unmarried mother. Doesn't that shock you?"

"It should I suppose, especially since it wasn't that long ago that I proposed to you, but I'm not totally naïve. These things happen. You'll be getting married then I suppose."

"That's not an option anymore. He's long gone and apparently he's moved on with his life."

"Abby I'm so sorry. You don't deserve this."

"How am I going to raise a child on my own? I don't know the first thing about babies. And how will I pay for everything? What am I going to do?" she cried as she buried her head in her hands.

"You don't have to be alone," he said so softly she didn't hear him at first. "Abby . . . " he said reaching for her hand, "you don't have to be alone. We can get married."

Raising her head she looked back at him through tear stained eyes not quite believing what she had heard.

"I mean it," he insisted. "We can get married this weekend, right here in the house if you like, and I can be the baby's father. You know I always wanted a lot of kids and we already have the house and no one would ever have to know."

"Robert that's so sweet but I already told you I'm not in love with you."

"I know that obviously but it doesn't matter to me. I'll be a good husband and a wonderful father and I promise you'll be happy. Oh Abby please say yes. Let me give your baby a father."

Overcome with all the emotions and stress of the last month, the word just slipped out of her mouth . . . "Okay."

In an instant Robert was at her side, crushing her in an embrace so strong she couldn't breathe before she slowly pushed him away to see a look of joy on his face.

"There are conditions to my agreement however," she said slowly. This time more than ever she wanted there to be no misunderstanding between them.

"Whatever you want," he said happily.

"Robert this is serious. I want to make sure you understand completely."

"Anything my love."

"First and most importantly you will never ask me anything about my baby's father. Not who he is, where he lives, or anything."

"Agreed."

"And second, if we get married, I promise I will be a good wife to you and I will make a happy life for us both, but there's no guarantee I will love you. Can you accept that? I mean really accept that?"

"Abby, I would do anything for you and I know that in time you will grow to love me. You just need to give us a chance."

"That's not good enough . . . you're doing such a wonderful thing for me I don't want to hurt you. Can you truthfully say that you can spend the rest of your life with a woman who isn't in love with you?"

"I love you enough that even if we are nothing more than friends I will never regret marrying you. Is that all of your conditions?"

"Yes."

"I agree. So, will you marry me?"

"Yes."

•   •   •

Robert wasted no time arranging for a private wedding ceremony and by the end of the following week they were married and had moved into Robert's new house. Friends and family were shocked by the sudden marriage but none more so than John. The scowl on his face had been there for days and she dreaded the confrontation that would eventually come. It took a week before she could no longer avoid his anger.

"Don't you think you owe me an explanation?" he asked as the two worked alone together in the kitchen late one Sunday afternoon.

Although they had been together all day most of it had been spent in tense silence as Abby waited for his anger to erupt.

"Would it do any good?" she said as she wiped her hands on her apron and poured herself a glass of water. Since becoming pregnant coffee no longer seemed to agree with her.

"That depends what you're going to say. Why did you do it Abby? Why marry someone you don't love?"

"It seems I didn't seem have a choice." she said sadly, unable to look at him. "I'm pregnant."

The kitchen was so quiet they could hear the gentle hum of the cooler. When John had no response to her announcement she looked up to see tears rolling down his face.

"I see," he said finally before turning his back on her.

"It's not what you think."

"I know I'm an old man but believe me, I know exactly what it is. I guess I'm just surprised that you slept with Robert especially knowing how you felt about Theo."

"Sleep with him?! Of course I didn't sleep with Robert!" she exclaimed.

"Well then who.." he asked before the light bulb went off. "Oh, Theo's the father."

"Yes."

"As much as I didn't trust that boy when he arrived I never took him for the kind of man who would turn his back on his own child."

"He didn't. He doesn't know."

"Why in hell not? Abby what were you thinking? No matter what you feel about the boy he deserves to know he's going to be a father."

"He's moved on. I found out he's seeing other women and I haven't heard from him since getting back from the lake. And even if he wasn't he made it perfectly clear to me that he has no interest in having a child. It's over between us so there's no need to tell him."

"I don't think he would see it that way. Does Robert know about Theo?"

"No. I made him promise that he would never ask about the child's father and I want you to promise me that you will never mention Theo's name to anyone. As far as anyone in town knows Robert will be this baby's father. Theo is out of our lives and I don't want to even think about him anymore."

"But . . ."

"No buts. It's over. My life is with Robert now and I don't want to talk about it anymore."

Chapter Twenty-Two

With so much changing in Abby's life in the span of just a few months and the stress she was under, she might have been forgiven for withdrawing from everyone around her, but that wasn't the case. Once people stopped gossiping about her sudden marriage, her life went back to being status quo at least during the day. It was only late at night, with Robert sleeping soundly next to her, that thoughts of what might have been invaded her mind.

Months had gone by with no letter from Theo and she doubted there would ever be another. At first Abby vowed not to write him either but missing him and trying to cope with the difficult adjustment to marriage with a man she didn't love drove her to put her thoughts down on paper. Serving as a journal of sorts, long narratives of her daily life and her thoughts about where her life had ended up filled pages that were carefully sealed in envelopes never to be sent. She wrote as if speaking to Theo, finding solace in sharing her thoughts with him, even if he would never see it while the baby growing inside her served as a constant reminder of what they had once shared.

A knock on her office door brought her out of her daydreams.

"Abby?" Susan's quiet voice asked.

"Come in."

"Sorry, I thought you were gone for the day. The Post Office called and asked you to stop by before you go home."

"That's odd. Did they say why?"

"Nope. Just asked you to stop by."

"Okay thanks. Would you please let John know I'm leaving for the day and I'll see you tomorrow?"

Grabbing her things, she walked out the front door with a heavier step than usual. The continual morning sickness was becoming less frequent, but in its place was a never ending fatigue that left her drained by the end of each work day. Even so the walk to the post office took just a few minutes.

"Hey Abby, thanks for stopping in," the Postmaster said. "I have letters for you that wouldn't fit in your box."

As the man disappeared from view, Abby's heart leapt. The only person who would send a letter to her post office box was Theo. Was it possible he had written again? Quickly reappearing the Postmaster placed a shoebox full of letters on the counter in front of her.

"These are all for me?" she asked in surprise.

"Addressed to Miss Abby Peterson." he said with a laugh. "Apparently the people who sent them didn't hear about your wedding. Congratulations on that Mrs. Ward."

"Thank you."

Grabbing the box and hurrying out of the building, Abby's heart began to beat so fast she had to sit down on a nearby bench. She wanted to immediately open the letters but with her emotions running wild she was afraid she'd burst into tears at what they might say. Privacy was what she needed and there was only one place left to her that would allow the privacy she needed. She made her way to the now vacant and as yet unsold Victorian she had called home before her marriage.

Taking a seat at the kitchen table, she took a deep breath before opening the box and spreading the dozen or so letters in front of her. Theo's familiar handwriting on the front warmed her heart before she opened the first envelope to discover nothing about Theo's feelings for her had changed. Each successive letter was as full of love for her as ever until she got to the most recent. Jumping to the same conclusion she had when she failed to receive a letter from him, the most recent letter was filled with questions on why she had stopped writing and why her phone had been disconnected. Finally he asked point blank if she no longer shared his feelings.

"I don't know what I did to make you stop loving me, but don't worry, I got the message when I discovered you have disconnected your phone. If you loved me at all, if there is even the tiniest of those feelings still in you, won't you please contact me and tell me what I did to make you stop loving me? Meet me at the lake, call me at the number below, or even write a letter. Don't I at the very least deserve an explanation?"

His final letter was unsigned and Abby instinctively knew he was saying good-bye. Had a few misdirected letters really changed the course of both of their lives? Thinking he no longer loved her Abby had married a man she didn't love leaving no way out for either of them. Would contacting him now make any difference? There were still the other women to consider after all.

Of course she still loved Theo, but even if he still loved her contacting him would truly break his heart. There was no way to keep news of her marriage to Robert from him but more importantly he would learn about a baby he had never wanted. Should she simply let him go to save him from the heartbreak?

Long after she should have been home she sat in the empty house struggling with the dilemma of her own doing before tears mixed with anger and resignation ended in a decision. Theo deserved an answer whether he would like what he heard or not. He needed to be free of her and only she could give him that freedom. Springing the news about her new life on him in a letter would have been easier, but difficult or not, she vowed to call Theo the very next day.

•   •   •

Waiting until Robert had left for work the next morning, her nerves on edge like never before, Abby picked up the phone to make the call. It was quite early in California and Theo would most likely still be asleep, but it was now or never.

"Hello", a not quite awake Theo said as he answered the phone.

"It's Abby."

Instantly more awake, she could almost hear the smile in his voice. "Oh my god Abby, where have you been? Why haven't you written?

Why did you disconnect your phone? I thought you didn't love me anymore."

The questions tumbled out one after the other as her eyes flooded with tears at the agony in his voice.

"I'm sorry," she said simply, too overcome with emotion to say much more.

"I've been writing for weeks with no response. What is going on?"

"I don't know what happened, but I got about a dozen letters all at once just yesterday. When you didn't answer my letters I thought you had stopped loving me," she cried.

"Well that's the Post Office for you," he said with a laugh. "But at least I know you're okay. How have you been? Are you well? Are you happy? I have so much to tell you about Hollywood and the movie and my life out here and I don't know where to start."

"So you're happy?"

"Happy? I'm over the moon. I just wish you were here to share it all with me. I miss you so much."

"Please don't say that. It just makes this harder."

"Makes what harder?" he asked hesitantly. "Abby what's going on? Why did you disconnect your phone?"

"I can't see you anymore," she said softly.

"Don't say that," he said now with more than a touch of anger and hurt in his voice. "Please don't say that."

"I'm sorry Theo, but there's somebody else."

"But you love me. You promised to never stop loving me!"

"It would never have worked between you and I. We're too different and our lives are in separate parts of the country. You have to see that."

"What happened to you? Just weeks ago you told me how much you loved me. What could possibly have changed in such a short amount of time? Abby what the hell is going on?"

"I'm sorry but I am with someone else now and it's only fair to tell you, I'm married."

"What!" he screamed into the phone. "For God's sake Abby what is going on? Why would you lie about something like that? No one gets married in just a month. Who is this guy?"

"It's Robert . . . the man I dated before meeting you."

"The soldier? You married the soldier? But you didn't even like the man. Why in hell would you marry him?"

Each bit of news was ratcheting up Theo's anger and Abby's hands began to shake knowing she hadn't dropped the biggest bombshell yet. Taking a deep breath, she finally said the words.

"I'm going to have a baby," she said bluntly. "We're going to have a baby."

His anger was palpable. "So you left my bed and went straight to his is that what you're telling me? My God Abby, that's not you. I know that's not you. You don't love him and do you know why I know that? Because I know you and I know that you love me and you will always love me. Why would you throw away whatever chance we could have had for a wonderful life together?"

"I'm sorry . . . "

"Sorry for what?" he spat. "Sorry for tossing me aside? Sorry for breaking your promise to me? Sorry for marrying a man you don't love simply because you got pregnant? I would have married you. I would have been father to your child but you never even gave me a chance. My God Abby what has happened to you since the lake?

"Theo, I.."

His deep sigh interrupted her.

"No, I don't want to hear your excuses. What's done is done. I hope you have a very happy life together you and your new family. But remember this. I will never stop loving you. Think of that the next time the man you married takes you into his arms. I will never stop loving you."

Without another word he hung up on her.

His anger had been expected and even justified, but it was his pain that tore her apart. She could hear it in his voice and in the words he shot back. He had promised John not to hurt her but in the end she had been the one they both should have worried about.

•   •   •

Robert realized something had changed in his new bride but he chalked it up to pregnancy hormones as the months went by. Abby was spending even more time at work when she should have been taking things easy and once home she was quiet and withdrawn and easily brought to tears by the most innocent of comments. Still he was as attentive as ever, going out of his way each and every day to do something nice for Abby as her pregnancy progressed.

What he couldn't know and she left unsaid, was his extra effort to make the pregnancy easier for her was actually making things worse and she was consumed with tremendous guilt. Robert had been nothing but kind and caring and seemed happier than he had ever been while Abby struggled each day to justify what she had done not only to Robert, but Theo as well.

Understandably since the phone call, she and Theo had not had any contact and she was working hard to put all thoughts of him behind her even as his child grew within her. She owed Robert as much and yet each time someone congratulated him on becoming a father she found herself filled with resentment at his obvious joy. Unable to see her own feet, back aching, and hormones causing frequent mood swings, only her desire to finally hold the baby in her arms was getting her through it all.

The moment came almost two weeks later than expected when a tiny, red faced, screaming child was placed gently in her arms.

"She looks just like you," Robert said quietly as he put his arm around them both and softly kissed the top of the baby's head.

Unable to stop staring at her new daughter, Abby knew better. Every feature of the child was the spitting image of Theo and Abby began to cry yet again. Frequent mood swings attributable to the flood of pregnancy hormones were not unexpected and had become a good cover for what Abby was really feeling . . . missing Theo more than ever.

"Have you decided on a name yet?" the nurse asked as she adjusted the blanket covering mother and daughter.

"I thought we could name her after my mother," Robert suggested.

"It's Deborah," Abby said firmly. "Deborah Krista Ward after my mother."

She had been thinking of it for some time. Deborah after her own mother, and Krista after Theo's.

"Krista?"

"It's lovely don't you think?"

"Of course my dear. Whatever you want."

Later, the baby safely back in the nursery, Robert sat at Abby's bedside holding her hand.

"Why don't you go home and get some sleep?" she suggested. Her room had been a revolving door of visitors and she just wanted some time alone with her own thoughts.

"I will but I wanted to give you something first," he said as he pulled a small box out of his jacket pocket and handed it to her.

"What's this?"

"I wanted to give you something to remind you of how much I love you. How much I will always love you. Open it."

Lifting the cover Abby's eyes opened wide at the beautiful sterling silver locket with the finest filigree covering the piece.

"Robert it's beautiful but you didn't have to do this."

"Oh but I did," he told her. "Look inside."

"Inside?"

"There's a photo."

Carefully opening the locket to find a small photo of Robert in his Army uniform, Abby finally understood. Today on the birth of her daughter by another man Robert was reminding her where her future lay.

"You can put a picture of the baby on the other side when we get one. So you'll always remember your family."

For the first time since she had agreed to marry him she truly understood the sacrifice he had made for her and she vowed to never forget it again.

"I understand. Will you put it on me?" she asked.

As he did so, the smile on his face said more than words could. Gathering his things, he prepared to leave before she reached out to stop him.

"Robert?"

"Yes dear?"

"Thank you . . . for everything."

Chapter Twenty-Three

Krista couldn't have been more shocked by the startling revelation in Theo's story, but it wasn't until he paused to look at her that the full impact of what he had told her finally sunk in.

"The baby. Abby's baby with you . . . that's my mother isn't it?"

"I'm afraid so." he admitted. "Abby admitted the truth to me just a few years ago."

"Does my Mom know?"

"Abby thought so, but we're not sure. Deborah had some health issues when she was a teenager and the Hospital discovered her blood type was such that she couldn't possibly have been Robert's daughter. That was about the same time the difficulties between mother and daughter began and Abby suspected Deborah might have overheard their conversation with the doctors. But neither one of them ever actually talked about it and since your grandfather already knew the truth and Deborah recovered, there was no reason to bring it up again."

"No reason!" Krista said louder than she should have as they walked slowly around the park, "I think Mom had a right to know who her father is don't you?"

"Certainly, and when I found out I was beside myself. How Abby could have kept that secret from me for so long I couldn't imagine and we almost ended our relationship because of it, but in the end I couldn't stay away from her. She made me promise never to tell Deborah the truth. She believed that with all of Deborah's insecurities it was more important for her to think of Robert as her father then a stranger she had never met and in the end I agreed with her."

"And if you are Mom's dad, then that makes you . . . "

"Your grandfather, yes," he said before stopping to look at her. "That is if you are willing to accept me as such."

"Of course I can, but what about Mom?"

"That's the million dollar question I think. I promised Abby I would say nothing, but now that she's gone and you know the truth, I think I owe it to Deborah to also tell her the truth. But before we go there do you want to know the rest of the story?"

"Honestly? After this surprise I'm not sure I can take any more. But I am curious how you and Nan got back together."

"Ah . . . but for a series of misunderstandings, all of our lives might have turned out very different. So where was I? Abby's marriage…"

•   •   •

The week's following Deborah's birth were among the happiest Abby could remember. Robert doted on the child and while neither parent got any real sleep, Deborah was a joy to them both. The only thing marring Abby's joy was knowing Theo had a daughter he knew nothing about. Riddled with guilt, she struggled with how to tell him knowing she owed him at least that much but finally, unable to face the thought that he would reject their daughter, she kept her silence. Robert would be a good father, of that she was certain, and as unfair as she knew it was to Theo, someday she vowed to tell her daughter the truth. Until then it was Theo's face she would see each time she held her daughter in her arms and that would be punishment enough for her deception.

"Robert, if you don't put the baby down you're going to be late for work," Abby said with a smile as she walked into the kitchen, still in her night clothes.

It was the same each morning. Robert was the one to give Deborah her morning bottle leaving Abby with a few precious extra minutes of sleep before he gave them both one last kiss and dashed off to work. Having taken time off from the restaurant Abby was working harder than ever before. Between caring for the baby, the extra loads of laundry, and seemingly not having even time for a shower, she was more tired each day than she could imagine. Still, she wouldn't trade being a mother for anything.

"You're right but it's so hard to go to work and leave this precious bundle all day," Robert said as he reluctantly passed Deborah to her mother before bestowing kisses on them both. "I'll be home right after work. I love you."

"I know, I know," Abby said with a laugh as she shooed him out the door before mother and daughter settled into the rocking chair.

It was in those quiet moments, when the neighborhood hadn't quite woken up and Deborah began to drift off to sleep in her arms, that the memory of Theo invaded her mind. It had been months since he said good-bye to her and yet her love for the man was still firmly rooted in her heart. She dreamt of him more often than not, remembering his whispered words of love during the good times between them. Deborah was a constant reminder of what they had meant to each other and Abby finally had admitted to herself she would never stop loving him. But daydreams and reality were two different things and with a heavy heart, she began her day.

Being cooped up at home, even with a baby as precious as Deborah, was just not in Abby's nature and on such a beautiful day Abby decided to show her daughter off at the restaurant. The normally quick walk took much longer than usual as neighbor after neighbor stopped them to see the baby. It was no different once the pair arrived at the restaurant. The entire staff swarmed around them with Susan quick to claim the honor of holding the baby.

"I think she gets more beautiful every day," she exclaimed as Deborah curled her little hand around her finger. "You know, at first I thought she took after you, but now not so much."

"Look at that little nose," Doris said. "That's Abby through and through, but you're right. She must look more like Robert's side of the family."

Nervous about the direction the conversation was going, John stepped in. "Babies look like themselves," he said as he held his arms out to hold the baby. "All that matters is she is going to grow up to be as beautiful as her mother."

"Thank you John," Abby said as she gave him a kiss on the cheek. "But I never realized how tiring it is to have a baby and doubt I'll ever get a good night's sleep again. Still I wouldn't trade it for anything."

"Isn't Robert helping out?" Susan asked.

"Oh my yes. He's been wonderful and he adores Deborah. I don't know what we'd do without him."

"John, it's my turn to hold her," Doris claimed.

"Only because I have a couple of things to go over with Abby," he said before handing the baby over. "I was going to stop by the house tonight but now that you're here maybe we can talk in the office for a bit," he said mysteriously as he steered Abby to the office.

"I'm sorry you've had to take on all the extra work while I've been out . . . " Abby started as John closed the door behind him.

"It's not that. I have a message for you."

"A message?"

"From Theo."

Nothing that came out of his mouth could have been more unexpected and Abby's knees went weak before she collapsed into a chair. Stunned into silence she could only look at John with tears in her eyes.

"I shouldn't tell you, hell it's probably better that I don't, but I did promise him."

"What is it?"

"Abby are you sure? You have a new life now, a new family. There's no need to open old wounds. Just think about it for a minute."

"Please John, I know you don't approve of him but I have to know. What's the message?"

Taking a deep breath before he spoke, he pulled up a chair for himself and took Abby's hands in his own.

"He's been calling every few days trying to reach you. Thank goodness I've been the one to answer the phone each time he has called."

"John please . . . what did he say?"

"He said . . . *remind Abby of her promise. She'll know what I mean. Three weeks from now.* Just what does that mean? What happens in three weeks? "

"Nothing. I made him a promise before any of this happened. It means nothing now."

"I don't think Theo sees it that way."

"It doesn't matter what he thinks. You're right. I have a family to consider now. Nothing else matters. So, just forget that and tell me how things have been going here."

John was confused by her answer but if Abby wasn't willing to clue him in on what was going on it wasn't his place to question her further. They spent the better part of the next hour going over the restaurant's books before Deborah's hungry cry interrupted them.

"Time for her afternoon bottle," Abby said as she closed the books and turned off the desk light. "If there's anything you need just give me a call at the house. I should be back to work in another month or so."

"And if Theo calls again? What should I tell him?" John asked.

"Nothing. The message has been delivered and that's all he needs to know."

"If you say so. Now don't worry about this place. Enjoy your time with your daughter. You only have these moments once you know."

"Thanks John. It means the world to me that I can count on you to run this place and . . . well you know…"

"I know. But can I ask you one thing before you go?"

"Anything, you know that," Abby said with a warm smile.

"Do you still love him? Do you still love Theo?"

"I know what you meant and heaven help me, I can't imagine loving anyone else."

•　　　•　　　•

Maybe Abby should have heeded John's warning about Theo's message but once she had heard it she couldn't get it out of her head. How he could possibly hold her to such a promise now that so much had changed in their lives was beyond her but in spite of knowing that she couldn't help but feel a tingle of excitement at the possibility of seeing him again. Of course, she could never go. How could she possibly explain to Robert that she was going to leave him alone for an entire week with a newborn and wouldn't be telling him where she was going or what she was doing?

As the March days passed Abby was fighting a losing battle with her conscience but it wasn't until the day before she knew Theo would be at the lake waiting for her that she made the decision. She was going.

Within just a few short hours she'd arranged for Susan to spend each day with Deborah, found a fill-in waitress for the restaurant, and packed her bag. All that remained was telling Robert.

"What do you mean you're leaving for a week?" he said in surprise. "Where are you going?"

"I just need a break," Abby said. "It's no big deal. I'll be back next Sunday."

"But what about Deborah? Are you taking her with you?"

"No, but Susan is going to take over for me here at the house. She'll do whatever is needed to help you out. She loves Deborah and Deb loves her."

"And what about me? If you wait a week or two I can get some time off and we'll go together." The desperation in his voice was building.

"I'm sorry, but I'm going alone. We'll take a family vacation this summer I promise. But this time I need to go alone. I know you don't understand the need to be alone but I just need a little peace and quiet. I'll come back a whole new woman."

"I happen to like this woman," he said before his arms snaked around Abby's waist. "Please don't go."

"I'm sorry, but I have to," she said as she peeled his arms away.

The look on his face before he turned and walked out of the room had been indecipherable; something she was becoming all too used to. It seemed the man was truly incapable of showing any type of strong emotion. She knew she had hurt him beyond measure but the need to see Theo again was overwhelming.

That night, for the first time in their abbreviated marriage, tension ran high and silence reigned until it was time for her to leave early the next morning. Holding Deborah in his arms Robert watched silently as

Abby gathered her things, placed a soft kiss on the baby's forehead and turned to her husband for the same before he pulled away from her.

"I'm not going to ask why you insist on going but I will ask one thing of you . . . remember you have a family who loves you."

Stunned beyond words at the power of his words, Abby simply nodded and walked out the door with Robert's words echoing in her head. It was clear he suspected what she was doing and who she was doing it with and still he hadn't stopped her; instead choosing to remind her that her duty lay with him. Guilt weighed heavily on her and on several occasions during the trip she stopped with the intention of turning back, but Theo's face always came to her and so she continued on becoming more of a jumble of nerves with each passing mile until she felt physically ill at the prospect of facing him.

Could he possibly still love her after everything she had done? She destroyed the love they shared and she alone deserved every bit of anger he would surely heap upon her, but could some small part of him still love her? The need to know was what drove her on.

A few miles before her destination she pulled to the side of the road and removed the silver locket she hadn't taken off since the birth of her daughter, trying not to think of the photos inside, before looking at her wedding band. A symbol of her commitment to Robert, its removal seemed the ultimate betrayal and the thought almost stopped her, but not quite. Abby slipped the ring off, wrapped both pieces in a tissue and placed them in the glove box leaving Mrs. Abigail Ward behind. It was Abby Peterson who drove on to meet the man she loved.

Nearing the cabin she slowed the car to scan the long drive for some sign of life and saw nothing. There was no car in sight. Theo wasn't there. Pulling to a stop, the crunch of gravel the only sound in the secluded spot, she started to weep as she finally admitted to herself the real reason she was here. This trip, for her at least, had always been to rekindle the love they shared and to beg his forgiveness for everything she had put him through; to satisfy a deep yearning to feel Theo's arms around her, his lips on her own as they whispered words of love to each other and he wasn't even here.

She knew what she needed to do – turn the car around and go back to her husband, beg him to forgive her and put Theo in her past where he belonged - but movement in her peripheral vision interrupted her thoughts. There on the lake a boat was speeding into shore, the sole occupant waving furiously. As the boat drew closer, her heart stopped beating. It was Theo.

Every thought in her head froze at the sight of him as he pulled the boat to the dock and carefully secured it before walking slowly towards her. Clad in t-shirt and jeans, the sun glistening off his dark hair, he seemed different somehow. Still as handsome as ever, something had changed in the way he carried himself. He stood taller, more confident, with a swagger to his step that hadn't been there before. The only thing that hadn't changed was the unexpected smile on his face as he reached to open the door and offer his hand to help Abby out of the car. Confused by his seemingly warm welcome Abby didn't know what to say as they stood mere inches apart.

"I didn't believe you would come," he said softly as he continued to hold her hand.

"I wasn't sure I would," she replied unable to meet his gaze as she stared at the space between them.

"How was your drive?" he asked before dropping her hand and grabbing her small suitcase.

"Fine."

"You look well."

"I am."

The stilted conversation, so unlike their last time at the lake, put Abby on edge as she waited for Theo to unload his fury. Out of the corner of her eye she tried to find some hint that it was coming, but saw nothing even while knowing his non-descript treatment would most certainly change.

"There have been some changes since last year. They added a garage, we'll put your car there later next to mine, and the cabin now has another bedroom at the back. I'm in that one and I've readied the upstairs bedroom for you. I know how much you like waking up to that view."

A wave of relief washed over her. As much as she wanted to feel his arms around her, it would have meant cheating on her husband and she had been struggling with the thought. Theo had made the decision for her.

"Thank you," she said simply.

"Why don't you go up and get settled while I put together some lunch for us? I had hoped to have fresh fish, but didn't have much luck on the lake this morning."

"Thank you," she said again before climbing the stairs.

In the relative privacy of the upstairs bedroom Abby placed the suitcase on the floor and tried to gain control of her chaotic emotions. Her reflection in the mirror was that of a scared woman on the verge of tears; a rabbit ready to take flight at the first sign of danger. She froze where she was listening to Theo whistling while he worked in the kitchen below, seemingly without a care in the world. What was going on?

Her eyes landed on the large expanse of the bed and she caught her breath remembering it was there the love she and Theo shared had created a daughter. Her hand went to her throat to touch the locket, a habit she had long ago acquired when she needed to calm herself, before remembering it wasn't there. The unexpected reminder of the life she had left behind and her guilt overwhelmed her. Her decision to come to the lake was wrong by every definition, but she had let her desire to see Theo control her. She needed to get back in her car and go back to her family. Grabbing her suitcase, she started down the steps just as Theo called out to her.

"Abby, lunch is ready when you are."

Just hearing his voice was enough to pull her back. Taking a deep breath she took one final look in the mirror before putting the suitcase down and going downstairs.

"I wasn't sure how hungry you are, but we have sandwiches and salad," he told her as he placed the food on the table. "Please sit."

"Thank you."

Taking a seat opposite Theo, Abby finally looked into his beautiful eyes and felt her heart melt with desire when he smiled back at her.

"I was wondering if you would ever look at me," he told her, his eyes crinkling in amusement. "It's wonderful to see you."

Reaching across the table he covered her hand with his own before she pulled hers back and put it in her lap.

"I'm sorry, I shouldn't have done that. I forgot myself for a minute there. So how have you been? Tell me about your new life."

He seemed determined to act as if nothing had changed between them and she didn't understand it. If the shoe had been on the other foot she wouldn't have been able to contain her anger and hurt, but he was acting as if he felt nothing.

"I'm fine thank you."

"You said that earlier but you forget I know you too well and saying you're 'fine' is not an answer. How is married life and, more importantly, how is it being a mother?"

Having left her family to be with him Abby had no intention of discussing them with him now, but she did want answers of her own.

"Theo, what am I doing here? Why did you insist on holding me to the promise?"

"Because I wanted to see you again of course. Because I think of you every day."

"Why do you think of me at all?"

"How could I not? Every day I go to the set and get to do the thing I love most in life and it's all because of you. I wouldn't have the life I have now if it weren't for you so of course I think of you."

Subconsciously hoping he would declare his never ending love for her Abby felt more than a sense of disappointment. He no longer loved her.

"Oh."

"What did you think I was going to say?" he asked softly, his eyes boring into her. "Did you think I was going to say I think of you because I'm still in love with you? Since you're married to someone else that would be rather foolish don't you think?"

His words cut her to the quick but there was no animosity in his statement, just the truth.

"Of course. That would be foolish."

Determined to steer the conversation away from what she had done to him she asked about the movie. It had been months since he started the film.

"It's a long process with even longer days and it can wear on me but for the first time in my life, I can't wait to get up in the morning and I'm disappointed when the day is over. There was a lot to learn at first as it's nothing like being on the stage, but I think my work is good, at least I hope so, and I'm really enjoying it."

Little did he know Abby knew full well just how much he was enjoying himself but now was not the time to bring it up and she remained silent as they ate and he talked about his career. By the time lunch was over the sense of impending doom was lessening. It was the old Theo who sat across from her and his excitement about his life was infectious if only she could let herself enjoy their time together.

"So what would you like to do this afternoon? We could go fishing, or we could take the canoe out . . . I know how much you like that."

"I'd love to get out on the lake if that's okay with you, but maybe the boat rather than the canoe."

"The boat it is then," he said as they walked down to the dock.

Minutes later they were motoring slowly out onto the calm waters of the lake as a flood of memories rushed back to her . . . the smell of pine in the air, the slap of a large fish as it breached the surface of the water creating a cascading series of ripples before once again disappearing below the surface, the warmth of the late spring sun on her face and the breeze whipping her hair in a frenzy of tangles as the boat moved across the lake. Suddenly she remembered the one thing she missed the most, the loons. She scanned the lake searching for them.

"What is it?" he asked. "What are you looking for?"

"The loons."

"I've been here a couple days and haven't seen or heard them yet. Maybe they didn't come back this year," he said as he killed the motor and let the boat drift. At this early part of the season, their's was the only craft on the lake.

"But I thought they come back to the same lake every year," Abby said as she continued to scan the horizon. "What if something happened to them?"

Something about the birds had been magic for them the last time they were together. Their absence now only seemed to mirror their own broken relationship.

"I'm sure they're fine," he said. "But like people there might be things beyond their control that pull them apart. We just have to hope they find their way back to each other."

Every fiber of her being knew he wasn't just talking about the loons.

"Yeah, we have to hope," she said softly as she trailed her hand over the side of the boat in the cold water. "I don't remember it being this quiet here."

"Not exactly what you're used to," he said with a chuckle. "Between the restaurant and a new baby I'll bet your life is one big noise."

"Theo please don't," she asked before sitting up and looking at him. "What?"

"I'm not going to talk about my family with you."

"Why in the world not? Are you ashamed of them?"

"You know it's not that. It's just . . . "

"It's just what? Don't you talk to your friends about your husband? Don't you talk to your friends about your baby? I don't even know if you have a son or a daughter. As your friend don't I get to know about your life?"

"You know we're more than just friends...or at least we were. I didn't come up here to talk about my family."

"Why did you come here?" he asked with the first hint of anger Abby had seen from him. "You didn't come just because you made me a promise a year ago, we both know that. So just why are you here Abigail?"

Abby had learned long ago that use of her full name signaled his anger.

"I don't know."

"You need to do better than that," he spat. "I deserve better than that."

Struggling with how much to share of her internal battle she tried to explain.

"I owed you. I owed you the chance to pay me back for hurting you. I owed you an explanation."

"And? No woman leaves her husband and baby behind to meet a man just to provide an explanation that could just have easily been said in a letter or on the phone. So, I ask again . . . why are you here?"

"To say good-bye," she said softly as tears began to fall.

She hadn't intended to say it but she knew it was for the best. Theo would never be out of her life if she didn't and she owed it to Robert and her daughter to put him in the past. Deborah's parentage would remain a secret from Theo because it was the way it needed to be.

"When did you get to be such a liar?" Theo asked before he started the motor and turned the boat back to the dock. If Abby had been able to look at him her tears would have been reflected in his own.

Chapter Twenty-Four

Three days had been spent together at the lake in virtual silence. As uncomfortable as it was becoming, neither seemed willing to just give in and go home. Theo was as cordial as ever, treating Abby the same way he would any other guest, but it was far from the closeness they had previously shared. Early each morning, thinking Abby was still asleep, he quietly left the cabin and spent time alone on the lake – the boat always within eyesight of the cabin - while Abby watched from the small balcony wrapped tightly in a blanket to ward off the early morning chill.

What was the point of having left her family behind if they couldn't even talk to each other? Watching him on the lake each morning she vowed to pack her things and go home but then he would come back and stop briefly to look up at her with a smile that tore at her heart and so she stayed. After a year apart, being able to see him was enough it seemed.

The day had been particularly warm, unusual for April, and the cabin had turned stifling hot before Abby, dressed in cut offs and a bikini top, made her way down to the dock to dip her toes in the cool water as Theo read a script on the patio. Flashes of lightning were beginning to dot the horizon heralding an approaching spring storm and she knew she would be safer inside, but inside meant being subjected to another tense evening. A creak of the dock boards announced his arrival.

"I hope I'm not interrupting your thoughts," he said softly before he sat down next to her and put his own feet in the water.

"It's fine," she said without looking at him.

The tranquility she had been feeling had instantly been replaced with nervous energy. Sitting side by side on the narrow dock they were closer than they had been all week and she could feel the heat coming off his body sending her desire into freefall.

"I've missed this you know," he told her as they watched the stormy sunset together.

"I suppose LA doesn't have too many lakes," she said with a nervous laugh.

"I wasn't talking about the lake Abby. I miss spending time with you like this. I miss us."

"Theo, I . . ."

"Please, let me say what I need to say."

She couldn't look at him, but knew that he was studying her closely with that intenseness she remembered.

"Do you love him?"

"You wouldn't understand."

"Try me."

"He's a good man and he's making a good life for us. But I'm not in love with him."

"Then why are you with him? You deserve to be with someone you are madly and passionately in love with. You deserve to love a man whose face you can't get out of your mind. A man who will spend all night and every day showing you how precious you are to him."

"And is that you?" she asked sadly. "Are you telling me you still love me after everything I did to you?" The wild pounding of her heart made her feel dizzy and she tightened her grip on the dock lest she fall head first into the water as she waited for his answer.

"Of course I do. I will never stop loving you and I think you still love me or you wouldn't be here."

He was right of course, but to admit it would hurt yet another man who loved her.

I'm here because I owed you an explanation. To try and atone for what I did to you and for how I hurt you. That's it."

"Maybe you truly believe that but you're lying to yourself and you're lying to me."

"Theo you don't know me as well as you think you do. I've changed. My daughter changed me and there's no going back to the way things were."

"So it's a girl."

"Yes. I have a daughter."

"What's her name."

"Deborah, after my mother," Abby told him. She prayed he wouldn't ask the child's middle name.

"Does she look like you?" he asked softly. "I'll wager she's beautiful like you."

"She looks just like her father."

"Oh," he said with disappointment as Abby turned her head to hide her tears. It would have been the perfect time to tell Theo he was a father and yet she couldn't do it.

A sudden clap of thunder shook them to their core.

"I think we better go inside," Theo said as he got to his feet and held his hand out to her just as the sky opened up above them.

Gale force wind began to blow the freezing rain sideways forcing them to hold tightly to each other as they raced for the cabin. Slamming the door shut behind them, Theo hurried to close the downstairs windows against the fierceness of the storm while Abby did the same upstairs.

"Theo help me," she shouted. "I can't get this window closed."

Taking the stairs two at a time he went to her side where she struggled to close the last window against the rain lashing her face. As they did so the sudden quiet enveloped them as they stood face to face shivering in their wet clothes.

"This brings back memories," Theo told her as he reached up to gently move the wet hair out of her eyes before taking her face in his hands.

The look of desire in his eyes, a look she thought she would never see again, flamed her own desire and she didn't dare move for fear of what she might do.

"Theo please don't."

"Abby I know you love me. I can see it in your eyes every time you look at me."

"I can't. I'm a married woman," she pleaded with less conviction than she felt as her body began to tremble in anticipation.

"But you don't love him and you're here with me, the man you do love . . . the man you promised to love forever."

"*I carry your heart...*" she said softly as she looked up at him with tears in her eyes.

"*I carry it in my heart,*" he completed before covering her lips with his own in a kiss she thought would never happen again.

The floodgates of her heart opened and she gave herself freely to him; the chill of the sudden downpour overtaken by the heat building between them as their kiss grew deeper and more passionate. Abby molded herself to his body as her legs threatened to give way. Only Theo's sure embrace kept her upright as he slowly began to remove her clothes and his hands began a slow and sensual exploration of her nakedness; his touch leaving a trail of fire on her skin before her own hands mirrored his actions.

She remembered without fail the outline of every muscle stretching across his taut belly as her lips tasted the sweet sensation of his skin, teasing and taunting until he moaned in ecstasy. Reaching down he lifted her from her feet as she wrapped her legs around him.

"Love me," she whispered into his ear as he placed her gently down on the bed, covering her body with his own.

Their year apart had stoked their desire for each other and they joined together in an explosion of sensations. Neither had forgotten how to pleasure the other and there was little sleep to be had as the storm raged outside and their love for each other manifested itself in every sensual way possible. Sunrise found them cuddled together as the first pink light of morning enveloped the room.

"Beautiful," Theo said with a yawn before pulling Abby even closer to him.

"Storms lead to the most beautiful sunrises," she told him.

"I wasn't talking about the sunrise," he said with a laugh and a kiss on her bare shoulder. "You're beautiful."

"And you're a charmer as I already knew," she said as she turned to face him. "But something's different and I've been trying to figure it out all week."

"I don't know what you're talking about. I'm still the roguishly handsome man you fell in love with," he teased.

"That you are, but it's not that. There's an air about you that's different. A new found confidence or, I know it sounds old fashioned, a certain kind of swagger that wasn't there before. Maybe I'm just imaging it."

"No, you're not," he admitted. "My Mom told me the same thing when I visited last month. She told me it's because I have found my place in life and I've become the man I was meant to be."

"Is it true? Are you the man you were meant to be?"

"It is, with one exception. I was meant to be with you."

"And I ruined it," she said sadly.

"Abby this is not your fault. Fate conspired against us. I get that you thought I had abandoned you. You turned to Robert. I can't fault you for that, but it doesn't have to ruin the rest of our lives. Divorce him and we can still be together. I can learn how to be a father to your daughter."

They had spent hours talking that night about what had led them to this point and still she had withheld the biggest lie of them all, but seeing how happy he was she just couldn't bring herself to admit Deborah was his daughter. Nothing had changed in his desire for children and the scandal would ruin his career just like it had so many others in Hollywood.

"I can't divorce Robert," she said simply.

Theo's views on marriage and religion were far different than her own. For her divorce just wasn't an option. She had made vows before God and nothing would ever change that.

"Can I ask you something I have no right to?" he asked as he intertwined his fingers with hers.

"You're going to ask if we sleep together, Robert and I."

There was no pretense between them and she knew it had been on his mind.

"Yes. Do you?"

"I know what you want my answer to be, but Theo I can't tell you that. We're married after all."

"I'm sorry I asked, but I understand."

"What about you? I suppose there is someone special in LA right?"

"I'm not a saint Abby and I'll admit it. When I found out you married someone else, I went a little crazy and there were a number of women in and out of my bed, but they never lasted because they weren't you. I can't imagine loving anyone but you."

"Thank you for your honesty but where does that leave us now? Is this all we have, these few days together?"

The thought of losing him again after reaffirming their love was more than she could bear and she started to cry before he reached out and wiped her tears away.

"We still have our promise to always love each other and to meet here once a year. And of course we still have our letters. That is if it won't cause problems with your husband. I've missed your letters."

"As I have missed yours, but it's not fair to you."

"Nothing about this is fair to either of us but if it's all we can hope for I say we grab what happiness we can for as long as we can."

It was settled then or at least as settled as an illicit affair could be but Abby couldn't have been happier. Their remaining few days at the lake were like the first time around and they laughed and loved and talked and held each other knowing that soon enough they would each go back to reality. The final night, holding hands as they sat side by side on the patio watching the calm settle over the lake, the haunting call of the loon echoed around them.

"They're back," Abby said with a happy smile.

"Didn't I promise?" he said.

•   •   •

The couple that said good-bye the next morning was different from the one who had met a week earlier. Secure in their promises to each other they were each returning to their separate lives and the secret between them until the next year when they would meet again.

"Are you going to be all right?" Theo asked as they held each other close one last time.

"Now that I know you still love me, I can face anything," she said with a smile.

True love, the kind she shared with Theo, had given her more strength than she ever could have imagined. Knowing he carried her heart in his own was the only reason she could return to her loveless marriage.

"I'll miss you every day and I'll write as often as I can," he assured her.

"And I'll do the same," she promised before hesitating. "But before I go I need to ask you something."

"What's that my love?" he said as he nuzzled her neck in a particularly sensitive spot.

"Tell me you forgive me. Tell me you forgive me for hurting you," she said desperately.

"There's nothing to forgive. We hurt each other and it's over now. Someday, when we're both old and gray, we'll tell the story of this crazy love affair to our grandchildren and they will realize, like I've always known, that you and I were meant to be. *I carry your heart . . . "*

"I carry it in my heart."

Chapter Twenty-Five

Pulling up to the house after her week with Theo, but remembering Robert's face when she had left, Abby wasn't sure what kind of a reception she would get. The one thing she wasn't expecting was to see him come out of the house, Deborah in his arms, in welcome. She slipped on her wedding ring and the locket just before exiting the car.

"Welcome home," Robert said as he gave her a chaste kiss on the forehead.

Still consumed with her feelings for Theo, Abby steeled herself to not pull away from him. She hadn't realized until that moment how hard it would be to accept Robert's affection once again.

Deborah began to cry. "There, there now sweetheart," he said as he rocked her in his arms. "Mommy's home now."

"I'm glad to be home," Abby said as she reached for her daughter.

Robert hesitated for just a moment before handing the baby over. Once in her mother's arms she quieted and they walked into the house.

"So how have you been?" Abby asked as she put Deborah gently down in her cradle and turned towards Robert to find she had been speaking to an empty room. He was gone.

It seemed the welcome home had been nothing more than a charade for the neighbors and he was still angry with her but she couldn't blame him for it. Walking around the house she finally spotted him through the window, furiously attacking weeds in the garden. This was the reaction she had been dreading and it was best faced head on. With a quick check on her now sleeping daughter she walked slowly to his side. There was no way he could be unaware of her presence yet he said nothing.

"I'm sorry," she said finally as he knelt in the dirt, violently pulling weeds from between the rows of newly emerging vegetables. "Robert will you please say something?"

Standing up he clapped his hands together to remove some of the dirt before slowly turning to look at his wife; once again sporting a face showing neither anger nor disappointment.

"Do you really want to have this discussion here where all the neighbors can hear?" he whispered at her. "At least do me the courtesy of waiting until we're alone. But that will have to wait. I'm going out for the day."

He dusted off his trousers, walked into the house and out the front door before he drove away in a most unusual display of backbone for a man who barely left the house at the end of his work day. But where did he go? Although he had many friends, they were all married and on a Sunday would be spending time with their family. For just the briefest of moments, Abby wondered if he was leaving for good before she brushed the thought away. His family, flawed as it was, meant too much to him to just walk away.

Yet the longer he stayed away the more of a reprieve Abby had. High on Theo's love her mood was light and when Deborah finally woke the baby kept her laughing for hours. In just a week's time she had changed and her resemblance to Theo was even more pronounced. Holding Deborah in her arms, staring at the miniature version of the man she loved, Abby vowed that somehow she would find a way to make the crazy situation they found themselves in work.

Robert had a right to his anger but as the hours passed she was beginning to worry until finally, around midnight, the sound of his car pulling into the driveway got her out of bed. Pulling on her robe, she headed downstairs just as an extremely intoxicated Robert stumbled in the front door and slumped to the floor. She was stunned by his condition but hurried to his side to help him to his feet.

"Come on let's get you to bed," she said before he jerked away from her touch.

"Do you really think I'd share your bed after what you've been up to?" he snarled. "Get out of my way."

Pushing past her he made his way clumsily up the stairs as she stood open mouthed below. It was his first true acknowledgement of what he suspected. As she watched he stumbled past the door to their bedroom at the top of the stairs until she heard the slam of a guest room door. Startled out of her own sleep, Deborah's cries pierced the night.

Of course he knew what she had been up to. He was too intelligent to not understand it but he had kept his promise to ask no questions leading her to believe there would be no consequences for her absence. Obviously that wasn't the case and she couldn't fault him for it. If the tables were turned she would not have been as gracious. Tomorrow, when Robert was thinking clearly, they would have to settle some things. Until then, she could only go to her daughter and calm her cries.

•   •   •

While the excessive drinking of that night would not be repeated, Robert sleeping in another room was. In some respects not sharing a bed with him was a relief for Abby but she also knew it couldn't continue forever and when the time came that he once again claimed his place in their bed she would not object. For now at least the best she could hope for was being in the same room without angry words between them and going back to work made even that less of a challenge.

Deborah was safe at home under the care of a neighbor which made the transition back to work easier. The restaurant was where she belonged – where no one judged her – and it was like coming home and so she returned with a smile.

For the most part everyone assumed her smile was happiness at the birth of her daughter. Of course that was true, but John ferreted out the other reason for her happiness. Surprisingly, he was happy for her as she told him about her recent week at the lake.

"If this is what happens when Theo is in your life, I think you need to find a way out of your marriage," he said as they worked together in the kitchen. "I've never seen you so happy."

"Did you really just suggest I get a divorce?" Abby said. Her spatula stopped in mid-air above the cake she had been frosting as she looked back at him in shock.

"I know your feelings about divorce," John said quickly, "but you shouldn't be married to Robert and we both know it. Did you ever stop to think that maybe you deserve happiness too?"

"I am happy," Abby assured him. "Of course I'd love to be with Theo all the time, but that's not how things worked out for us. Robert's a good man. We'll be fine. Besides, I can't leave him now. I'm pregnant again."

There was silence in the kitchen at her announcement.

"Theo's?" John finally asked.

"No, obviously it's Robert's. I went to the doctor yesterday and he says I'm about two months along."

"Congratulations I guess," John said hesitantly.

"This is a good thing," Abby assured him. "Robert will be over the moon."

"And Theo?"

"He understands about my life here."

"Understanding and accepting are two different things, but you know him better than I do. If you're happy I'm happy," he said sincerely.

"Let's just keep the pregnancy news between us I until I have a chance to tell Robert okay? We haven't spent much time together since I got back but he needs to know before the whole town does."

"I wouldn't wait too long for that conversation if I were you."

John was right. The longer Abby waited to share news of her pregnancy the more likely it would be that Robert would jump to the wrong conclusion about the father. He needed to be told right away.

He had been working longer hours than normal since she returned, most likely in an effort to avoid being with her, and she took the extra time that evening to prepare his favorite dinner. With Deborah down for the night, Abby slipped into Robert's favorite dress and waited for his arrival.

"What's all this?" he asked as he walked into the house and found her in the dining room where the soft glow of candlelight reflected off their wedding china.

For the first time since she returned home she noticed wrinkles lining his forehead and the gauntness in his cheeks. He looked like a man with the weight of the world on his shoulders; a weight she knew she had caused.

"I wanted to do something special for you to show you how much I appreciate what you do for our family," she said with a smile. "Why don't you go upstairs and get cleaned up and I'll put dinner on the table?"

"Deborah?"

"Already fast asleep. Now hurry before it gets cold."

He still looked like he didn't quite trust what she was saying. His demeanor towards her had been so cold all week Abby hadn't been sure he would join her but before long, he was back downstairs, hair slicked back, chin freshly shaven, smelling of his favorite cologne.

Taking his seat at the table, he looked up at her with the first real smile she had seen from him as they filled their plates and started to eat; their conversation filled with the mundane discussion of any married couple.

"Thank you for the meal but you didn't have to do all this," he said as he pushed his now empty plate away.

"Of course I did. You do so much for me and our daughter and I needed you to know what you mean to me."

"Well it was wonderful. Thank you."

"There is something else I wanted to tell you though."

As if a switch had been flipped his expression went from satisfaction to wariness in a second.

"What is it?" he asked hesitantly.

"I'm pregnant," she said quietly, her gaze never leaving his face. "We're going to have a baby."

She could tell he was doing a quick calculation in his mind and she hurried to clarify. "The doctor said I'm about ten weeks along."

The frown quickly disappeared as he realized what she was telling him. The baby was his.

Gathering her in his arms he lifted her to her feet, peppering her face with kisses before he finally came back to earth.

"But you haven't been sick. With Deborah you were always sick."

That fact hadn't escaped her notice either and she was quick to assure him she was healthy and feeling well.

"I was feeling quite tired, but having a week off seemed to resolve that."

Instantly she regretted bringing up her time with Theo and she waited for his reaction.

"So that's why you left? Because you were fatigued? Why in heavens didn't you just tell me silly? I thought.. Well never mind what I thought. This is the best night of my life...well next to marrying you and Deborah's birth. I'm going to be a father...well and truly a father!"

Stunned that he had jumped to the wrong conclusion about her week away, Abby didn't know what to say but she knew enough not to dissuade him of his fantasy. News of the baby had chased away the demons she saw in his eyes and instantly the old Robert was back.

"This time it will be a boy, I just know it," he exclaimed as together they worked to clear the table. "It's just the start you know. We have to fill up this big house with children. It's what I've always wanted."

"I know, but let's take this one at a time," she asked with a kind smile.

She would love a big family too. It was the greatest difference between she and Theo. She wanted nothing more than to come home to a house full of children that would surround her when she was old and grey. The only thing he wanted was Abby and his career. As difficult as it had been to make choices that hurt him, it appeared she was right where she was supposed to be and this baby would prove it.

"Are you ready for bed my dear?" Robert asked as Abby hung up the dish towel and turned to him.

The look on his face told her she wouldn't be the only one in their bed that evening.

Chapter Twenty-Six

"That chapter in your Grandmother's life was a particularly happy one. We had started to exchange letters again on a regular basis and I was lucky enough to sneak in a few phone calls to the restaurant when the timing was right. The letters of course were a great source of comfort to both of us, but there was something about being able to hear Abby's voice that made me come alive again."

"To me being apart from each other again would have been torture," Krista said as she and Alex held hands under the dinner table. The pair had spent the day at Abby's house, finally finishing their work to clear out the attic while Theo took a much deserved break from the story to catch up on things back home before joining them for a late supper on the back deck.

"It was of course, but at the time and in those difficult circumstances, we were just happy to have any contact at all. Of course the right thing would have been to end our affair, but we were both too weak to do it."

"Don't be too hard on yourself," Alex chimed in. "You were two people in love. I'm not so sure I could have walked away either."

The look of adoration he directed at Krista caused a wave of heat to go through her and she squeezed his hand just a little tighter.

"Let's hope you young ones never have to face that kind of dilemma," Theo told them with a smile.

"Did you know about Nan being pregnant with Uncle Matt?" Krista asked.

"Oh yes my dear. There were no more secrets between us. Abby was a wife to your grandfather in every way. I had no illusions about that and I knew Abby loved children. Truth be told, every time she was pregnant, I could hardly contain my jealousy towards your grandfather. He shared something special with Abby that I thought I never could…well at least until finding out about your mother. It was much later when I found out your grandfather and I shared more than Abby's love."

"What do you mean?" Krista asked in confusion.

"Abby and I had continued our annual promise to meet at the lake and for many years Robert had been as accepting of it as he could, until one day I called their house by accident. I had the number in case of emergency, but had always called the restaurant. This time though I dialed the wrong number from my address book and your grandfather answered. Hindsight being twenty-twenty I should have just hung up but as soon as I asked for Abby I could tell he knew who I was even though we had never met."

"Wow! That had to be some conversation," Alex said as he leaned forward in his chair.

"Not at that moment, but when he realized who I was, or rather who I was to his wife, he wanted to meet."

"You said no didn't you?" Krista asked, her eyes wide as saucers.

"On the contrary, I agreed to meet him in Chicago."

"Were you scared?"

"Apprehensive is a better word for it, but I figured I owed it to him to hear him out so we agreed to meet in a bar where I figured he couldn't kill me and when I walked in, there he was in a booth in the back corner, nursing a beer. I had never seen a photo of him, but knew instantly it was him from the look of determination on his face. At first he didn't say much, and we stared at each other for the longest time. Of course by that time I was pretty well known but he didn't seem to recognize me even though I looked every inch the movie star with an expensive suit and a gold watch while he looked like any other working man.

"And?" Alex asked.

"And, it was nothing like I expected."

"In what way," Krista asked. "Was he angry?"

"Not that he showed. He asked me if I was kind to her and if I truly loved her. It was the one thing we both had in common – our love for her. By that point he realized his marriage to Abby was never in jeopardy. They were going to be together forever. I got the impression he just needed to satisfy his curiosity about me."

"That's it?" Krista asked. "Didn't he even try to make you stay away from her?"

"Quite the opposite. He asked me to promise him that if anything ever happened to him that I would marry Abby. He said he cherished her and their children more than his own life but he knew he was living what should have been my life with her and he was grateful to me for loving her."

"Nan was always the most important thing in Pops' life," Krista said as a single tear rolled down her face.

"It was at that moment I stopped thinking of Robert as a rival for your grandmother's affection. He loved her as much as I did and knowing what he did, I realized he was a much better man than I."

"Did he know you were famous?" Alex asked.

"I'm not sure, but even if he did, I'm not sure it would have made a difference to him. More than anything I was the man his wife was in love with. Being famous didn't enter into it."

"Did Nan know about the meeting?"

"No, we had agreed to keep it between ourselves. I never saw him again and of course they shared many, many happy years of marriage together after that."

"Did you know how ill Pops was at the end? Did you know how Nan devoted her life to him?"

"Not at first, but as time passed and I saw the toll it was taking on Abby I finally got her to admit it. She told me that Robert had suffered for years from pain and illnesses they finally linked to exposure to Agent Orange while he was in the army and eventually he was forced to retire early in the hope that they would be able to spend quality time together in their waning years. "

"But that didn't happen," Krista said sadly as she remembered her grandfather's suffering.

"No, it didn't. From what I understand their lives were consumed with doctor visits, hospital stays and Abby becoming Robert's round the clock caregiver. At one point, seeing the toll it was taking on her, I offered to pay for round the clock care but she wouldn't accept. She told me it was the one wifely duty she could do for him and she was happy to do it. They had a wonderful life together and Abby told me that the night before Robert died he told her to marry me. He told her that he loved her more than anything in the world and she had made him happier than he deserved and then – and I'm not so sure if our places had been reversed I could have done this – he made her promise to marry me."

"So why didn't you and Nan get married when Pops passed away?" Krista asked. She had spent days thinking about that question. He had been gone for several years before Theo showed up.

"It was a matter of respect," Theo told her. "When your grandfather passed I would have married Abby right away, but we were of a different generation and it wouldn't have been proper. I pressed her over and over for a wedding date after a proper amount of time had passed…one year, two years, it didn't matter to me, but for the first time in her life, she couldn't make a decision. I suspect it was because she felt such guilt over what she had put Robert through. In the end though I finally got her to agree we would marry in a private ceremony on her eightieth birthday."

At his words a surprised gasp escaped Krista's lips and she looked back at him in shock before a smile appeared on her face. Nan hadn't lied. Her birthday celebration was going to be the best ever.

"So that's what she had planned!" she said happily before realizing Theo must have been devastated. "That also explains the dress I found in her closet still in the garment bag with tags attached. It must have been her wedding dress." Seeing the look of sadness on his face, she realized what she had done. "I'm so sorry," she said quickly.

"Thank you," he said sadly. "We had been calling each other for days before her birthday and had planned to meet at the lake for the ceremony. Abby was insistent we be married there and I had everything all arranged for our big day. But then she didn't answer my calls to her cell phone and I knew something was wrong. She had been so excited about the wedding and to stop taking my calls meant something had happened."

"Oh my God," Krista said suddenly remembering Abby's cell phone buried beneath the clutter on her countertop where it had been charging for days. "I can't imagine what you were thinking when you didn't hear from her."

"At first I thought maybe she got cold feet, but that just wasn't Abby. We had waited a lifetime for a chance to be together as man and wife. It had to be something more. Never in my wildest dreams did I think she would be gone."

"I'm sorry you had to find out the way you did. If I'd only known . . . " Krista said before getting up and hugging Theo.

"Thank you my dear. It was devastating of course, but at least I have the consolation of getting to know my granddaughter and spending these last few days with you. It has brought Abby back to life for me to be with you and that has eased my grief more than you know."

Alex had told her the same thing many times and Krista looked at him with a smile.

"So now what?" Alex asked.

"I don't quite know. You know the story so I suppose it's time for me to go back home."

"We're not the only ones who need to know your story," Krista said quietly as she looked at Theo in anticipation. "I think there's someone else who needs to hear it even more than me."

"Your mother."

"Yes although I warn you she's going to flip out. She loved my grandfather...sorry," she said casting a guilty look at Theo. "She loved Robert more than anyone else and she's going to be devastated to find out he wasn't her father."

"Nonetheless, I agree she deserves to know the truth. Not only that, but so does the rest of the family. How do you suggest we approach it?"

"Actually I've spent a lot of time thinking about this. Mom shouldn't be blindsided by it. If you are okay with it I suggest I approach her first. I'll show her the letters and we can read them together. Then, I'll arrange a family dinner at Nan's house…one final hurrah before we sell the house now that it's all cleaned out and we can introduce you to the whole family and tell them an abbreviated version of the story. Whether Mom will come to that dinner or not remains to be seen but I think it's the best way of introducing you to the family don't you think?"

"You're a very intuitive young woman and I trust your judgement. I do need to fly back to California for a few days to take care of some business ventures, but I can be back in two weeks. Would that work for you?"

"We'll make it work," Alex promised for both of them. "I have an overnight shift tonight so I better get going. If I don't see you before you leave, I'll see you when you get back. It has been a pleasure sir," he said before offering Theo his hand and the two men walked to the door.

"Don't make the same mistakes I did son." Theo said when they were out of Krista's hearing. "Marry that girl before someone else does."

"Already on it," Alex told him with a warm smile as he pulled a small ring box out of his pocket. "Just waiting for the right time."

Chapter Twenty-Seven

With Theo briefly back in Los Angeles, Krista started her plans and immediately sent out dinner invitations she had no doubt would be accepted. That was the easy part however. Figuring out how to break the news to her mother was proving much more challenging. Any advance warning of what was to come would cause Deborah to dig in her heels. She needed help if her plan was to succeed and with that thought in mind she joined her father for a cup of coffee at the coffee shop.

"I've been thinking about inviting Mom to a special mother-daughter weekend in the city before the school year starts," she told him.

It was something the pair had always shared when Krista was a child...a weekend of school clothes shopping in the big city followed by a special dinner in a fancy restaurant and a night at the theater.

"You haven't done that for years and I'm sure she would love it. But why now?"

"I'm hoping the weekend will help us find our way back as mother and daughter. These past few years have been miserable and I'm afraid if we don't reconnect now we never will."

"There's more to it than you're letting on isn't there? We got your invitation to the dinner at Abby's. You discovered her secret didn't you?"

There was no point in lying to her father about it and she nodded her head affirmatively.

"We did and while I think it's wonderful I'm not so sure others in the family will see it that way."

"You mean your mother right? She's the one that is not going to be happy."

"I'm afraid so and it impacts her more than anyone, but she has a right to know. I thought it would make more sense to tell her before I share it with the family."

"Have you ever heard the phrase *don't kill the messenger?*" he asked as he reached across the table to take Krista's hand in his own. "I don't want you to be hurt."

"Dad, I have to do this. Even if she never speaks to me again I have to be the one to tell her."

"If you're sure then I'll make sure your mom shows up. Now, as long as we're here let's order lunch. I'm starving."

•　　•　　•

True to his word in a week's time Steven had delivered Deborah into Krista's care and it wasn't long before the pair were in a luxury hotel room in the city. Krista had been a bundle of nerves on the drive up, but surprisingly, Deborah had been more than cordial almost to the point where Krista felt guilty about what was to come. After a nice dinner and a day of shopping, the pair returned to the hotel, slipped into the plush robes supplied by the establishment, and opened a bottle of wine to enjoy on the large balcony.

"It's been years since we have done something so special," Deborah said as she gazed at the stars that were barely visible through the light pollution of the city. "I'm glad you suggested it although I think this room is a little much."

"A bit pricey maybe but we deserve to be pampered," Krista replied before falling silent.

"Why are we really here?" Deborah asked suddenly. "Does it have something to do with your grandmother?"

Deborah had always been quite astute but her question startled Krista nonetheless.

"I'm sorry and I don't want you to be angry but I did want to talk to you alone about this."

"What if I don't want to hear it? Do I have a say in the matter?"

"I suppose but as angry as you might be I hope you will let me say what I came here for."

"What is it then?" she asked without a trace of warmth.

Gone was the open and loving mother who had been enjoying time with her daughter. In her place was a sullen woman rebuilding a wall around herself brick by tiny brick.

"I have a story to tell you...about Nan and about the man she loved."

Rising to her feet she went back into the room to dig through her suitcase before coming back with a package she unwrapped on the table in front of her mother.

"What's this?" Deborah asked without moving a muscle.

"They're letters that tell a love story - Nan's love story - and I think you should read them. Nan loved a man long before she met Pops and it didn't end when they got married."

"So my mother had an affair," Deborah said with more restraint than Krista thought possible. "I knew it."

"Mom, it wasn't just an affair. Please read the letters. I think when you do you'll realize it was so much more than that."

"What an ungrateful child you are," Deborah spat at her daughter. "To lure me up here under false pretenses and then throw this in my face. How dare you."

"You might not believe this," Krista said gently, "but I'm doing this for you. Because you deserve to know the truth and because next week when everyone is at Nan's for dinner they are going to know it too. I respect you enough to tell you in private. Please just read the letters," she begged.

"I will not and I am never going to forgive you for this. I want to go home."

"Please Mom, please read them. When you're finished if you want I'll take you home."

"I said no. If you won't take me home then tomorrow morning I'll take the train and leave you here. Now if you'll excuse me, I'm going to bed."

Draining her glass of wine, Deborah cast an angry look at her daughter before going back inside, turning off the bedside light, and crawling into bed. Having failed to convince her mother to read the letters Krista knew their relationship would never be the same. She sat on the balcony with her thoughts for a long time before finally giving up and going to bed herself. She had failed Theo and herself and now her mother might never know the truth.

•   •   •

Both mother and daughter slept in the next morning and while Deborah still wouldn't talk to her, Krista noticed she could barely keep her eyes open on the long, tense drive home. Any attempts to engage her mother in conversation had been met with stony silence and finally she just gave up. By the time she had dropped Deborah off at home Krista actually felt a sense of relief that was only enhanced by the sight of a smiling Alex sitting on her front steps waiting to welcome her home.

"So how did it go?" he asked as he helped her inside with her small case.

"Exactly how you would expect," came her sad reply. "She wouldn't read even a single letter and that was the end of it. There was no more discussion."

"So what now? Are you going to cancel the dinner? What about Theo?"

"Even if Mom doesn't show up the dinner is going ahead as planned and Theo will fly in the day before. I know he'll be disappointed not to meet her after all this time but I hope he understands I did everything I could."

"Have you considered the possibility that everyone else may react the same way your mother did? It's not every day kids find out their mother has been having an affair for sixty years."

"I've thought about it of course but even if they don't accept Theo as part of Nan's life at first I know them. Eventually they will come to love him as much as I do."

"He's right of course. You are so very like Abby and that's probably why you like him so much."

"It's more than that. I think even if I didn't know he was my grandfather I would feel a connection to him. We just clicked immediately. I don't know how you feel about it but he's going to be in my life from now on no matter what the rest of the family feels about him."

"What about me?" Alex asked as he took her into his arms.

"I already know how you feel about him," she said with a smile.

"That's not what I meant. Am I going to be in your life from now on?"

Dropping to his knee, he took Krista's hand in his own and looked up at her with adoration. "I know this isn't the most romantic setting, but I've carried this around with me long enough."

Reaching into his pocket, he retrieved a small box and held it out to her.

"The one thing I learned from all this is that two people who are meant to be together should actually be together. Abby knew it and so did Theo, but they didn't act on it and suddenly it was too late. I don't want it to be too late for us. Krista, I love you with all my heart and I can't imagine going through life without you. Will you marry me?"

Chapter Twenty-Eight

It was a busy day before the dinner. As expected everyone had accepted the invitation with the sole exception of her own mother and Krista was busy with preparations while Alex collected Theo from the airport. He was the first person to learn of their engagement.

"Congratulations," Theo said with great enthusiasm. "I know that somewhere above Abby is smiling down on you both and I hope that you will share as much love as she and I did."

"Thank you Grandfather," Krista said as she hugged him. "I just wish she was here with us."

"As do I my dear, as do I. And your mother? Does she know?"

"About the engagement? No, she doesn't. We thought we'd announce it when everyone is together tomorrow."

"Sweetheart I think Theo might be asking if your mom knows about him," Alex suggested.

"Oh. Unfortunately that's not such good news. The answer is no and my attempt to tell her your story blew up in my face. I doubt she'll show up tomorrow but Dad will be there. Maybe he can get through to her later. I'm sorry. I know how much you wanted to meet her."

"Honestly, I expected as much and I can't say I blame her. Finding out about me will be a big disappointment I'm sure."

"If she could only get to know you the way we have, I think she'd feel differently," Krista said. "I'm hoping the rest of the family will meet you with an open mind though."

"So they are all coming?" he asked.

"The house will be full. Just the way Nan liked. Now while you get settled, Alex and I have a lot of work to do to get ready for tomorrow. I'll be back in time to make us all dinner though."

"If you don't mind I'd like to help. It will make me feel like part of the family."

"That would be wonderful. If you're ready, let's go."

The trio spent the afternoon setting up for the dinner in the now empty house using Abby's finest tablecloths and place settings; unpacked once more from the boxes that had found a new home at Krista's. If there was one thing Abby loved it was a family dinner and they were determined to do her proud this one last time even if Krista was becoming a jumble of nerves and it showed.

"Honey let me take those plates from you before you drop them," Alex encouraged with a smile as Theo walked back to the car for another box. "What's going on? It's not like you to be this jumpy."

"I guess I'm just nervous for tomorrow. I so want everyone to like Theo as much as I do and I'm afraid they'll react like Mom."

"They aren't your mother and it's going to be fine. Sure they're going to be surprised –who wouldn't with that kind of news – but they are going to love Theo."

Pulling her into his arms for a kiss they were interrupted by Theo's return.

"What's the phrase they use these days? Get a room?" he said with a laugh before they quickly pulled apart. "I didn't mean to interrupt. That's the last box from the car."

"Well I think that's all we can do for today guys. Thanks for your help. I think tomorrow will be interesting to say the least," Krista said.

"Give your family some credit," Theo encouraged as they walked back to the car for the short trip to Krista's. "I believe everything will work out just the way it's meant to."

After a quick supper, Alex headed to work leaving grandfather and granddaughter alone again. Krista's quiet demeanor hadn't escaped Theo's notice.

"What's on your mind little one?" he finally asked.

"Last night I read the letter you sent Nan after winning the Oscar and realized you hadn't told me that part of the story."

"Didn't I?" he asked in surprise. "Don't see how I glossed over that part since it was such a surprising moment in my life. Would you like to hear it now?"

"Of course," she said with a smile.

"Filming the movie had ended well over a year before my performance was nominated for the Academy Award and by that time I had moved on to other projects so it was a huge surprise when I got the call. Naturally Abby was the first person I needed to tell and she was even more excited about the nomination than me......"

•　　•　　•

Oscar night was finally here and Abby was beside herself with barely contained nerves she tried desperately to hide from Robert. Her insistence that they watch the telecast had been a surprise to him as she usually preferred other ways to spend a Sunday evening, but there was no way she would miss seeing Theo on television. Since his nomination weeks earlier she had been on pins and needles waiting for this night. Theo had managed one quick call to the restaurant earlier that day and she knew he was as nervous as she was although he was trying hard to downplay it.

"Do you have your acceptance speech prepared?" she asked in an effort to calm him down. Surrounded by a room full of people as he prepared for the night's activities he had been talking so quickly and quietly she could barely understand him.

"There's no need. I'm not going to win," he told her. "It's just an honor to be nominated."

"Isn't that what everyone always says?" she asked with a chuckle or two. "You're a shoe-in to win. Your performance was really wonderful and you deserve it."

"Be that as it may people don't win on their first nomination. I just need to concentrate on not looking overly disappointed when they announce someone else's name."

"I don't know. I just have a feeling about tonight. Do me a favor and when we get off the phone please just jot down some notes. It's better to take a few moments now than stand on that stage in front of the whole world and not know what to say."

"I suppose you're right," he admitted. "But then again there really is only one person I need to thank if I do win and that's you."

"Theo how can you even say that? You're surrounded by people who have helped you get to this point and they need to be acknowledged. Whatever small part I might have played in this is nothing compared to them."

"Stop being so humble Abby. You are the only reason I'm in this business and you know it. If it wasn't for you . . . well I might be one of those guys driving taxis you used to talk about. I'm sorry, but I have to go. The car is waiting for me downstairs," he said even as she could hear people calling his name in the background.

"Break a leg tonight my love. I'll be watching."

•　　　•　　　•

In an effort to hide her agitated state from Robert Abby had invited a group of their friends to watch the telecast with them. Deborah and Matthew had been tucked in for the night and as the show began the men slowly began to drift away to a game of cards in the dining room leaving the women glued to the television to watch all the celebrities. Theo had been gone for several years and no one in the room seemed to recognize the man on the screen as the handyman who had painted fences and mended staircases not so long ago leaving Abby free from worry that someone would connect the dots and clue Robert in.

The wait until the Best Supporting Actor category was interminable and Abby could barely sit still. Finally the prior year's Best Supporting Actress appeared on stage as Abby tuned out the discussion around her, concentrating only on the screen and listening closely as the woman read off the names of the nominees. Theo was last on the list and as the camera panned in for a close-up shot she noticed how tense he was. The smile he offered the camera was barely there but her breath caught at the sight of the suave and debonair actor in his tuxedo.

"And the Academy Award for Best Supporting Actor goes to . . . Theo James!"

Without being conscious of it, Abby erupted in cheers and applause as Theo got out of his seat to shake hands with the man next to him before making his way to the stage; accepting congratulations from everyone along the way as the audience hooted and hollered their support. The smile on his face was finally at full wattage and Abby couldn't have been happier for him. Placing the golden statue on the podium he reached into his breast pocket with a shaky hand. The auditorium quieted again before he spoke.

"Thank you so much. I know everyone says this, but this is really unexpected. Someone I am very close to told me today that I should have a speech ready and right now I'm so glad I listened to her. I'd like to thank . . . "

Theo thanked a lengthy list of people including his manager and his family before he paused.

"There's someone else I owe all this to. You have been an angel since the moment I met you and none of this would be possible without your love and support. I love you," he said before blowing a kiss that left Abby speechless.

"I think we can safely assume he was your choice right Abby?" Jennifer asked with a laugh. "Hey I would have voted for him too. He's so handsome."

"My daughter has seen the movie five times already," another woman said. "Apparently all the girls in her school have a crush on him."

"I don't know. Don't you think he's too good looking?" Tammy said. Robert's sister, Tammy had only been invited at her brother's insistence. The two sisters-in-law had never developed a family bond. "I mean men who are that handsome…there must be something wrong with him. I was reading in one of the tabloids that he is never seen with a woman and you know that that means."

"No," Abby said heatedly. "Just what does that mean?"

"Well obviously if he's that good looking and isn't married, he must be . . . a homosexual. Hollywood's full of them you know."

Abby burst into laughter at the absurdity of the thought and soon the other women joined in with her.

"So you're saying the person he said 'I love you' to is a guy?" Jennifer asked with a laugh. "What celebrity would take a chance like that? You're just being spiteful because the guy you wanted to win is a loser."

"Enough you two." Abby interrupted. "The next category is coming up soon and I can't wait to see who will win. Does anyone want something else to drink?"

Refilling drinks gave Abby the chance to escape to the kitchen where she said a silent prayer of thanks for Theo's big win that meant so much more to him than recognition from the industry. Theo's father had steadfastly refused to accept his chosen profession, but now with such public acknowledgement of his success, Mr. James just might change his mind. The statue was nice to have, but his father's acceptance would mean more to Theo than any award ever could.

By the end of the evening Abby was happy but drained. Leaving Robert to watch the late newscast she slowly climbed the stairs to the guest bedroom closing the door softly behind her before opening the heavy bottom dresser drawer and moving winter clothing aside to uncover one of the many shoeboxes holding Theo's letters.

She was aware of the danger of keeping the letters, but had been unable to part with a single one and the boxes continued to multiply as new letters arrived. It wasn't until recently, when she discovered Robert going through the closet in the very same room that she realized she needed to find a more secure location for her treasures. When the opportunity presented itself, she would move them to the far corner of the overly full attic.

Thumbing through the letters, stopping at the one containing the news of his Oscar nomination, she pulled it out and read it yet again. Wishing more than anything they could have been together for Theo's special night, she clutched the paper to her chest, gave it a soft kiss and put it carefully back where she had found it before heading to bed with a smile and a longing to feel Theo's arms around her.

The soft creak of the bed springs as Robert joined her later interrupted her daydreams of Theo. Married or not, for this one night at least when her thoughts were on the west coast with Theo, she couldn't bring herself to be a wife and as Robert reached for her, she feigned sleep before he finally turned away from her.

● ● ●

It was a short two weeks later when the package arrived at the restaurant. Expecting a delivery of new menus, the box sat untouched on the floor of Abby's office until the end of what had been another busy day.

"Are those the new menus?" John asked nodding towards the box that took up a large portion of the small office.

"I think so," Abby replied without looking up from her paperwork. "I was thinking we'd roll out the new menu at the first of the month. What do you think?"

"You're the boss so you keep reminding me," he teased. "Seriously I think that's a good plan. It'll give us a little time to advertise the changes. If I know our customers, they're going to need time to adjust."

They had been talking for some time about changing things up. While their current menu was well received, Abby was anxious to try new recipes.

"You're right about that. Are you heading out for the day?"

"Yes. Me and the missus have a date tonight. It's our fortieth anniversary and it's the first one I've remembered all on my own," he said proudly.

"That's wonderful! Congratulations. Give Malinda a kiss for me will you?"

"Thanks and see you tomorrow bright and early." Soon a chorus of good-byes could be heard from the dining room as Susan and Doris joined him.

Closing her eyes, Abby let out a long sigh and leaned back in her chair. Instead of dawdling she should be on her way home for some play time with the children before Robert got home but it had been another long day and she was tired. Up well before dawn to get the kids up, dressed and fed before their babysitter arrived, these days she was tired before she even got to work. If you added in all of her charitable endeavors in the community she was worn out. Only the promise of her upcoming week at the lake with Theo was getting her through each day.

It would be their third year at the lake and after a rocky couple of years, Robert hadn't even batted an eyelash when she reminded him of this year's trip. Whether he knew she was meeting Theo or not remained a mystery to her and he had had nothing more to say about the annual trips since that first time he had come home stumbling drunk. In fact, since that time he had welcomed her home from each trip with open arms before life went on as before. Either he was the most accepting man she had ever met, or he truly didn't have a clue.

For years guilt over the duplicitous life she led was constant until she acknowledged the effort she put into keeping both of the men in her life happy. A dutiful wife and mother who worked hard for family, friends and sometimes complete strangers, the only time she ever put herself first was the one week in April when Theo became her whole reason for living. Safe in his arms, the love between them renewed yet again, she became another woman and at the end of their time together, she returned to her family refreshed, rejuvenated, and ready for whatever life sent her way. With all that in mind, she let the guilt go. Still daydreaming about the upcoming rendezvous with Theo wasn't going to get supper on the table and she put her paperwork in the desk drawer and reached for the desk light as the phone rang.

"Abigail's" she said cheerfully.

"Just the person I was hoping would answer," came Theo's dulcet voice in her ear.

"I was just thinking about you," Abby said excitedly. It was the first time they had talked since the Oscar win. "Have you come down from cloud nine yet?"

Her comment elicited a hearty laugh from him. His Oscar win behind him, doors that had never willingly opened for Theo now came wrapped in Oscar gold and his letters were full of news about the new opportunities. Producers, directors, and even studio heads stumbled over each other to get the suddenly popular actor in their films and Theo was working harder than ever.

"Not quite. My agent wants me to ride this high as long as I can and I've been swamped with offers. I can't remember the last time I got even four hours sleep."

"Ah the price of fame," Abby said with her own laugh. "Hey wait a minute! You're not calling to back out of next week are you?"

"Not a chance," he quickly assured her. "I just wanted to know if you got the package."

"What package?"

"I sent you something and thought you'd have it by now. Are you sure you didn't get it?" he asked anxiously.

"No, but I did get new menus today and I'm sitting right here looking at them. They are addressed to me from...wait a minute...these aren't menus." For the first time since the package had been delivered Abby finally noticed the California return address and she placed the box on her desk and reached for a letter opener. "What did you send me?" she asked excitedly.

"Open it and find out, but do it carefully. There's some pretty precious cargo in there."

Being careful to not damage the contents, Abby slowly opened the seal and removed the large amount of packing material to reveal a beautiful, and quite heavy, mahogany box.

"Theo the box is beautiful, but what is it?"

"Open it and see," he said mysteriously.

Removing the wooden box from the cardboard she placed it carefully on her desk and slowly opened the lid before being stunned into near silence. There, nestled in dark blue velvet was the shiny golden Oscar statue she had last seen in Theo's hands and a single red rose.

"Oh my God, Theo! I can't believe you sent me your Academy Award!"

"I know it's not a Tony like I promised, but I hope you'll accept it anyway," he said with a laugh.

"But why? Why send it to me? It should be front and center on your mantel at home."

"I was going to give it to you at the lake, but I couldn't wait. I was so anxious to get it to you, I didn't realize the Academy was expecting me to have it engraved with my name and category. Someday we'll have to add that, but you know what it's for."

"Of course I do, and it's so thoughtful of you, but I can't keep it."

"Of course you can. You might not be able to put it out on display, but its' yours. Without you I wouldn't even be in this business, much less have won an Oscar. You deserve it more than I do and I want you to have it. Besides, I fully intend to add another to the collection sometime in the I hope not too distant future."

"You're too good to me my love." Abby said with tears in her eyes. As much as she appreciated the gesture, ideas were flying through her mind of how to keep the gift from Robert. "Just remember this belongs to you. For now I'll keep it safe for you until you're ready to reclaim it."

"If you didn't notice, there's more to the box," Theo told her. "Take out the statue and remove the wooden panel beneath it. There's a hidden compartment where you can store my letters." He already knew Abby kept his letters just as he did hers. "I would imagine that shoebox of yours has seen better days after all this time."

"This is perfect! Thank you for thinking of it. Just another reason why I love you so."

"Well, I suppose I better let you go, but I can't wait to see you next week. I love you Abby."

"And I love you."

After a quick look at the clock and some even faster calculations in her head, Abby knew she would have to hurry if she was to get the Oscar home and secreted away before Robert walked in the door. Placing the wooden box back in the cardboard one she hurried to do just that, transferring all of the old letters carefully into the hidden compartment before carrying the whole box up to the attic. Her secret safe once more, she gave the box a final pat, before going back to reality.

Chapter Twenty-Nine

A summer of discovery had come down to this final day when the entire family would learn of the secret Abby and Theo had kept for the past sixty odd years and Krista woke with an unexpected sense of sadness. The excitement of learning about Theo and Abby had dominated her summer and soon it would be over. All that was left now was to hope the rest of the family would embrace Theo the same way she had.

Of course it wouldn't be the same for them. None of the aunts, uncles or cousins had the same direct connection to him and she wondered not for the first time if that was the only reason she was so taken by him. He was charming and witty and distinguished, but beneath all that was his undying love for her grandmother. The man had waited six decades for the woman he loved and now he just wanted to get to know the daughter he hadn't known about. Could anyone in the family fault him for that?

Her mother certainly had. Since their return from the disastrous weekend trip to the City, Krista had heard nothing from her mother even though she had left message after message on her cell phone. Being part of this day was an opportunity not to be missed, yet it appeared Deborah would be doing just that. She might not realize it, but both she and Theo deserved more.

"Good morning Grandfather."

"Ah there you are my dear. I hope I didn't wake you," he said in return. As usual, he had been enjoying a quiet cup of coffee while reading the morning paper.

"Not at all and to tell you the truth I didn't get much sleep last night." Krista poured herself a cup of coffee and joined him at the table as he set the paper aside.

"Worried about your mother?" Theo asked gently.

"A bit, but more worried about you."

"Whatever for?" he asked with a laugh.

"My family is wonderful and I hope you'll discover that for yourself today, but I'm worried that the news of your love affair with Nan will be too big of a shock for them. I don't want anyone to be mean to you."

"Nonsense," he assured her. "There's nothing they can say to me that Abby and I didn't say to ourselves at some point in our relationship. I'm not naïve my dear. Learning about Abby and me will be a shock and I expect your aunts and uncles to be angry with me; after all they are Robert's children. But I hope that in time, they will come to see that everything we did was out of love for each other. I am not expecting to be accepted by them, but I am hoping."

"Well at least you have Alex and me there with you and we both love you very much."

"Thank you my dear and I love you also. That alone makes all of this worthwhile."

"Oh my!" Krista exclaimed with a quick look at the kitchen clock. "I didn't realize it was so late. I better get cleaned up and start taking things over to Nan's. I decided to make the ham in her oven today. Everyone is bringing one of Nan's favorite recipes today…to honor her memory and all."

"That's a lovely idea," he said with a warm smile. "A ham dinner will take me right back to where it all started."

"I know," Krista said with a smile before bestowing a quick kiss on the top of his head and rushing upstairs to get ready.

•   •   •

By the time the family started to gather at Abby's house for their farewell dinner, it had started to look and feel like Thanksgiving. Everyone came loaded down with dishes, some already prepared, some ready to be baked, and laughter filled the house. While their numbers remained one short with Deborah's absence, the house was full.

Alex's presence was accepted without question although Uncle Matt began to tease Krista unmercifully about it.

"Nobody said boyfriends were invited to this shindig," he whispered as he stood behind her in the kitchen. "Does that mean he's more than a boyfriend?"

To keep the focus of the day on Theo, she and Alex had decided to not share their news until they had a better idea of how the day would go. Her engagement ring was hidden away on a chain around her neck.

"I don't know what you're talking about," she said before moving away from him but he followed her again.

"Mom always hoped the two of you would get together. She said she saw a spark between you. I know you've been spending a lot of time together so is there going to be some big announcement today or what?"

He had always been able to read her like a book. "Today is about Nan and her life Uncle Matt. You know that."

"Is it maybe about the old guy who has been staying at your house?" he asked quietly. Theo had yet to make an appearance and she was surprised Matt knew about him. It's not like they had been flaunting his presence around town, but then again it was a small town and everyone knew everything.

"You'll just have to wait and see," she told him with a mysterious smile just as the doorbell rang. It was Theo and he had perfect timing.

Charlie was already opening the door and the room quieted as the family turned to look at the late arrival. Krista hurried to the door to welcome Theo and introduce him to everyone.

"Everyone, this is Mr. Theodores James and I've invited him to join us today."

One by one her family stepped up to welcome Theo even as they cast confused looks her way. Alex made his way to Theo's side and parted the crowds so Theo could have a seat front and center near the fireplace. As he did, Krista asked everyone to take a seat in the large living room before she found her own spot in front of the fireplace and took a deep breath.

"Thanks for coming today everyone," she told them. "The last time we were all gathered here, it was the day of Nan's funeral. I didn't think we would have a repeat of that gathering again, but here we are and honestly, I'm not quite sure where to begin." Her carefully planned speech flew right out of her head in the face of dozens of family members staring back at her.

"Sweetheart take your time and just say what's on your mind," her father encouraged.

"It's just us Krista. Don't be nervous. We all know why we're here," Matt encouraged with a smile. "Mom's already gone so it can't be worse than that."

"Okay, well, do you remember when Uncle Kevin was telling us about the condition in Nan's will? The part where I had to go through the house? She said '*In this house you will discover the story of my life and the love we shared.*'"

"And did you find it?" Aunt Mary asked. "And does it have something to do with our guest?" All eyes turned to Theo as he smiled back at them.

"It took some time, but yes, I did and yes, it has everything to do with Theo. Alex would you get the box for me please?"

All eyes on him, Alex retrieved the mahogany box from Abby's bedroom where it had been deposited just that morning and placed it on the coffee table in front of Krista. He gave her hand a quick squeeze of encouragement, before sitting back down next to Theo.

"This is what I found," she said before slowly opening the box to reveal the Oscar. As the room erupted in oohs and aahs, she lifted the statue out of the box and set it on the mantel next to the picture of Abby.

"Is that thing real?" Uncle Kyle asked. "Where did it come from?"

"Wait a minute," Matt exclaimed as he turned to look directly at Theo. "I just realized why you look so familiar to me. You're Theo James the actor aren't you? Mom loved your movies."

"Guilty as charged," Theo said smoothly.

"Then the Oscar is yours?" Matt asked hesitantly as he looked back and forth from the mantel to Theo.

"It is."

"But why did Mom have it?" Mary asked innocently.

"Well Aunt Mary, that's why we're here today." So caught up in the drama of the Oscar being revealed, few had noticed as Krista had taken the letters out of the box and arranged them on the coffee table. "But the story is about so much more than the Oscar. It's about a love that spanned decades. These letters are what gave me the first clue and you can read them later if you'd like, but for now, I hope you'll all keep an open mind as we tell you about Nan and the man she spent her life loving. Theo, if you please . . . "

Rising to his feet with more agility than they had seen from him all summer, Theo stood before the family and began to tell the story of how he and Abby had met. His voice was strong and his gaze direct as he spoke with a smile on this face that was quickly replaced by tears in his eyes as his emotions surfaced once again.

Everyone sat enthralled by the story and Krista watched their faces carefully for any hint of anger or rejection. While they were all visibly shocked to learn Abby had such an unexpected past, more than a few had tears in their eyes as the true depth of Theo's feelings for Abby were conveyed in his words.

What had taken all summer for Krista to discover was condensed into just over two hours and not a soul had moved during the entire time. It was only towards the end when Krista realized her mother was standing silently in the back of the room listening to every word with tears streaming down her own face. It seemed none of them had noticed when she slipped in. While Theo finished the story, Krista made her way to her mother's side. So captivated by what they were hearing, no one else in the room paid the pair any attention.

"So now you know the secret Abby and I shared for so long," Theo said. "Telling you isn't a plea for your forgiveness. That's between me and my God, but Abby wanted all of you to know who she really was. She cherished each and every one of you and except for that one week a year when we were lucky enough to be together, she put you first in everything her entire life and if she was still with us today, we would have shared this secret with you together. I can only ask that you try to accept that she did the very best she could in an exceptional situation because of how much she loved you. All this might have been different if we had been able to marry, but it was important to her that you know and understand what we felt for each other."

The room was silent for the longest time as each family member tried to take in everything they had heard. Exchanging glances with each other, it seemed no one knew quite what to do next until Matt stood up and extended his hand to Theo.

"Thank you sir. That couldn't have been easy to share. I for one don't quite know what to say. Knowing Mom loved another man wasn't something I was prepared to hear today and obviously I have a lot of questions yet, but I appreciate that you were willing to come here and tell us about it."

Matt's acceptance of Theo seemed to break the ice with the rest of the family and he was soon surrounded by everyone anxious to ask the questions they had held during the retelling of the story. It was the break Krista needed. Leading her mother into Abby's bedroom, they took a seat on the bed.

"I'm sorry Mom. I didn't want you to find out this way," she said tenderly.

"I didn't", Deborah told her. "I read the letters that night in the hotel after you went to bed. I stayed up all night reading them and then reading them again."

"Why didn't you say something?" Krista asked in surprise.

"I needed time to process it all I guess. It's one thing to suspect your father isn't really your father. It's quite another to have the evidence in front of you in black and white."

"You knew?"

"Not officially, but I knew my mother better than anyone. We had always been extremely close and while she and Dad were happily married, there were telltale signs here and there of someone else. I tried not to let on that I suspected, but teenagers have a hard time letting go of something like that and I was angry. I was too young to understand that the world isn't always just black and white and I took my anger about it out on Mom without even giving her a chance to explain."

"If you knew the truth would things between you and Nan have been different?" Krista asked.

"I'd like to say yes, but truthfully I don't know. I was young and stubborn and it was easier to blame all of my unhappiness on her and it compounded year after year until it was at the point where I just couldn't let go of it even after she was gone. Now I'll have to live with that regret for the rest of my life."

"So now what?"

"What do you mean?" Deborah asked as she dabbed at the tears in her eyes.

"I mean Grandfather. He's desperate to get to know you, but said he would understand if you weren't ready."

"Would you think less of me if I told you I'm scared to death?" she asked her daughter. "Obviously he knows how cruel I was to Mother. Maybe he won't like me?"

"Honestly Mom, I think he's terrified himself, but I'm pretty sure the only reason he's hung around this long is because he wants to get to know you. He's the most caring man I've ever met and after Dad and Pops, that's saying a lot. You have your entire family here to support you and that's got to mean something. Just come out and let me introduce you. That's all I ask."

"Okay, but give me a minute to compose myself then I'll be right out."

Giving Deborah an extended hug, Krista returned to the living room surprised to see how easily her family had embraced Theo. He continued to be surrounded by both generations and in spite of her worries about what was yet to come, she was proud of her family. Her father joined her as she surveyed the room.

"Where did you sneak off to?" he asked as he put his arm around her shoulder.

"Mom's here." The look of surprise he gave her wasn't unexpected. "She's in Nan's bedroom. Did you know she read the letters?"

"I suspected, but wasn't brave enough to push her on it. I think we both underestimated your mother unfortunately. Something has changed in her these last few days. I just don't know what."

"She wants to meet him," Abby said with a slight smile. "I promised it was just a meeting. If she is uncomfortable she doesn't have to stay, but I'm hoping she will."

As she said the words, they both turned at the sound of the bedroom door opening and Deborah walked up to them.

"I'm glad you came sweetheart. I'll be right at your side," Steven told his wife as he took her hand.

"Me too Mom. Now, are you ready to meet your father?"

Krista took her other hand and together the family made their way to Theo's side as the room quieted and Theo turned towards them. Krista could feel her heart beating furiously as her Mom squeezed her hand so hard it hurt.

"Grandfather, I'd like you to meet my mother – Deborah."

The pair stared at each other, each unsure what to say, until finally Theo spoke softly.

"I've waited a lifetime for this moment my dear. I'm so very sorry I never knew."

As tears rolled down Theo's cheeks and everyone waited for Deborah to respond, others in the room began to cry too. Krista held her breath praying that above all, Deborah would accept this moment for the wonderful thing that it was, when finally she spoke.

"Hello father."

Just two simple words that conveyed more than years of anger at her mother ever did and a collective sigh of relief was released before everyone began talking at once. For Theo and Deborah however, there was only one thing to do and as one, they moved into each other's arms. Krista could see Theo whispering into his daughter's ear, and whatever he said seemed to be accepted as Deborah nodded her head and for the first time in months, a smile lit up her face; timid, but a smile nonetheless.

Krista's work on behalf of her grandmother was done. The Ward family had all finally discovered the secret. The story of Abby's life and the love she shared with Theo was now part of all of them and nothing would ever be the same. The day had been a wonderful tribute to the family Abby had created and no one wanted to see it come to an end.

As Krista had hoped, no one in the family hesitated to share stories with Theo and to an outsider it would have appeared he had always been part of them. As the day went on even Deborah, who had continued to be a bit more reserved than the rest of the family, finally joined in. It warmed Krista's heart to see the smiles exchanged between father and daughter and she prayed that with the passing of time and with her mother's heart finally opened to the truth, Deborah may yet surprise them and form a loving bond with Theo. Only time would tell, but for now, at least they were no longer strangers.

Alex and Krista tidied up as the family said their good-byes to Theo until only her own parents remained. Watching through the front window, they were shocked when Deborah reached up to hug her newly discovered father before they walked to their car and Theo came back into the house.

"Did my mother just hug you of her own accord?" Krista asked excitedly.

"I'm happy to say she did," Theo told her before collapsing into a chair. "You know her better than I my dear. Do you think that means she might eventually accept me as her father?"

"I'd say that's a safe bet," Krista said as she and Alex took their own seats on the sofa and joined hands.

"Thank you my dear. I owe all of this to you," Theo told her. "Just like your grandmother, you opened your heart and home to me and now I have a family of my own. I can't thank you enough."

"Actually I think we owe all this to Nan. If she wouldn't have fallen in love with you, all of our lives would have been much different. But what's next with Mom?"

"We're going to take things slowly. She wants to get to know me a little better and I'm happy to do whatever she asks if it means I will have a small part in her life. We're going to meet for coffee tomorrow so we can talk."

"That's wonderful sir," Alex said. "We're both very happy for you."

All eyes settled on the Oscar which still kept watch from its' place on the mantle.

"I suppose it's time the Oscar went back to its' rightful owner," Krista said sadly remembering Nan's promise to return it to Theo.

"I don't see why," Theo said with a smile. "I have a matching one at home and besides, it belongs here with you both.

"Speaking of your home," Alex said with a quick look at Krista. "We wanted to run something by you. We've both become very fond of you . . ."

"We love you..." Krista interrupted to clarify.

"Yes, we love you. Thank you sweetheart. Anyway, we were wondering if you might consider staying here in town, with your family." The couple had spent days talking about it, only hesitating to bring it up because they were unsure how Deborah would react.

Knowing Krista's sentimental attachment to Abby's large house and with hopes for a large family of their own Alex had suggested they purchase Abby's home for themselves. That idea had then grown into the suggestion of Theo moving to Krista's smaller home. It made perfect sense and was a great way to keep her new-found grandfather in her life. Alex quickly outlined their plan.

"We know Krista's house isn't the size you're used to out in California, but you can't beat its' proximity to your daughter and granddaughter!"

"Does your mother know about this plan of yours?" Theo asked with a raised eyebrow. His relationship with his daughter was still in its infancy and he didn't want to do anything to jeopardize it.

"She doesn't, but I can guarantee you she won't object," Krista assured him.

"Let me think about it," Theo told them as he gazed at Abby's photograph. "It would be wonderful to spend the rest of my life surrounded by memories of her."

Chapter Thirty

Watching Theo pack his things a few days later, Krista couldn't stop the tears from gathering as he prepared to head back to California.

"Are you sure you can't stay a little while longer?" she asked as she sat gingerly on the side of the bed.

"I would love to, but if I'm going to be able to come back in time for your wedding, I have business that needs to be tended to," he said with a gentle smile.

She and Alex had finally broken the news of their engagement to the rest of the family and thanks to her rediscovered relationship with her mother, wedding plans were well underway. Since acknowledging Theo as her father, Deborah had undergone a dramatic change. To everyone's surprise and excitement, her progressing relationship with her father had brought the light back to Deborah's soul. Each day she became more and more like her own mother and it was rare to see her without a joyful smile on her face. They had much more to discover about each other, but in finding Theo, Deborah seemed to have found herself.

"But you'll think about our offer right?"

"I might as well tell you my dear," he said as he sat down next to her and took her hand in his own. "I'm going back with the hopes of a quick sale of my own home. I think your idea is wonderful. I want to get to know my great grandchildren when they come along and this house will be perfect for me. But we can sort out the details later. I better finish packing or I will miss my plane."

"Alex won't be here for another half-hour or so. You've got plenty of time."

"Actually I asked him to come a bit earlier. There's something I need to do before we leave for the airport. Something I should have done weeks ago."

"What's that?" Krista asked in confusion.

"I need to say good-bye to your grandmother."

•   •   •

Driving through the gates of the cemetery the mood in the car turned somber. Maybe it was reverence for the souls there or an understanding of the importance of the moment, but none of them said a word as Alex parked the car and they walked slowly to Abby's grave. The man who had appeared so virile and strong just hours before seemed to whither a bit with each step he took and Krista cast worried glances his way wondering if this would be too much for him. She kept a careful hold on her grandfather's arm just in case. The headstone in sight, with Abby's name prominently displayed, they stopped a short distance away before Krista and Alex walked forward and she knelt down to place a bouquet of lilies at the base of the headstone. Her lips moved in a silent prayer as the men watched a single tear roll down her cheek. Her prayer completed, Alex helped her to her feet and they walked back to Theo.

"Do you want me to go with you Grandfather?" Krista asked. The flowers in his hand had begun to shake and she worried for him.

"Thank you my dear, but can you give me this time alone with Abby please?"

"Are you sure?"

"I am. I'll join you back at the car."

Giving his hand an encouraging squeeze and reaching up to kiss his cheek, she nodded before she and Alex walked back to the car.

Unsure he would have the strength to say goodbye, Theo took a deep breath and surveyed Abby's final resting place. A cool breeze cut through the hot August sun ruffling the leaves in the maple tree nearby. Abby loved these types of days and a smile came to his face as he remembered the joy she found in everything about her life. As difficult as it had been for them to live such divergent lives, she never complained; instead finding happiness in each stolen moment they shared. She was one of a kind and no other woman had ever come close to the perfection he saw in her. Never a religious man, for the first time in his life he prayed there truly was a heaven and that someday he would be reunited with her to share eternal love.

Seeing her name there in the cold hard granite, he moved forward, reaching out an unsteady hand to trace each letter with his finger before dropping suddenly to his knees, hands in his head as the tears began to fall in earnest.

"I should go to him," Krista said anxiously before Alex pulled her back into his arms. They had been watching the scene unfold.

"No Krista. He needs to do this himself. It will be okay."

As they watched, Theo's tears turned into sobs and his whole body shook with his grieving. Finally he raised his head and reached out once more; his hands tracing the phrase engraved at the bottom of the stone.

Krista had forgotten about the special engraving containing the words of e.e. cummings, but seeing him touch the stone so lovingly, she remembered exactly what it said. At the time of Nan's death none in the family had understood the significance of the phrase; it was only since meeting Theo and hearing the story that Krista understood and she began to cry softly as Alex held her close. If she had ever needed proof that true love existed she had only to look at the devotion exhibited by her grandfather. Their love had spanned a lifetime and would not be separated even by death. She and Alex could only hope to be so lucky.

"Thank you my love for giving me such a wonderful life," Theo said softly as he wiped his tears away. "Thank you for your wisdom in bringing me together with my daughter and granddaughter. They are the living, breathing embodiment of you and I will spend the rest of my life cherishing each of them as much as I loved you. Until we meet again, know that I will love you forever."

Leaning over to place one last kiss on Abby's name, he struggled to his feet, unsteady at first as if the good-bye had taken more out of him then he had to give. With an inner resolve only Abby had been privy to, he straightened his shoulders and stood up straight giving one more look at the gravestone *"I carry your heart . . . "* he whispered.

As he turned away, the wind in the trees seemed to whisper back..."*I carry it in my heart."*

In memory of my dear friend Krista Witty Amos. Her smile could light up any room and I miss her every day . . .

About The Author

Barbara A. Luker is a life-long resident of Saint Peter, Minnesota and as a certified Municipal Clerk, Luker utilizes her writing skills working for the City of Saint Peter. A devoted fan of the Minnesota Wild and a supporter of several animal rescue organizations, she lives that passion in part through adoption of her polydactyl rescue cat Annie. Her first published novel, *Remembering You*, was released in 2020.

Note From The Author

Word-of-mouth is crucial for any author to succeed. If you enjoyed *I Carry Your Heart*, please leave a review online—anywhere you are able. Even if it's just a sentence or two. It would make all the difference and would be very much appreciated.

Thanks!
Barbara A. Luker

We hope you enjoyed reading this title from:

BLACK ROSE
writing™

Subscribe to our mailing list – *The Rosevine* – and receive **FREE** books, daily deals, and stay current with news about upcoming releases and our hottest authors.
Scan the QR code below to sign up.

Already a subscriber? Please accept a sincere thank you for being a fan of Black Rose Writing authors.

View other Black Rose Writing titles at

Made in the USA
Middletown, DE
27 August 2022